SHIFTING RESOLVE

— 5 —

SHIFTER LORDS

S.E. BABIN

CHAPTER

One

No one ever noticed a wren.

I could have become a snake or a rat or even a tiny gnat, but those were all scary, annoying things people noticed right away. But a pretty bird with a stunning song? Even if they noticed, no one batted an eye, chalking the presence up to a random blessing or a spot of good fortune.

It helped that I was shadowed underneath a lush canopy of leaves and branches, perched in an abandoned nest. If anyone questioned the presence of a wren at night, the nest made it all make sense.

As long as they weren't an ornithologist, but since we were spying on one of the Lords, I thought we could skip that fear. For now.

Caelan was somewhere close, crouched low to the ground, ears pricked in anticipation of this going to absolute shit.

To be fair, when I was involved, the odds of something going to shit were approximately 80 percent in favor of the shitshow.

One of the Lords had encroached on the territory I'd claimed after our battle with Donovan. I wasn't all that mad about it because what was I going to do with pieces of several states when I had enough shit keeping me busy here?

Caelan was not of the same opinion. Thus, why we were here spying when I would rather be snuggled up against my Lord. His take was we kept the territory until we got a good read on the other Lords. Then, if I was ready to give it up, we could pass it to the one least likely to use it against us.

My argument was that I only liked Rowan so far. Soren was up in the air, but Moira was still pissed off at him, and it was friend code that I had to be pissed off too.

I'd only give the territory to Rowan, but he was entirely uninterested.

Caelan and I had gone back and forth over this until we agreed to see for ourselves what was happening.

Technically, no Lord could "steal" the land I'd claimed. It wasn't mine in a legal ownership way, but every time I claimed land for my own, it boosted my power. I was pretty darn powerful on my own, but when I was on land soaked with my magic, I had the advantage over most opponents who challenged me.

Caelan had tracked the encroacher to this massive mansion on a large plot of land in Montana. It was cold as fuck out here, and if I had teeth, they'd be chattering.

There weren't that many trees on the property, making it difficult to disguise ourselves, though it was easier for me than Caelan. A big ass wolf was a little harder to hide than a tiny bird, and we were on the eastern side of the state, where wolf sightings weren't as common as in the west.

And since this Lord was being shady, he'd no doubt be on the lookout for the other Lords, especially Caelan. I could sneak in much easier than he could since I had the ability to shift into pretty much anything.

But I also didn't want to tangle with another Lord. To be honest, I was sick of the Council and sick of every Lord except Rowan and Caelan. Stealing the land was par for the course with these asshats, and I had to agree with Caelan on one point.

Encroaching on claimed land was the Lord thumbing his nose at me and my power.

I'd questioned Caelan about how a Lord would know about my claim, and he told me they could feel my magic. Every time he stepped on my land, he knew the ground belonged to me.

Odd, but I believed him, which meant one of these assholes was playing a dangerous game. Had they learned nothing from the last time? We weren't sure which one of the Lords, if any, had betrayed me, or if the fae had done all that on their own. I suspected Ethan because he was a massive dick, but Caelan told me that was too easy.

What did I know? Someone lured me to the Hall of Fae, attacked me and my father, and while we were distracted by that, they tore down my property wards and had the Lords square off against Caelan, Rowan, and Ben, while another forced a spelled crown on my head that damn near killed me.

Smelled like collusion to me.

We'd been trying to find the culprits since and kept hitting a dead end around every corner. But Caelan and I kept trying, the Lord maybe a little more than me. Watching me die had broken something inside him, and he was out for blood.

I still mostly wanted to be left alone, but I'd come to the conclusion that wasn't in the cards for me. Not since Cernunnos had claimed me as his heir and I'd destroyed a sacred fae tree.

Okay. *The* sacred fae tree.

Cernunnos was the only fae that I knew of who could travel to all the realms. Everyone else relied on the tree's power like a magical elevator. Even when the tree died, it left a seed behind with someone worthy who would then plant it. Rinse and repeat.

Tree dies. Seed grows. Yay, another tree.

Except it didn't count on one Evie Quinn (meeeee) swallowing the seed, which pissed off ancient powers and ancient fae, and said seed decided to come out in an untimely manner and way, leading me to give birth to a tree on Caelan's property.

Then someone or something decided the best way to kill me

was to force me into the tree where my powers could slowly be drained over eternity. Except...they didn't know about the Chimera part of me or expect my sheer will to survive. Not only had I come out of the tree furious, I'd burned the thing to the ground, not giving it time to produce a seed.

Ding dong. The wicked tree is dead.

Now I was the gate to the other fae realms. Whether anyone realized it yet was up in the air. I could transport people over before the tree had decided to go all supervillain on me, but I'd absorbed even more of its power.

No fae had been brave enough to approach me yet. Especially not with the new and handy burn-things-to-an-unrecognizable-crisp power I'd discovered once the tree was forced to spit me out.

Things had been suspiciously quiet for months now, and even Caelan was getting antsy.

The Lords hadn't moved against us, and they'd stopped pressuring Caelan to "get me in line." Laughable of them to think he ever could, though I was way more willing to play ball with Caelan than any of the other Lords.

Except Rowan.

Besides Caelan, he was my favorite.

But before my time in the tree, Rowan and Caelan were neck and neck for my favorite.

Now Caelan was far ahead of the pack. He'd changed. I'd changed.

We'd both stopped being neurotic overthinkers and possessive nutcases (ahem, Caelan) and realized we were better together.

I hesitated to claim things were good, really good, because that's when the sky would open and rain holy mortal hell down upon us.

The house looming several feet away was a three-story monstrosity, complete with those old columns typical of a southern home by the front door. White and marble, they rose from the porch to the roof. Sometimes they gave a house character. Other times, as was the case with this house, all they did was add to the aloofness of the place.

This was no home. The landscaping was covered with a fine dusting of snow, but even underneath I could tell there were no well-loved plants here, only the builder's landscaping. Whatever was cheap and easy to maintain, the builders had placed it and whoever bought the house never bothered to change anything.

No hanging baskets hung from hooks on the large porch. No rocking chairs or side tables or planters beckoned a welcome for guests. There wasn't even a welcome mat, only a generic fiber mat to wipe your shoes.

This place was stark and bare. A pretty home when you took a critical look at its bones, but devoid of soul.

A perfect home for someone like Ethan.

Caelan had cautioned me against assuming Ethan was the Lord who lived here, but this house practically screamed his name. Devoid of personality, icy, and not a spot of color in sight…

Yup. That's Ethan.

No one had moved for an hour, and I was freezing my tail off. With a whisper of wings, I flitted from the nest to the roof. I knew where Caelan was lying, but he was so well blended into the brush I couldn't make him out. I hopped over the top of the roof and down the back to see what kind of patio the house had. It wasn't common for a bird like me to be out during the winter, so I didn't want to get caught, but most people wouldn't think too much of a bird sighting.

If I were an actual fairy wren, I wouldn't even be in this country.

When a quick peek over the side of the roof revealed lots of cozy places to hide, I took a chance and hopped onto the large smoker, quickly disguising myself behind a large grill glove.

Still no sign of movement.

A bad feeling was building in my gut. I poked my head up and looked through the gauzy curtains. Wealthy people rarely thought about the back view when it came to people looking in.

They felt safe and secure in their bubbles. I could see into most of the downstairs area.

The living room was a large, open space, furnished with high-end, modern couches and what looked like a carved, solid-wood coffee table. A television was on, but the sound was off. Fresh flowers sat on the dining table, a mix of expensive peonies and dahlias dotted with the occasional white lily.

But that wasn't the most interesting thing about the scene. As my eyes trailed over the living room and dining room, I blinked in stunned shock at the scene I spotted next.

Ethan sat in a chair in the kitchen. Unremarkable unless you counted the fact that he was tied and gagged. I took a step back and almost fell off the smoker.

Throwing out a wing to balance myself, I flitted closer, perching on the arm of the wicker patio couch. Ethan's eyes were wide with horror, his feet planted firmly on the floor, but his body pushed back, as if he were trying to get away from whatever or whoever stood in front of him.

There was no way for me to get closer to see who it was without giving myself away.

I leapt off the couch and flew as fast as I could, my heart beating a hundred miles a minute as I searched for Caelan.

The wolf, seeing my frantic dash, rose high enough for me to spot him. I dove and shifted, crouching low to the ground.

When I shifted to my fae form, my clothes stayed on. When I used my chimera magic to fuel a shift, bye bye clothing. No rhyme or reason to it, but I made sure I either shifted in the nude or didn't care about what I was wearing. Tonight was a little different. We were in Montana in December, and it was colder than a mofo out here.

Using my wren form was advantageous for spying, but I could keep my clothes on when I did. The thought of being naked out here sent a shudder down my spine.

"Ethan is in there," I said. "Someone or something has him tied up."

Caelan's eyes flashed gold. Seconds later, he shifted, reaching for the bag that had fallen from around his neck. "He's not trying to get away?"

I'd thought of that, too. "No. I'm not sure if someone is using magic to keep him in the chair or if he's too afraid to try to escape, but we need to decide what we're going to do."

Caelan's teeth flashed in the dark. "You think we should leave him there?"

My first instinct was to say yes. The asshole had damn near gotten me killed a few months ago.

Caelan's wicked chuckle made me grin. "I didn't think you had it in you."

"How bad would it be if we did leave him there?"

Caelan shrugged. "We're already down an extra Lord without Donovan. No one has moved to replace him yet. Ben is brand new. If Ethan gets taken out, it could signal a breakdown in leadership."

"Which means someone might step in and try to start some trouble?" I finished.

"Exactly. I won't say no if you want to leave. No one knows we're here, so no one will know we saw him."

I sighed. "Dammit."

Caelan dressed quickly, but the clothing he had was not suitable for the weather. Wolves were naturally resistant to the cold, shifters even more so, but we lived in Texas, and the cold there was not the bone-deep chill of a Montana winter.

I chewed on the edge of my thumb. "Will he owe us a favor if we help him?"

Caelan glanced at me with surprise. "The time in that cursed tree has changed you, Evangeline."

Not a hint of disapproval in his tone. The opposite, in fact.

"The only Lords who gave a shit about me disappearing were you and Rowan. The rest can go fuck themselves."

He snagged me with an arm and pulled me into an embrace.

"Don't count Thorvin out so fast. He has grieved from the moment you went in."

I stilled. "He doesn't even know me."

"Doesn't mean he wanted to do you harm." He pressed a kiss to my temple and pulled away. "Thorvin is a complicated individual."

"If you say so," I grumbled, glancing over at the house. "Think he's dead yet?"

Caelan snorted. "It's hard to kill one of us. If you'd like, we can time it."

I snickered. "Let's go save Ethan's sorry ass."

CHAPTER
Two

I followed Caelan's lead, staying low to the ground and hidden in the shadows. When we reached the patio, Caelan gestured for me to stay around the corner. I hunkered down at the edge of the house, hands buried deep in my coat pockets.

It didn't take him long to return. "I can't see who has him."

"But he's still alive."

Caelan nodded. "Unfortunately."

We grinned at each other.

"How do you want to play this?"

He glanced up. "Two fireplaces. One goes to the living room. The other goes to the master, I bet. We can try shimmying down that way, but I'm too large. You'll have to do it and open the window. Then we can try to take them by surprise."

"Sounds like a lot can go wrong."

"True. But we don't know what we're walking into. Ethan hasn't struggled or tried to free himself from his bonds, which tells me he knows exactly what that person is capable of, and it isn't good."

It made sense. "If we go in headfirst, we lose the element of surprise, and we'll have to hit them hard and fast."

"Preference?"

"I'm not a warrior like you. I'll always choose stealth. But I'll let you lead this one. This Cagney and Lacey stuff isn't in my wheelhouse."

Caelan scratched his chin. "Or we could split up. You take the fireplace. I'll wait for your signal, then go in. You'll act as backup if I get in a pinch."

"How will I signal?"

He pointed to a second-floor window. "Up there. Flash the lights twice, then start heading downstairs. Ready?"

I nodded, my heart pounding. "Ready."

He brought me in for a hard and fast kiss, then slapped me on the ass. "Start shimmying, flower girl."

I rubbed my bottom cheek. "You're having fun," I accused.

"It's been a while since one of us has been in trouble. I'm looking forward to Ethan getting bent over a barrel."

I grinned. "Me too." Calling up my Floromancy, vines slid from the earth and wound around my legs and abdomen. Once they were steady, I tapped a thick vine around my waist. A second later, I was in the air, Caelan gaping at me from the ground.

I winked and let the earth carry me to the roof, where the vines gently deposited me and slowly sank back into the ground. On silent feet, I made my way to the second chimney and peered inside. I couldn't see any blockages, but the space was tight enough to make me worry. Although I was much smaller than Caelan, at five feet seven, I couldn't be considered petite.

Reaching into the chimney, I carefully extricated the screen and perched on top of the stone. Calling more vines, I wrapped one around my wrist and called the other down to steady my waist. Then I carefully scooted off the edge, allowing the vines to take my weight.

Controlling the vines with a slow but steady pace, we moved down the chimney until my feet were an inch below a pile of wood. Careful not to disturb it, I stepped over until I was on the stone floor and released the vines once more.

I let out a relieved breath and hurried to the window. Caelan stood right outside, expression tense until he spotted my silhouette. I reached over and flashed the lights twice, then went to the door, easing it open before peeking out to ensure I was alone.

Voices came in from the kitchen.

"We can sit here all night, Lord," a feminine voice said. "Where is my cousin?"

I froze. The voice was familiar. But it was the second voice that piped up that gave me pause. I'd left my cell back in the vehicle because phones were expensive and I wasn't sure it'd survive the shift.

Shit. I snapped out a thin thread of magic to get Caelan's attention before he barreled in and screwed us all. Pressed against the wall, I moved the small vine to wrap around the Lord's ankle and gently tug. He was smart. He'd know to wait.

After a tense moment, I realized he'd gotten my message. Creeping back into the room, I shut the door, cracked open the window, and took my wren form. Seconds later, I met Caelan outside.

Once I shifted, he came closer. "What is it?"

Even I had trouble believing what I saw inside that house. "Donovan is in there."

Caelan froze. "Impossible."

I'd agree but there was no mistaking that weasel's voice. "Not only that, so is Nadia."

Of all the people who might take Ethan hostage, Nadia wouldn't have been in my top five. The woman was on a desperate search to find out what happened to Gianna. She knew she was dead, but she didn't believe the "official" story, which wasn't much of a story at all.

I didn't blame the woman. Gianna had died a terrible death.

He swore quietly and scrubbed a hand over his face. "Donovan is dead."

"I didn't see his face," I whispered. "But that was definitely his voice."

"You think the fae resurrected him?" His face was a mask of

confusion. I'd seen the battle, seen Donovan go down. I assumed he was dead, too.

The fae could do a lot of things, but I'd never heard of one being able to resurrect the dead. It wasn't outside of the realm of possibility, but I'd never met anyone who could do it.

"Are you sure he was dead? Fae can heal even the most grievous wounds."

"I didn't take a pulse," he growled as he took me by the elbow. "Let's get the hell out of here."

"You don't want to help Ethan?"

"It's not that simple anymore. We can't let Donovan know we're onto him. Let's get back to the car, and I'll make a call."

We hauled ass back to the vehicle we'd parked half a mile away. As soon as we were in, Caelan turned the heat up to full blast and called 911. As soon as it was done, he broke his phone in half and tossed it out the window.

"Clever but expensive," I drawled.

"The Keep has a stash of them for occasions just like this."

"For when other Lords get kidnapped and tied to a chair for interrogation?"

"You'd be surprised how often people want to tie us to chairs." His eyes sparkled.

"Perv," I said fondly.

A minute later, sirens appeared in the distance, screaming past us in a cacophony of sound. "They'll either kill him or haul ass out of there."

"Not the best odds," I mused. "Are you going to tell Ethan you know?"

"The Lords have a meeting next week. If Ethan divulges that Donovan is still alive, I'll think about it." From the look on his face, he'd have to really think about it.

"I still don't understand why he didn't lose his position over everything." He was at the forefront of the Lord and fae incursion of my land and had been gunning for me ever since I'd gotten tangled up with Caelan. My stringing him up with vines and beating him a little bit because he called me a slut had not helped matters.

No regrets.

Caelan reached over and took my hand. "I voted against him multiple times. Because Titania had influenced the others, there was no proof she hadn't done the same to him. When directly asked, Ethan did not admit one way or the other whether he'd acted of his own volition."

His voice deepened several octaves, the animal inside him close to the surface.

"Because you would know he was lying."

Caelan nodded. "He's always been a slippery bastard. The other Lords had to vote to keep him in because of the lack of concrete evidence against him. There's no law against being an asshole."

True. If there were, I knew a lot of people who'd be in the clinker. "What are the odds he makes it out of this one?"

His lips twisted. "High, unfortunately. You said they're still interrogating him?"

I nodded. "They want to know what happened to Gianna."

Caelan snorted. "Donovan is still playing both sides."

"And he knows exactly what happened to her." Donovan had been working with Rhona, the Chimera involved with Finn, in an effort to destabilize Caelan's region, and used Gianna, a swan shifter, to help. But for reasons unknown, Rhona murdered Gianna and stepped into her place. In an effort to get rid of me, she and Donovan had planted Gianna's body on my property, probably to "uncover" at a later date, so I could go down for the murder.

They didn't count on Cernunnos popping into the wedding and refusing to bless the union, thus ruining Rhona's plans before they'd even begun, or expect my father to step in and tell me about Gianna's death. I might have discovered it on my own during my upkeep of the land, but I'd been so busy I'd gotten a little lazy about caring for my property the way I should have been. Once Cernunnos showed me what they'd done, I'd disposed of Gianna's body permanently.

"But he can't pin it on you because the body is gone." He chuckled. "I would have loved to be a fly on the wall when he realized that."

I leaned back and grinned. "Yeah. I can see him going full Rumpelstiltskin."

Caelan pulled into the parking lot of the hotel where we were staying. "It'd be a lot easier if he stayed dead. If he starts throwing accusations out about your involvement, things might go sideways." He shook his head. "I don't understand how this happened. I would have bet money the guy was dead."

"Maybe we should have stayed and waited for the police to arrive." Hindsight was always twenty-twenty. "Then we could have seen for ourselves."

"Getting caught would have been worse."

Caelan opened the room door and held it open. "If you say it's Donovan, I have to believe you. I'll check with the Keep mage when we get back."

I shrugged off my jacket and tossed it onto the chair. "What do we do about the land?"

"We go out first thing in the morning and stake your claim."

I turned to see him standing by the door, watching me with glowing eyes.

My heart skipped a little. No matter how many times I looked at him, he always stunned me. Tall and lean, dark hair and stormy eyes that turned gold when he was experiencing high emotion, Caelan took my breath away. We'd started off rocky and stayed that way for months.

He came on too strong, and I was a paranoid little rabbit constantly overthinking things. But when I'd finally gotten out of that cursed tree and got a second chance, none of that small shit mattered anymore. Rowan had already knocked some sense into Caelan before my forced disappearing act, but he never got the chance to talk to me before I was gone.

Caelan felt the same way when I made it out. None of it mattered to him either, but he did stop trying to rope me into marriage, and the guy had become a serious snuggleholic. I was not upset about it.

In fact, I'd sent Rowan a big ass package of hybrids and new plants I thought he might like, along with a year's membership to a fancy whiskey club. The other Lord was going to make some woman very happy.

My thoughts had scattered the second I looked at Caelan because the guy was looking at me like I was the only thing on an all-you-can-eat buffet.

"Um." All the thoughts were falling out of my head, so I had to ask about the land now before I lost all train of thought. "How do we stake my claim?"

He stripped his shirt off. "We can talk about it tomorrow."

"Err. Okay."

Caelan grinned, the edge to it making me a little nervous. There was nowhere to run, and he was looking decidedly predatory. I took a step back when he prowled my direction.

He untied the drawstring of his joggers.

Everything tightened. "Are you taking a shower?" My voice came out far huskier than I intended.

"Nope." The grin widened.

"Huh." I said. "Whatever shall you do?"

"I have a few ideas."

Caelan pounced.

Three

We spent the next few days driving as we traced the outline of the claimed land. When we finally made it back to the starting point, I was feeling a little ill.

"It's too much." Total understatement. I had no idea how I'd managed to claim that much, but I'd stopped counting at six states.

Caelan had his arm on the back of my seat, fingers toying with a strand of hair loosened from my ponytail. "You took as much property as you could claim."

I slid him a look. "I didn't mean to take anything. Can I sign it over to you or something?" I rubbed my forehead. "Or lease it to you for like a dollar?"

He chuckled. "Depends on whether you're in this for the long haul. I'll manage the territory until you decide what to do with it, regardless."

I frowned, not loving his word choice. "Wait. Are you not in it for the long haul?"

A gentle tug on my hair and a reproving look. "I'm in this forever, flower girl."

My eyes narrowed. "Then why'd you say that?"

He snorted. "Because just a few short months ago, you were doing everything you could to haul ass from me."

I didn't say anything for a long moment. "To be fair, you were freaking me out."

He dipped his head in acknowledgment. "I'm aware."

"Something has changed?"

"Not at all."

I crossed my arms and glared. "Then why are you asking me if I'm in it for the long haul?"

Caelan laughed. "Evie, if you wanted to get married right now, I'd skid this vehicle into the court parking lot and drag you inside. I'm here for you as long as you want me to be." He pulled off the side of the road and stopped. Turning to me, he gently gripped my chin in his hand. "Stop overthinking."

He was right. I was overthinking. "You haven't asked me to marry you in months," I grumbled.

"Do you want me to start again?" His eyes glimmered with amusement.

"No," I grumbled. "But maybe ask me once. Later."

Caelan's eyebrows flicked up. "Oh?"

I nodded.

"When the time is right."

I nodded again.

A thoughtful look crossed his face. "Alright then. When the time is right." He pulled the vehicle back onto the road. "Then I suppose your answer is 100% yes, you're in it for the long haul."

"I'm going to punch you," I growled.

Caelan's laugh filled the air and settled the knots twisting in my stomach. "We'll work everything out when we get back. In the meantime, I think we should talk about building a house."

I blinked. "Here?"

"Mmm hmm. We'll need to visit periodically to keep up appearances and dissuade others from encroaching."

"Like Ethan."

He nodded. "And we should start soon. I'll handle Ethan."

"A house," I mused. "How much land?"

Caelan chuckled. "As much as you want, darling."

He was really good at being a boyfriend. Or whatever we were. Boyfriend didn't feel like the right term to describe what he was to me.

I wound my fingers in his. "Can we design it ourselves?"

"I'll never tell you no, Evie."

I glanced over. "What if I want a pony?"

"I'd ask you what kind."

I snickered. "Wait until you see the house plans I come up with."

He picked up our joined hands and pressed a kiss to the back of my palm. "Do whatever you want. As long as I'm with you, I'd live in a hole in the ground."

Hot and occasionally spoke like a poet. How could I not swoon over him?

DRYADS WERE GENTLE CREATURES, but cross one at your peril. One of our more difficult customers was learning this as Moira and I sat back and stayed the hell out of it.

I'd gotten back the night before, reluctantly saying goodbye to Caelan from the vehicle. It was getting more difficult to separate from him, and while that was scary, I realized I was maturing.

Many things had changed since I'd escaped the tree. I no longer took things or people for granted. And the people around me had done the same. My magic was more balanced, and I no longer had to siphon as much.

Rowan's theory about being touch-starved had been spot on. As outlandish or odd as it seemed, the moment Caelan had stopped hounding me about marriage and we started forming a stronger, more intimate connection, something inside of me had clicked.

Moira and Ash had always been affectionate, but they'd stepped it up a little. Enough to let me know they cared, but also enough to not make it weird. Even Tess was trying, though she had her own issues to deal with after singlehandedly destroying a powerful fae in an effort to save my life.

Ash was always the one to put a comforting touch on my shoulder or brush a hand over my hair as he passed, and I'd always thought he was the gentlest of all of us.

He'd blown that theory to smithereens today.

The woman was someone we hated seeing come in, but her money was spent as well as anyone else's, and she hadn't done anything over the top. Until today.

"*Excuse* me?" Her voice was right on the cusp of a screech.

Ash's look could have shriveled even the most violent heart. If they were smart. Which this woman obviously was not.

"Ma'am, we all watched you walk out of here with a stunning bouquet. Every flower was at the peak of health."

"I beg your pardon." She could not have sounded more offended if she'd tried, but Ash was right. If someone purchased a bouquet more than a day old, I personally touched it up before I let it go out the door. Less than a minute prior to the sale, I'd inspected and boosted every flower and greenery in the crystal vase.

Ash didn't give an inch. "Your item was in pristine condition when you walked out of here, and our guarantee is the flowers will stay that way for a minimum of seven days."

A hint of craftiness glinted in the woman's eyes. "That's exactly what I'm saying. Several flowers died the same day!"

"And you didn't think to bring it back?" Ash said, one eyebrow raised.

"Well, it's heavy…"

"No photos either?" Ash pressed.

"I didn't think to take any. I mean, I'm a long-time customer and thought my word would be enough."

Ah yes. We'd officially moved to the guilt portion of the argument.

"I'm sorry, ma'am," Ash said. "Like I said before, we cannot offer a refund to merchandise that's not returned to our location so we can inspect it."

That bouquet had been two hundred and fifty bucks and took hours of work to put together.

If this had been a one-time deal, we would have been more flexible, but this was the third time the woman had requested a refund, and Ash, more so than the rest of us, was over her shenanigans.

"Further," Ash continued, "this is the third time you've been dissatisfied with our work. This begs the question of why you continue frequenting our establishment if we can't seem to serve your needs."

The woman blinked. "Well, I'm *trying* to give you a chance to rectify your mistake—"

Ash snorted. "The only mistake here is that we didn't ban you the second time you asked for a refund."

She gaped like a fish before her face turned bright red. "This is appalling treatment! I'll tell everyone what you're really like. You just wait."

"And we will put a sign on the door with a picture of your face on it to warn other local proprietors away from your scams."

I winced but didn't interfere.

The woman paled. She took a step backward. "You wouldn't."

Ash crossed his arms over his chest. "I certainly would. In fact, I bet if I went out right now and asked around about you, I'd find at least two other businesses tired of seeing you come into their shop, too."

Her eyes slid my way, her face taking on a beseeching look.

She'd get no help from our corner. I hardened my expression and stayed silent.

"Fine," she snarled. "Wait until you see my online review."

"Oh no," Ash said with mock horror. "Wait until you see our rebuttal."

Moira covered her face but couldn't stop the sound of her snicker.

The woman turned on her heel and sailed out the door, two spots of color high on her cheeks. Ash's shoulders slumped.

I walked over to him and slipped my arm around his waist, giving him a gentle squeeze. "She deserved it."

"Yeah," he said with a sigh.

"You alright?"

"I'm fine," he mumbled. "Mostly annoyed."

I studied his face, the tight jaw and tired eyes. Concern flared in me. I'd seen Ash tired, but never at this level of bone-deep exhaustion. "Need a break?"

"No, but I may work in the back for a while if you don't mind." He relaxed a bit and leaned into my embrace. "How are you?"

"I'm good. How about you head there, and I'll make you some tea?"

"Don't bring me anything without milk and sugar," he said with a shudder.

"I did that one time," I groaned.

"And may you never live it down." He scooted out of my embrace and headed to the back. Moira's eyes trailed him until he disappeared behind the doors.

"You think he's okay?" she asked.

"He will be."

"He's better than he was. Things with him and Tess are close to normal again." Their breakup wasn't as disastrous as it could have been, but Ash had taken it much harder than Tess, resulting in some disruptions for the shop, and to our interpersonal relationships. We were slowly getting back on track, though I doubted Ash and Tess would ever fully recover the friendship they had before.

"Maybe he's lonely."

Moira uncrossed her lean, slender legs and rose, stretching and yawning. "I'll check on him in a little while. In the meantime, I'll drop off Hattie's delivery."

We upped our game for her regular order. This week's

bouquet was a red, white, and green extravaganza, complete with glitter, bells, and candy canes. "Think it will give her a heart attack?"

"Nah," she said with a laugh. "Hattie is a feisty thing. I don't think anything we did would be too outrageous for her."

"Good." Hattie was a spry elderly woman and one of our favorite regulars. She had a standing weekly order for seasonal flowers, with the instruction to be as creative as we wanted. Keeping in mind her age and the style of her house, we dialed our antics down some, but we always made sure we went for creativity and flair.

Hattie had never made a single complaint. The opposite, in fact.

Tess floated over. "I made her some cookies if you don't mind taking them with you."

Moira eyed the plate of what appeared to be chocolate chip cookies. "Just for her? None for us?"

Tess smirked. "There's a full plate in the kitchen."

"May the gods bless you," Moira said, taking the plate from Tess's pale hands.

As she scooted away, I called out. "Bring me two back!"

"Depends on how many Tess brought," Moira sang as she disappeared around the corner.

"I brought a lot," Tess said, then frowned. "But Moira can eat her body weight in snacks."

A surprised laugh broke from me. Despite what happened with Ash and then Titania, Tess had come through it okay. She still had moments where she became paralyzed with intrusive thoughts, but after everything, Tess had come out better for it. She was a little more self-deprecating with her humor and a little more adventurous than she had been, telling me she only had one life and needed to make the most of it.

Wise advice from our young banshee, and something all of us should take to heart.

"Thanks for thinking of us."

Tess shrugged. "I don't have a boyfriend anymore, so I can make cookies and do whatever I want."

I laughed again. "True."

Tess settled onto the stool behind the register and pulled the order book over.

I eyed her. She'd always be pale. Her heritage as a banshee required it. But there was a happy flush in her cheeks and a sparkle in her eye where there'd been none before. As much as it pained me to know Tess was doing far better than Ash, her glow up made me ecstatic. "You know," I ventured, "when you find that perfect person, you can still make cookies and do whatever you want."

Tess waved a casual hand. "I know, but then I have to make sure I have extra time for them, and I have to split my time between what they want to do and what I want to do." She shook her head. "I don't want to make decisions like that right now. If I want to see an afternoon movie, I can just buy a ticket and go. If I want to make chocolate chip cookies, I don't have to worry about scheduling the time between a date or an event."

I blinked. "Fair enough," I murmured. "Being single can be a ton of fun."

She smiled. "So far it's wonderful!"

I was glad Ash was in the back because ouch.

The shop bell rang. Power swept into the room, a tingle of awareness making the hair on the back of my arms stand up. A man entered. Tall, lean but built with muscle, sharp jawline, but a shaggy mess of blond hair at odds with his mostly clean-cut appearance. He wore a pair of gray slacks and an emerald-green pullover sweater. Handsome and well-dressed, I automatically assumed he was here to buy something for his girlfriend or wife.

I rose from the worktable, taking a clean towel with me to wipe off the remnants of plant material from the display I was working on. "Welcome to Little Shop of Florals. Shopping for a significant other today?"

The man's gaze landed on me. I almost sucked in a breath at

the intensity of his bright blue gaze but managed to control myself. "Are you Evie Quinn?" A crisp English accent in a deep voice would have melted me a few years ago, but I was made of sterner stuff now.

I tilted my head. "I'm afraid I'm at a loss here. Who are you?"

A devastating smile. "I'm Barrett Masters. We should have met years ago, but you managed to elude my notice for far too long."

My eyebrows went up. "I'm not sure what you mean."

A sheen of crimson rolled over his irises. I took a step back and pulled power in anticipation of a strike. Another Chimera. Perfect timing. Not much of anything interesting had happened in a few months, so naturally, it was time for the sky to fall.

He held up a placating hand. "Peace, Miss Quinn. Contrary to what you've seen from our kind, not all of us are bloodthirsty monsters. I'm here to make you an offer."

"And if I don't want to entertain any offers?"

Barrett's smile reached his eyes. "Your reputation is well-earned, I see."

"Reputation?" I frowned.

"Word of your exploits has reached across the globe. Though I can't say I fault you for your responses to anything in the past, if what I'm hearing has happened to you is true."

Moira came in from the back and halted, eyes narrowing as she spotted Barrett. Without a word, she came up to stand beside me.

Barrett's eyes briefly flicked to her, dismissing her as a threat. I almost smiled. Moira might not get involved in a lot of scuffles, but I had no doubt she could hold her own if she were ever pushed.

"Exploits?" I echoed, even as anger filled me at his words. "I wouldn't give a shit if you faulted me or not."

His smile widened. "Forgive me. Poor choice of words. My understanding is one of our kind, Rhona to be specific, intruded on your territory and tried to stake an...ill-advised claim on you."

"True," I acknowledged though I didn't expand on what I'd done to her afterward.

Barrett's blue eyes sparkled. "Death was a light sentence for Rhona. And I already know what Finn did to you." His expression sobered. "If I had known years ago, I would have ensured he never caught up to you."

He gave me a slight bow. "The making of—" He paused, his eyes lighting on Tess, then Moira.

"They know," I said shortly.

He dipped his head in a slight nod. "The making of a new Chimera is a sacred thing and not something our kind takes lightly."

Moira stiffened. "It wasn't her fault," she snapped, her voice heated.

Barrett focused his full attention on her. "If I thought it was, we'd be having a much different conversation right now."

Moira snorted. "You have no idea what kind of storm you'd get caught up in if you came for her."

A thin smile. "I'm afraid I do." He gestured toward the seating area. "Please. I'm here only to talk. May I sit for a while?"

I thought about rebuffing him, but he'd made no aggressive moves and appeared to be here for a discussion and nothing more. "Please," I said after a moment of tense silence. "Would you like some coffee or tea?"

"Coffee, please."

I turned to make a cup for both of us, but Moira laid a hand on my arm. "I'll get it. Go have a seat."

"Cream and sugar?" Moira asked, her voice a little too sweet.

"Neither," Barrett said, eyes narrowing a hair, as if he heard it too and realized he should be suspicious.

She flashed a friendly smile and walked away.

Barrett leaned forward and lowered his voice. "Do I need to worry about poison?"

"Umm."

"No!" Moira shouted back but added an ominous disclaimer. "Not this time."

His lips twitched. "I like her."

"Me too." I crossed an ankle over my knee and waited.

Barrett's power beat against my skin, and I took a moment to ponder if he knew what he was doing or if his magic was so immense he couldn't keep it completely contained. The thought made my heart skip a beat, and I studied him a little closer.

Moira interrupted with two steaming cups of coffee. "Poison free," she said in a too chipper voice.

He raised his mug in a salute. "Thank you."

Barrett didn't speak for a few moments. When he did, what he said took me by surprise. Hard to do these days.

"I've rented a house in Joy Springs for the next few months."

I tried and failed to keep the surprise off my face. "Oh? Any particular reason why?"

An amused smirk tipped his lips. "You."

Moira snorted from the worktable area.

I shot her a glare and chewed on the inside of my cheek as I tried to come up with a response to that one.

"I'm not sure I understand what you mean," I said after a long moment. "We've never met, and I do my best to keep my head down."

Moira snorted again.

"I get it, Moira!" I snapped.

The witch laughed out loud.

Barrett's lips twitched.

"I said I do my best," I grumbled.

He leaned forward, the coffee mug balanced on his palms. "Our people are broken and scattered across the world."

"For a long time, I thought I was the only one."

His eyes flickered. "Our numbers are low," he admitted. "We are scattered far and wide."

I noticed he didn't say what those numbers were. "You know

what the Chimeras have done to me. Why should I take you at face value?"

"You shouldn't," he said simply.

A faint smile curved his lips. "I've done my homework, Miss Quinn. You have yet to pick a fight, but you've proven victorious over everyone who's tried to engage you in conflict."

"Fuck yeah," Moira said quietly as she fist pumped under the table.

"Not without consequences," I said quietly, the memory of floating through a never-ending nothing sending a chill through my bones.

His expression sobered. "Few walk away without wounds of some kind." Barrett sipped his coffee. "I'm here only to help. You are a Chimera, Evie. Our powers are varied. While I don't know all that you are, my reports tell me you are tangled up with the fae. If you do possess fae blood and you carry the Chimera line…"

His voice trailed off. "Then your power may be endless. I'm here to show you what we can do."

"And if I don't want your help?" I knew there was still much to learn about my power, both Chimera and fae. But this man was a complete stranger, and there were few strangers bearing gifts who came without ulterior motives.

He shrugged. "Then I'll have a short sightseeing trip in Texas and return home in a week or two. No harm no foul."

My eyes narrowed, making Barrett laugh.

"I promise. You will have no quarrel with me."

"What do you want in return?"

When his eyes lit up, I felt vindicated. "I'm not marrying you," I blurted. "Or doing anything weird."

Barrett's mouth snapped shut for a long moment. A bewildered look overtook his expression. "Uh. I'm not in the market for a bride, willing or unwilling," he said slowly.

"Good. Because I have no desire to be a pawn in a game I don't understand."

He crossed his arms and eyed me, a thoughtful look on his

face. "I have a feeling Joy Springs might be an interesting place to be. For at least a little while."

Normally, this place *was* a fun, small town, but over the last six months, it had turned into a hotbed of fae and Shifter Lord drama. Only a few people knew my secret, but the more attention I brought to myself and this shop, the more likely that secret would be spilled.

If I thought I'd been in a world of trouble when I was stuck in the tree, I had a feeling it'd be nothing compared to an entire town chasing after me with fiery pitchforks. But all the activity on my land and at Caelan's Keep had begun to draw the curious.

Last week, Moira had shown me a Joy Springs gossip blog where speculation about me and the Shifter Lord ran rampant. They even had a wedding countdown clock.

Caelan asked me if I wanted him to have the writer take it down, but I declined. If we gave it any attention, people would double down and make it worse. I was all about ignoring my problems in hopes they'd go away. One thing we hadn't done was show off as a couple in town. To my surprise, Caelan was completely content to hang out at my house or the Keep, though I suspected he might like my place better.

Less demands on his time. Every once in a while, he'd smuggle Fee and Poe in, letting the raven and phoenix explore the territory to see if there was anything new to check out since the last time they'd been, though they had to keep relatively low to the canopy to avoid detection.

Fee was almost fully grown, in bird years at least. She glowed with a ferocious power that made her difficult to look at head on, though she dimmed her natural fiery glow when she wanted to be stroked.

Barrett grinned at my discomfited look. "All I want is for you to be more involved in diplomatic relations for our kind."

I blinked. "That's worse than marriage," I blurted. "Are you insane?"

"Not at all. It's time for our people to have a seat at the table."

I stared at him like he'd grown a second and third head. "Do you want me to die?"

He chuckled. "No one is going to die, Miss Quinn. Chimeras are far too powerful to die easily."

"Says you," I muttered. I'd almost died a few times since the Chimeras had come into Joy Springs. "We're the stuff of nightmares. Others use us as their bogeymen in bedtime stories."

Barrett's easy smile made me nervous. "Perhaps. But you know how we fix it?"

Moira had wandered over from the worktable and perched on the edge of the couch beside me. "If you say public relations," she drawled, "I'm going to punch you right in your pretty mouth."

A flash of teeth. "Feisty," Barrett murmured, his eyes heating as he stared at my friend.

Oh boy. Soren, the Shifter Lord currently sniffing around Moira, was going to love this development.

And I knew he'd blame me for this development.

"It's true," Barrett said after looking away from Moira. "Good PR can turn the devil into a saint."

Moira scoffed. "What about you?" She waved her hand in his direction. "You've got the look. Tall. Blond hair, blue eyes, sharp jaw. Television would love you."

"I'm a stranger to everyone here. Evie is well known."

I snorted. "Not really. Evie keeps her head down and tries to stay under the radar."

Moira patted me on the shoulder. "Tries is the right word."

"Shut it," I said under my breath.

"Everyone in this town knows you're dating the local Shifter Lord."

I shook my head. "No. They suspect. That's not the same as us popping downtown for dinner."

Barrett pierced me with his bright gaze. "Then why don't you?"

"She's shy," Moira said.

I sighed. "I'm not interested in being the face of anything, much less the Chimera awakening or whatever it is you're trying to do with your people."

"Our people," Barrett said. "And just because you don't want to doesn't mean it isn't necessary. We've been in the shadows for far too long. It's time we get a seat at the table."

It finally clicked. "You want to take power from the Lords."

Moira sucked air through her teeth.

"No," Barrett said immediately. "I'm not interested in taking power away from anyone. A single Chimera can devastate a city. We are our own power."

Ruling through fear was the worst way to stay in power. Eventually, the desire for freedom would lead to revolt.

"I see the doubt on your face. I have no desire to be feared, only the desire for a voice. That's all." Barrett rose and walked his mug over to the small sink.

Brownie point to him for washing it before he left. When he turned, he inclined his head. "I hope to hear from you." He rattled off an address and left after giving Moira a long look. "And you, too," he murmured.

The door closed behind him, and Moira sagged against me. "Man. Blonds aren't usually my thing, but he is preeeettty."

"And dangerous," I said under my breath. "That's definitely your type."

"What can I say? I have a type." She snuggled into me and inhaled.

"Stop smelling me. It's weird."

"But you smell like flowers and the outdoors. It's nice."

I ruffled her hair. Ash and Tess came out from the back.

"He smells a little bit like you," Ash remarked.

I eyed him. "I didn't know your sense of smell was that powerful."

He shrugged. "It's not. Chimeras have a specific hint of something other in their blood."

That didn't sound good. "Easily identifiable?"

It was one thing for the residents of this town to think there was something unique about my scent. But if Barrett and other Chimeras came around and revealed themselves, it would take no time for others to realize what I was. And I wasn't ready for that. I might not ever be.

"Maybe, but I've been around you for years now. It's as familiar to me as my own scent."

Moira nodded. "Ash is right. I'd recognize it, but my sense of smell is far more sensitive than either of yours. Any other shifter would find it unique but probably wouldn't peg someone who had it as a Chimera."

"Tess?"

The banshee lifted a pale shoulder. "I have a perfectly normal sense of smell unless it comes to death. You smell like Evie to me. No more, no less."

"Glad to know no one here is about to die again," Moira said.

"Give it time," I drawled. "The day is still young."

CHAPTER

Four

CAELAN

The air was cool and crisp, the scent of pine and the wild fresh in my nose. Evie's presence was a beacon to my senses, drawing me down the sidewalk and into her shop. Things were good, really good between us, and I was doing my absolute best not to fuck it up again.

Between Rowan's admonishment and Evie's disappearance into the accursed fae tree, my faith in myself and the world around me had been shaken to the core. Seeing her emerge, furious and naked, her magic, a thundering cloak around her body, made me see things in a different light and grasp at the second chance we'd been given.

But after rounding the corner and catching a glimpse of the sign hanging above her shop, something else caught my eye. A small group of men had gathered outside Little Shop of Florals, speaking in low undertones. Unfortunately for them, my hearing was keen, and I caught every word.

"I didn't expect her to be so hot," one of them whispered, a tall, lean, young…something. Not human, not shifter. He held a small bouquet of flowers in his hand. Sweat beaded at the top of his forehead, his jaw clenched with nerves.

"Yeah," said another. "She's smoking."

"I dunno, man," said a shorter, blond man. "I can feel her power signature all the way out here. I have no desire to be someone's bitch."

A frown creased my brow, but I kept walking. Maybe the witches were having one of their weird Beltane parties. Wait. No. That was in the summer. Winter solstice, then. They had copious amounts of sex at all times of the year, so maybe this one was… Yule.

Yep. Cernunnos would have a field day with this one if he happened to pop into the woods and stumbled upon a holly-themed orgy.

"Where'd you hear about her?" Another man asked. "A notice went out on social media from one of the Lord's pages."

My steps hitched. I slowed my pace and strained to listen.

"I don't know why someone that hot is having trouble finding a husband," the first one said.

My phone vibrated against my hip. I let it go to voicemail.

"I heard she has issues. Did you hear about the crazy shit with the tree?"

The blond snorted. "Gotta be hyperbole. No way a fae tree grew in the middle of a Lord's territory. Caelan would have killed her and scattered her bones."

My phone rang again.

They were talking about Evie.

"I saw some fliers posted in the local coffee shop. The dowry is enormous."

My fists clenched at my sides. I bit down my snarl of rage and stalked over.

My power reached them before I did. Every man gathered around turned.

All of them stilled, their eyes widening.

"Good afternoon, Lord," one of them said. "I'm surprised to see you away from the Keep."

"Are you speaking of Evie Quinn?" My voice came out rough, the wolf vibrating in my tone.

The dark haired one swallowed. "Yes. She put out a notice looking for a husband." He gestured to all of them. "We're all unmated and unmarried."

I could destroy every single man standing here and they knew it. One took a larger step back. "I'm out."

He spun on his heel and hurried down the sidewalk. Smart man.

"Evie Quinn is unavailable. She has never been on a search for a husband and is romantically entangled with someone else."

The blond, less intelligent than the others, snorted. "She's still unmarried. There's still a chance."

The dark-haired man's eyes flickered. "Mind if I ask who she's involved with?"

My smile was a thing full of teeth and violence. "Me."

A short nod from him. He held up his hands and gave me a sheepish smile. "I had no idea. No offense meant, Lord."

"Leave," I snarled.

Even the blond hauled ass away.

Goddammit. When I found out who was responsible for this, I'd tear them limb from limb.

I felt Caelan's fury before he entered the shop. Petals fell from my hands as I rose, grabbing a towel to wipe away the debris before hurrying toward the door.

I didn't get there in time. Caelan entered in a whirlwind of rage, his ever-changing eyes sweeping the shop before falling on me.

"Caelan?"

He stalked toward me, eyes glowing golden. One hand snagged around my waist, and he hauled me against him, lips claiming me in a fiery kiss.

My brain short-circuited. When we came up for air, his eyes had reverted to their normal stormy gray. He touched his forehead to mine. "Hi."

I blinked up at him, touching my lips with my fingers, unable to come up with a single word for that greeting.

Moira let out a wolf whistle. "I wish I had someone greeting me like that at work."

"No kidding," Ash grumbled. "What the hell, Caelan? Is everything alright?"

"Any of you heard about a dowry concerning Evie?"

The term made my brow furrow. Wasn't a dowry for a bride?

"A dowry?" Moira laughed. "Are we in the Victorian age or something?"

I took a step back. "Is that why you're so angry?"

His posture vibrated with tension. "Several men were outside discussing social media posts and fliers announcing you're in the market for a husband."

I burst out laughing.

"From your reaction, I suppose there's nothing you want to tell me." Caelan's lips twitched.

I stepped closer and brought him into a hug. "If I haven't married you by now, I can't imagine I'd marry anyone else."

He rubbed a hand over his face. "Gods," he muttered. "The Lords are at it again."

"I don't know why I'm such a hot commodity for them."

"You've been very clear about them leaving you alone," Caelan said. He shook his head. "Let me do some digging. I'll get to the bottom of things."

"They were waiting outside?" Moira asked.

Caelan nodded. "One of them had flowers."

Ash let out a shout of laughter.

"What kind of flowers?" I asked.

Caelan's eyes narrowed.

"What?" I said innocently. "There's a big difference between carnations and dahlias."

Moira grinned. "She's right. Carnations say fast food. Dahlias say fine dining."

"I don't know what kind of flowers he had. If they're smart, they're on the way out of town as we speak."

"Ooh," Moira said. "Your Lord got all alpha on them."

But Caelan had stopped listening. He sat up a little straighter, a tinge of gold in his eyes. His nostrils flared. "Who's been here today?"

"Besides Evie's harem?" Ash asked.

Caelan's hot glare made Ash's mouth snap shut.

I lay a hand on his arm. "He's talking about Barrett."

"He's…" His voice trailed off. "Like you."

I nodded. "He wants to bring the Chimeras out into the open."

"He wasn't here for the dowry?"

I rolled my eyes. "Not at all. He had eyes for Moira, though."

The vampire wiggled her eyebrows. "Sure did. Blonds aren't my thing, but I might give him a spin around the block and see if he can back up all that delicious power swimming in his veins."

I stared at my friend for a long moment. "Gross."

Moira cackled. She ruffled my hair and rose from the couch arm. "I'll be in back finishing up the new holiday arrangements. Don't leave before you come chat."

She blew a kiss at Caelan and went to the back. Tess floated to the register, and Ash went over to his workstation and settled in. His new project was a magnolia bonsai. I knew how to manipulate flora, but Ash's realm was trees. He'd been working on this one for months now, and every once in a while, he'd mutter fiery curses under his breath about stupid magnolias and their stupid, high-maintenance roots.

When I saw that particular bonsai on his table, I stayed away.

"Want some coffee?" I asked Caelan.

"Always."

I fixed us both a cup and handed him one. He'd sat down on the sofa and patted the space next to him. "Slow day?"

"Lunch is always a little slow. We'll pick up after two."

He checked his phone. "Good. I'll stay for a little while if that's okay."

"It's always okay."

He flashed me a gorgeous grin that pulled at my heart. "I want to bring Seymour and Hannah by this week if you don't mind."

"They're always welcome too. How are they doing?"

"If plants could mate, I'd guess Seymour and Hannah are about to get married." He shook his head and chuckled. "I can't move them apart without him trying to take a bite out of me."

"Aww. They're happy." I'd made the Venus flytrap in a fit of pique after Caelan pissed me off. But Seymour was no regular flytrap. I'd modified his traps to produce a paralytic that could take a shifter down in less than a minute, and he'd used it to take several shifters down, Caelan included.

But Seymour's occasionally bloodthirsty nature spoke to Caelan's, and to my surprise, now the two were…friends, as much as someone could be friends with a sentient plant.

I'd made Hannah for Caelan's boutonniere and toned her nature down a notch. She still had violent tendencies, but she had a sweeter nature than Seymour, something the male flytrap seemed to gravitate to.

"They keep sneaking out of the Keep. Garrett caught them once, Simone the next time. I caught them the third, right as they made it to the property line." Caelan grinned. "Pretty sure Poe and Fee are helping those little escape artists."

"How'd you get them to stop?" I curled my feet onto the sofa and soaked up his warmth. He ran several degrees hotter than me. Sitting beside him felt like cuddling up to a crackling fire.

"I had to promise visitation. Twice a week, they're coming over to visit you."

I laughed. "They're welcome to stay longer if they want."

"Is this how divorced parents feel? Seymour and Hannah go to you three days a week and stay at the Keep for four."

"Yes, well, you can come with them and stay if you want."

Caelan's chuckle sent shivers down my spine. "I like that idea even better."

I rose and whispered in his ear. "But you have to learn to be quiet. Honestly, Caelan. You're so *loud*."

He nipped my nose with his teeth. "Vicious woman."

The bell rang, and seconds later, three young women came in giggling over a private joke. One glanced over and spotted Caelan sitting next to me and gasped.

"Lord Caelan!" She was short, blonde, and curvy, and from the smile she bestowed on Caelan, very, very interested. "I'm so surprised to see you here."

Her gaze flicked over me and dismissed me in the same second. Anger sparked in my belly.

Caelan's expression didn't change. "I'm here all the time. My girlfriend owns the place."

I sucked in a soft gasp. *Girlfriend.* It felt right and wrong all at the same time.

When the girl's eyes widened, I held up my hand and wiggled my fingers at her in a mocking wave.

"I'm Evie," I said. "Welcome to Little Shop of Florals. Tess can help you if you're looking for anything in particular. I'm on break for another fifteen minutes."

Her eyes tightened at my abrupt dismissal.

One of the other girls, a shorter redhead, pressed her lips together and took a step away from the blonde, her eyes sparkling with amusement. "My mom's birthday is coming up. I'll ask Tess for help."

The other girl tugged on the blonde's elbow. "Come on, Courtney. Let's look around."

For a moment, I thought Courtney was about to make a terrible mistake, but eventually she turned and followed the redhead deeper into the store as Tess showed her the bouquet options.

"Girlfriend?" I murmured.

Caelan tugged me closer. "Weird word," he agreed. "You're so much more to me than just a girlfriend. I'll come up with a better word."

"What do you want me to call you?"

Caelan stilled, and for a moment I thought I'd said the wrong thing. "Flower girl, you can call me whatever you want."

I glanced up at him and narrowed my eyes. "Why are you being intentionally vague?"

He lowered his voice. "Evie, the moment you want to make this permanent, I'll fly in a minister and have you married within the hour. In the meantime, you can call me whatever you want."

"You always have a way with words." I squeezed his bicep. "Must be part of the required Shifter Lord training."

"Yes. Romance 101 is required coursework before we get our diplomas."

"I bet you were an A student."

Caelan grinned, making my heart skip a beat. "I'll show you exactly what kind of pupil I was later."

I snorted. "Want a refill before I have to get back to work?"

He took my cup and rose. "I'll get it. Half?"

I nodded and watched him walk away, which was one of my favorite things to do.

Things were good. Really good.

The dowry thing was weird, but I'd take a marriage proposal over attempted murder any day.

CHAPTER
Six

Caelan left after his second cup of coffee, saying goodbye with a kiss so scorching, Moira screamed she was going to get the fire extinguisher to break us apart. When the door shut behind him, I let out a satisfied sigh.

Moira came up behind me and propped her head on my shoulder. "I'm glad you're happy," she said softly.

"I am."

"Caelan seems to have gotten his shit together."

I laughed. "He hasn't asked me to marry him in months."

"Oh noes," Moira said lightly. "He must be cheating on you."

I swatted at her face. "He knows it makes me nervous."

"As it should. Proposals should happen once and only once. It loses its meaning if the guy keeps popping out from corners trying to rope you into matrimony."

"He wasn't quite a jack-in-the-box," I said, feeling the need to defend him. Caelan had gotten grumbly and possessive, but he'd turned over a new leaf after I almost died.

Moira grunted and craned her neck to keep watching Caelan. "Damn, Evie. Give that ass a nice smack for me tonight."

"It is a nice ass," I said wistfully.

"Can you please stop talking?" Tess muttered. "You're grossing me out."

Moira grinned and walked over to Tess to ruffle her pale hair. "One day you, too, will ogle your boyfriend as he walks away."

"I like the front better," she said in a serious tone. "My neck would hurt from looking down all the time."

"That's just part of the fun, dear," Moira said.

Ash finally raised his head from the bonsai and made his way over to us, stopping abruptly when we all shut up. He huffed a breath. "You're either talking about me or sex."

"Can't we be talking about both?" Moira said and batted her eyes.

Ash snorted and made himself a cup of coffee. "I don't like the look in your eyes. What are you planning?"

"Moi?" She lay a hand over her chest and let her eyes go wide. "Absolutely nothing."

"Mm hmm." He turned and leaned against the wall. "Do you need an alibi?"

Moira straightened. "Are you willing to give us one?"

"Us?" I asked, not having a clue what was going on.

"Depends on how bad it gets." Ash grinned at Moira's crestfallen look. He leaned over and tugged on a lock of her dark hair. "Of course I'll give you an alibi, but I hope after all these years I wouldn't have to. If you can't sneak in, screw shit up, and get out again without getting caught, are you even half the vampire you claim to be?"

Moira sniffed. "I don't claim to be anything other than what I am."

"Where are we screwing shit up at?" I asked.

"First, we need to go track down some of those fliers or online chat rooms announcing you're in the market for a husband. Then we need to find a witch."

I snorted. "You can throw a stone out the front door and hit a witch."

"A good one. Someone who can create a failproof locator spell."

My eyebrows lifted. "You want to go after the Lords." I mulled the thought over and decided I liked the idea.

"Quietly," she corrected. "I want to inconvenience the hell out of them. Nothing harmful, especially since you and Caelan are on steadier ground. We can't risk jeopardizing his position."

I chewed on my lip. "I can't use my magic. They'll know."

All the Lords recognized my magic and would peg me for the culprit the second they stepped outside. Plus, how many Floromancers angry at the Lords were currently walking around?

None.

"You won't have to," Moira said, eyes sparkling as she grinned. "I'll meet you at your house tonight at nine. You don't need to worry about anything other than bringing snacks."

"Can I come?" Tess asked.

"Absolutely. Bring a thermos of coffee."

"Done." Tess floated away, and Moira and I pretended not to notice Ash watching her.

Right before closing time, a delivery man carrying a long white box showed up. On her way out, Moira held the door open.

"Evie Quinn?" he asked.

She pointed in my direction. "At the register." One of her eyebrows went up. "You got it, Evie?"

I waved her away. "See you later."

She grinned. "Can't wait!"

He set the box on top of the desk and pushed a clipboard and pen over. "Please sign."

I frowned at the label on the box. "Someone is delivering flowers to a flower shop?"

The address was from the next town over, a small outfit run by a human. They did good work, but I hadn't a clue why they'd be delivering something to my place.

"I just drop the boxes," the man said, his expression flickering with annoyance. "Sign so I can get out of here."

I blinked. "Busy day, I take it?"

His lips thinned.

"Fine," I grabbed the pen and scrawled my name. "You win more flowers with honey, not vinegar."

"Good thing I don't give a shit about flowers," he said as he snatched the clipboard.

Ash barked a laugh.

The delivery guy gave him a little salute and sailed out the door.

I didn't say anything for a moment as I tried to wrap my head around the guy's behavior. "Yeesh," I muttered. "That guy was sour."

"Everyone's a little sour these days," Ash said, clipping off a tiny piece of a maple bonsai he was working on.

"True."

"What'd you get?"

"Something from a flower shop."

Ash's brow furrowed. He set his scissors down and came to stand beside me. "Now I'm curious."

"Me too." I reached for the box opener and cut the tape.

"Did you make them mad?"

I laughed. "Not that I'm aware of."

"Good." Ash touched the box. "I don't sense anything other than…flowers." He shook his head. "What in the world?"

"Exactly. What can they send me that I don't already have?"

The arrangement was wrapped in pretty white and gold tissue paper. A card in a heavy vellum envelope lay on top. I opened it and read the message.

"It might be cheesy to send flowers to a florist, but a little birdie told me it would be a great idea!"

"Noooo," Ash said, voice laced with horror. He put a hand over his chest and closed his eyes.

The note was signed *Your Secret Admirer*.

"If those are carnations, we're taking everything outside, including the box, and burning it." He shuddered. "Then we're going to sage the shop."

I snorted. "Anyone who knows me wouldn't dare send me carnations."

"A peasant flower."

"Ash!" I snickered. "Carnations get a bad rap, but they're a versatile flower and perfect for spring arrangements."

"This announcement brought to you by Big Carnation."

Shaking my head at his antics, I unwrapped the tissue paper.

To our mutual horror, a large bouquet of wilted roses and dyed carnations lay before us.

Ash's chest rumbled with laughter. "You should put this online and shame the poor bastard who thought this was a good idea."

I sighed and took the poor arrangement from the box. "It's not the flower's fault."

Holding them up to the light, I frowned. "These guys are in rough shape. I'll put them in some water and let them live out their natural life cycle."

"In the back, I hope?"

I laughed. "In the back. I might be a Floromancer, but I do have taste."

Once the arrangement was heavily watered and resting in a vase, I grabbed the rest of my stuff and headed out.

"Don't stay too late," I called to Ash as I was about to walk out. "There's more to life than work."

He waved me away, not even looking up from his bonsai.

Sympathy rolled through me. Tess had broken something within him. While I didn't think the two were ever end game, this might have been his first real heartbreak. Though I didn't fault Tess for not being as broken up as he was about the situation. Ash couldn't accept her as she was, and she had every right to move on as she saw fit.

I just hoped he'd stop beating himself up over how he'd handled things and move on, too.

A STRANGE CAR sat in my driveway. Rowan's guard, a young shifter, was long gone, pulled back by the Lord after my disappearance and never restored to duty. He was a good kid, but I liked keeping my private life private. In times like this, though, I missed having my own personal alarm.

The car was sleek and silver, the windows tinted too dark to see inside. While my senses were better than average, in human form I was somewhat limited. I could smell nothing but gravel from the driveway and the coolant dripping from the bottom of the vehicle.

Carefully pulling my magic taut in anticipation of a strike, I slid out of my vehicle and leaned against the driver's side door, waiting for the stranger to show themselves.

I didn't have to wait long. The top of a dark head revealed itself moments later, coalescing into a handsome but dangerous stranger.

A shifter of some kind, based upon the golden tinge ringing his eyes, but no Lord I'd seen before. Caelan would have told me if they'd replaced Donovan. But since we'd found out he was still alive, would they have done that already?

I crossed my arms over my chest and stayed silent.

A slight tug of the man's lips as he came around the car from the passenger's side.

Having a driver pegged him as either important or wealthy, the two not always related. I withheld judgment.

"Miss Quinn?" He wore a suit, light gray with a white button down underneath it, no tie. Dark belt, dark shoes, and, thankfully, socks, which meant I could take him at least partway seriously. There wasn't a man on earth I'd take seriously if he wore pants without socks. Fifty-fifty on the no-show socks.

Then again, it was winter, and the suit was too close to white. Maybe I'd judge him a little until I figured out why he was here.

"Depends on who's asking," I answered.

A flash of teeth, the amusement there and gone. "My name is Dario Sanchez. I'm here to introduce myself to you."

"Why?"

"Right to the point. Refreshing." He leaned against his vehicle, an action that took me by surprise. He didn't care if he got his fancy, pressed suit dirty. "I'm in the running for Donovan's former position, though my intel has given way to an...odd rumor."

"Oh?" Another new Lord. Goody.

He tilted his head and studied me. Dario was, like most shifters, very pretty. Olive skin, green-dominant hazel eyes, full lips, high cheekbones. Tall and with a swimmer's build, and a mop of unruly dark hair, Dario looked like he walked off the set of one of those circa 2000s teen dramas. Too pretty for my taste. I liked my men a little less polished and a lot more dangerous.

"You're a Floromancer, yes?"

"You're a stranger on my property, Mr. Sanchez—"

"Dario, please."

"Dario, you're a stranger to me. I'm not in the habit of telling strangers anything. And don't you know it's rude to ask someone about their magical heritage?"

He snorted. "They told me you could be prickly."

Anger sparked in my veins. "Insult me at your peril, *Dario*."

Brighter gold flashed around the ring of his iris. "Feisty," he murmured. "I see now why you've won the heart of a Lord."

"You've got about five seconds before I throw you and your fancy car off my land," I said in a low growl.

He laughed, the sound low and husky. "Forgive me, Miss Quinn."

I did not tell him he could call me Evie, so at least he wasn't reaching too far for informality.

"I'm here because you appear to have claimed Donovan's territory."

"And if I have?"

"I'm here to see what it will take for you to give it back."

I blinked. "Um. You aren't a Lord yet. Why are we discussing this?"

"My appointment is merely a formality. I hope you understand how stepping into a Lord's position without full dominion of his assigned territory could be detrimental to their rule."

"The Lord's problems have nothing to do with me. I claimed his land because I'm more powerful and the land responded to me."

His eyebrows flicked up with surprise. "Interesting." He crossed his arms over his chest. "Donovan's lack of strength aside, do you believe you are more powerful than the other Lords?"

I sighed. "I have no idea, nor do I care. I've asked the Lords multiple times to leave me alone, and they continually fail."

His eyes sparked with amusement. "And if they did succeed in leaving you alone?"

"I'd throw a big ass party." Adjusting my purse over my shoulder, I pushed off the car. "If you'll excuse me, I need to start dinner."

"Is Caelan coming over?"

"If you ask me another question like that," I warned, "I'll show you exactly how powerful I am."

Dario's laugh followed me all the way inside.

A shiver of trepidation crawled up my spine. Even as I watched his car pulling out of my driveway, I had a feeling the potential Lord was not finished with me.

Great. One new thing to worry about.

CHAPTER
Seven

Moira arrived right at nine p.m., dressed like a sexy cat burglar. Her long, dark hair was tucked into a beanie, and she wore little makeup. Black leather pants, a black turtleneck, and black lace-up boots completed her look, but she carried a black puffer jacket and a pair of leather gloves.

She sniffed the air as soon as I opened the door. "Is that Bolognese?"

"I kept it warm for you."

She pecked me on the cheek and dropped her stuff on the bench by the door before hurrying to the kitchen. Moira didn't say another word until she was half finished with her dinner. "I want this recipe."

I blinked. "I'm not sure if I should be happy you want to cook or upset that you won't be coming over to steal my food."

She waved her fork at me. "I shall always endeavor to steal dinner from your house, but you have Caelan now, and it might be awkward if you two are otherwise…engaged."

Moira wiggled her eyebrows and shoved another bite into her mouth.

I ignored that. "Who are we starting with?"

"I figured we could pay Thorvin back first. There are three

potions inside my backpack. They'll last two hours until we're forced back here."

My brows lifted. I wasn't surprised she'd finagled two teleporting potions, but they must have cost her an arm and a leg. "How—"

She held up her hand. "Don't ask. Just enjoy the moment. We need to leave our cell phones behind for plausible deniability, but I brought two burners."

"Of course you did."

Moira winked. "You ready to go?"

I glanced down at my dark clothing. My attire was less form-fitting but would do the trick for staying hidden. "Just waiting on Tess and the coffee. Snacks are in the bag by the door."

"Awesome."

A thought occurred to me. "I don't think Tess needs a potion, does she?"

Moira shrugged. "Don't want to assume. We can ask when she gets here."

The doorbell rang a few seconds later, but before I could get to the door, a semi-transparent head poked in.

"I'll never get used to that," Moira shuddered.

"Come on in," I called.

Tess started to enter but jerked abruptly as something hard clunked against the other side of the door. She tried again, only to clunk once more.

"Stupid thermos," she muttered. With a sigh, she disappeared and rang the doorbell.

Moira cackled.

Shaking my head, I opened the door. "Still haven't figured out how to take items with you?"

"Stainless steel continues to elude me. I can take flowers and animals, and I once was able to transport a roll of toilet paper, but steel is proving tricky."

"You nailed toilet paper," Moira said dryly, "what else is left?

It's the hottest commodity during an apocalypse, so you'd be fine."

"Just not hydrated," I added. "Which might make the point of toilet paper moot."

Tess stared at us. "I don't have to pee in my other form."

"Also making the toilet paper a moot point," Moira said.

I snorted. "Want some dinner?"

I peeked at the pan to make sure Moira left some. Not much, but enough to scrape up a small serving.

"No thanks. I had a date tonight."

Moira's mouth dropped open. "You did? Who? Where?"

Tess sank onto my couch and shook her head. "I want to keep it private for now."

Moira blinked. "What? You tell us everything! Now you're gatekeeping your date?"

I lay a hand on Moira's arm.

"I don't tell you everything," Tess said quietly. "You just talk enough for everyone."

I put a hand over my mouth to hide my smile.

"Tess!" Moira shoved a bite in her mouth and chewed furiously.

"Don't feel like you have to tell us anything." I shot Moira a quelling look. "Everything is still brand new." I gave her a hopeful smile. "But I hope if things progress, we'll have the opportunity to meet him."

Tess nodded. "If things progress."

Moira's nostrils flared, but she stayed silent, shoving food in her mouth as if to keep herself from saying something she shouldn't.

"Also," Tess said. "There's someone in the driveway. I saw him when I popped into the back."

My lips thinned. "I need to extend the wards again." Doing so would be a pain in the ass for deliveries, but random strangers dropping by unannounced these days might be worse.

"Could you tell who it was?"

She shook her head. "Male. That's all."

"Was he doing anything suspicious?"

"Nope." Tess yawned. "Leaning against your vehicle."

Moira scraped up the last of her Bolognese and washed her plate. "Ready when you are. Since someone is out there, using the potions would be suspicious. Let's go out and greet him first."

"Potions?" Tess yawned again and stood.

"You alright?" Moira asked. "Yawning does not signal an exciting start to a nighttime heist."

Tess blushed.

"Oooh," Moira said. "Maybe more went down than just dinner." She made a production of checking the time on her phone. "All before 9:30?"

Tess's blush deepened. "This is why I don't tell you anything," she grumbled.

Moira laughed and slung an arm across Tess's shoulders. "Good for you, banshee."

I grabbed the bag of snacks on the way out. As soon as I got halfway across the yard, I knew who was leaning against my car.

"Shit," I said under my breath. "It's Garrett."

Moira cursed softly. "We're going foraging."

"I don't have my basket."

"You're carrying a bag."

"Yes," I agreed, "but it's not my basket."

Moira let out an annoyed huff. "Can we pretend just this once that you aren't a neurotic weirdo and maybe pretend the bag is where we'll stick the imaginary mushrooms?"

"But it's not my basket," I whispered.

"For fuck's sake," she muttered.

Garrett pushed away from the car as we got closer. "Going somewhere?" he drawled.

Caelan's Second and I didn't get along too well, though things had thawed somewhat once he'd been put in charge of Thalia, a young and slightly odd Seer. Thawed, as in I didn't grow irrationally angry every time I saw him these days, and only because Thalia drove him batshit insane, which was fun to watch.

"Foraging," Moira said before I could say something stupid.

"Takes three of you, does it?" His eyes flicked to my canvas bag and back up to my face. "Where's your basket?"

"See?" I hissed.

Garrett's eyes glowed with amusement.

Moira's teeth clenched. "Goddammit, Evie. Can you be normal just once?"

"No," Garrett said solemnly. "She cannot. Your Floromancer always takes her basket when she forages because, and I quote, 'it's wide and flat on the bottom and has these little pegs built into the wicker so I can add a little shelf on for a double decker carry home.'"

"Okay, Rain Man," Moira muttered. "I'm ashamed as your BFF that I didn't notice quite how fucking weird you are."

I sniffed. "Then I trust you can see how this is on you. Double decker baskets are extremely hard to come by."

Moira shook her head. "What do you want, Garrett?"

"Who's the target?"

Silence fell.

Garrett sighed. "I know you're going after the Lords. Who's first?"

Moira's eyes narrowed. "Shouldn't you be more interested in plausible deniability?"

He scoffed. "I'm trying to keep you idiots from getting caught or killed."

"How'd you know?" she asked.

"Thalia," I said with a groan. "She's really getting in the way of our shenanigans."

Garrett nodded, his smile holding an edge of malice. "She foresaw tonight going one of two ways."

I gave my bag a mournful look. "Damn. I packed awesome snacks, too."

Tess shook her thermos. "And I brought Mexican coffee. It's caffeinated and sweet enough to put hair on our chest."

Moira snorted. "If we're going to get caught, why do you need to know who our target is?"

Garrett let out a resigned sigh. "Because Thalia saw if I went with you, things would go differently."

"And if we stayed home?" I asked.

His eyes flickered. "All I can say is don't stay home tonight."

I stilled. "Is something going to happen?"

Garrett grimaced. "I'm sworn to secrecy. It's nothing bad, just annoying, and Caelan will react…poorly."

I shook my head. "You'd rather we antagonize a Lord rather than let Caelan get annoyed?"

Garrett lifted a shoulder. "I like the other Lords about as much as you do. And," he said, his focus turning to Moira, "a little birdie told me you've managed to secure three extremely rare potions, and I want to know how you did it."

Moira's eyes narrowed. "You agree to help us escape notice, no matter what we want to do, and I'll tell you how I acquired said potions."

Garrett's nostrils flared. "Do you plan on killing anyone?"

I scoffed. "I am not a murderer!"

Lots of raised eyebrows.

"Fair enough," I grumbled. "I don't murder anyone who isn't actively trying to murder me first."

"No murders on the agenda," Moira said. "I can't make a firm promise because the night is still young, but I subscribe to Evie's philosophy. If no one tries to murder us, we won't try to murder them."

Garrett shook his head. "I've never in my life met such a chaotic bunch of goblins."

Tess let out a warbling sigh. "You get used to it."

"You're one to talk," Moira said. "Didn't you possess someone not too long ago and tear them apart from the inside out?"

Tess fidgeted nervously. "They deserved it."

"Exactly," Moira and I said at the same time.

Garrett scrubbed a hand over his face. "Fine. We try our absolute best not to murder anyone, and you tell me how you got the potions. Deal?"

Moira stuck out a pale hand. "Deal."

"Thorvin is first."

Garrett's brows drew together. "Seriously? I thought it'd be Ethan."

I glanced at Moira, willing her with my eyes not to reveal what we'd discovered about Ethan and Donovan. "He's right. Why aren't we hitting him first?"

"You have a lot to learn about the art of anticipation," Moira said. "We hit Thorvin first and Ethan will get antsy. People do hilarious things when they're nervous." She wiggled her eyebrows. "Then we hit Soren."

"Should we hit Soren?" I asked. "Rowan is not on the list, and Soren has been decent. So far."

"She's right," Garrett said. "Soren is as much of an ally as he can be."

"What about that Dario guy?" I asked.

Garrett's attention sharpened. "What do you know about Dario?"

"He stopped by for a visit."

Garrett swore. "Caelan will be furious. Does he know?"

"I haven't talked to him since I got home." We all left our cells in the house. Tess was the only one without one, but she could pop in and out wherever she wanted, so it was less important she carried a phone.

"Who's this Dario?" Moira asked. "Is he hot?"

"They're all hot," I said with an eyeroll. "He seemed alright, though he was nosy as all get out."

"What did he want?" Garrett gestured for my bag.

I frowned but handed it over. The shifter pawed through it and pulled out a fresh chocolate chip cookie.

"Info about Donovan's former territory."

His chewing paused. "He knows you claimed the area."

I nodded.

"Someone's talking when they shouldn't be." He took another bite. "These are good. I'd like to add a dozen of these to our deal."

I rolled my eyes. "I make them for Caelan all the time. He just doesn't know how to share."

"My own dozen," Garrett emphasized. "One I don't have to share with my boss."

"Can we go?" Tess said. "I'm tired."

"One does not attend a heist tired," Moira lectured. "You attend one hopped up on substances and ready for vengeance."

Tess gave her a dark look and stayed silent.

Moira grinned and reached into her backpack. She handed me a glass bottle filled with a shimmering blue liquid.

"Do you need one?" she asked Tess.

"No, but I'll pop into the place where Thorvin is, so if he's not home, I'll need his address so I can make sure I'm in the right place."

"Banshees have an inner GPS," Garrett mused. "Cool."

Moira rattled off Thorvin's home address. "Got it?"

Tess nodded. "See you there."

A second later she was gone.

Moira handed the third bottle to Garrett. "Bottoms up."

She uncapped hers and downed it in one go.

Shrugging, I did the same. When in Rome, right?

I t took a while for my stomach to finish emptying. Garrett wasn't in much better shape.

"Fucking hell," he growled, struggling to stand. "What was in that shit?"

Moira must be built differently because she sat with her back against a large oak tree, completely unruffled by her interdimensional travel or whatever the hell we'd just gone through.

I felt like every cell in my body had exploded like a supernova, then reknit itself, leaving out a few pieces. The world was still spinning, and I kept my face focused on a small white stone, hoping I wouldn't throw up again.

"Wimps," Moira said, not an ounce of sympathy in her tone.

"You suck," I groaned. "Why didn't you warn us?"

She lifted a shoulder in a careless shrug. "It was my first time using the magic, too. I had no idea what would happen."

Untested magic. Awesome.

Garrett was the first to sit up. "Two dozen cookies," he muttered.

"Don't talk about food," I wheezed. "I might hurl again."

Time slowed as the world slowly righted itself and I could take a full breath in without wanting to lose what little of my dinner was left. I sat up with a soft groan.

"Alright, mastermind," I said. "What's the plan?"

Moira wiggled her fingers. "I've been dying to test something new I've been working on. We try that first, then I thought we could do some old-fashioned sabotage. How long does it take for the scent of your magic to fade?"

I thought about it. "Depends on what it is. If I leave anything behind like new growth or seeds, it could take days to fade."

Moira's eyes gleamed. "What if you took out some pipes the old-fashioned way?"

I thought about it. "You mean like using some roots to tear some drainage up or something?"

Moira grinned. "Yup." She pointed across the large expanse of land. "There are two promising culprits not too far from the house."

I squinted as I searched. A large oak stood proudly on the left side of the house, and someone who was obviously very bad at gardening had planted wisteria less than ten feet from the right side.

Not just wisteria. "Chinese wisteria," I whispered, a slow grin sliding over my face. "I may not have to do too much at all if the stuff is true to form." But something didn't look quite right. "Why is it blooming in the middle of winter?"

Garrett answered my question before I could send a trickle of power out to see what was going on. "Thorvin pays to keep his gardens magically enhanced. He likes green spaces but has a brown thumb." He sighed. "You sure you want to do this? Thorvin isn't a bad sort."

"He a friend of yours?" Moira asked.

Garrett snorted. "Fuck no, but he's the least worst."

"Rousing endorsement," I drawled. "I'll look and see where those roots are. Since he's paid someone to keep the wisteria alive during the winter, I may not have to do anything at all. The root system will keep growing and it's probably already far closer to the house than it should be." I may have to give just a nudge and let natural chaos take over.

"Give me the chance to check his security first before you go into view. He's a Lord, and they're all paranoid fuckers."

Without waiting for a response, Garrett crept away.

Moira watched him with bright eyes. "His intensity is kinda hot."

"Don't you dare seduce Caelan's second. We're just now in a place where we aren't tiptoeing around each other like nervous cats."

"For the record," Moira drawled, "Caelan was never nervous around you. The opposite, in fact. He wanted to eat you alive."

"Still does," Tess said from behind us.

I let out a quiet screech. Moira jerked.

"Tess!" she hissed. "A little warning next time."

"Sorry," she whispered. "Thorvin is at a bookstore downtown. I waited around to see if he was going to head anywhere else, but there's some kind of signing going on. He'll be there for a while."

"The Lord reads?" I frowned. Caelan had mentioned Thorvin was the scholar of our group. Guilt settled in. I opened my mouth, but Moira put her hand on my face.

"Nope. We're here, and we owe that douchebag some payback over him throwing you to the wolves."

I grimaced. "Titania held them all in sway, Moira. Maybe we should—"

"I'm with Moira," Tess said. "Titania's powers were suggestive. If Thorvin wasn't already on the fence about what to do, he never would have allowed what happened."

Moira blinked owlishly. "Tess on my side? Will wonders never cease?"

I stared at the banshee, feeling oddly empty. "I don't know Thorvin, but knowing that hurts more than I thought it would."

"Good," Moira said. "You ready?"

In the distance, Garrett crept through the landscape, slowly making his way back to us.

I squared my shoulders. "Yup. Let's do it."

The shifter gestured for us to follow. We crept back to the edge of the woods.

"Cameras everywhere and two sentries patrolling."

"Child's play," Moira said.

He gave her a quelling look. "I can't be caught prowling any closer to the property without causing problems for Caelan." He pointed toward the front door. "Come in from the east and stop right behind that maple."

I spotted the maple in question.

"Does your magic work long distance?"

Moira grimaced. "Not as well as Evie's, but I can do a few things."

Color me curious. Moira rarely used much magic around the shop and played coy when I asked questions about what she could do. But lately, I was catching the odd…resonance from Moira, a hint of power I'd never sensed before. The magic was intermittent, and sometimes I thought I'd imagined the feeling, but I'd brought it up once and Moira shut my questions down immediately.

Something was going on.

Tonight I might find out what it was.

Garrett eyed her. "Vampires are good at blending in. Can you get closer without catching the camera's eye?"

A slow smile curved her lips. "I intend to find out."

Garrett's answering smile made me very nervous.

Tess's form went transparent. "What do you want me to do?"

"Keep an eye out for the sentries," Garrett said before Moira could speak. "You won't show up on the camera very well as long as you stay in that form."

"Good idea," I said. "I'll investigate the wisteria roots."

"Wait until the last minute before you trigger any disasters," Moira whispered. "I'll be back in a few minutes."

With a wink she was gone.

CHAPTER
Nine

MOIRA

I rarely used my vampiric powers. In a town like Joy Springs, there was little need. Evie got into enough trouble for both of us, and she always managed to get herself out without my help. Now was my chance to sow a little chaos into the world as payback for what he'd done to Evie.

And to me.

I moved through the yard like a wraith, speed flooding my veins. If the camera picked up anything at all, it would be short flashes of light streaking through the property. I stopped behind the maple and studied the lay of the land, picking out the best place to get inside the house.

This was part of the plan I hadn't told her about. Thorvin wouldn't know what would hit him immediately, but the next time he told a lie, well…

Things might get awfully shiny.

Satisfaction burned through my veins. A flicker of pale silver appeared from the corner of my eye. Tess waved frantically.

I took a deep breath and sped through the yard, a flash of light in the quiet night, and gripped one of the wooden posts on the porch. One long leap later, I landed on the roof, the soft thump as quiet as I could be. I hurried to one of the upper windows, tucked my hand in my jacket, and punched a hole through the glass.

A moment later, I was inside Thorvin's house.

I reached into my pocket and palmed the small container of enchanted glitter.

Show time.

CHAPTER
Ten

Garrett swore under his breath when he spotted Moira breaking into Thorvin's house.

"That wasn't part of the plan."

I gave him a look. "There is no plan when Moira gets involved."

I sank onto the ground and put my fingers in the earth. "Give me a moment."

"Take your time," Garrett said dryly, "there's nothing at stake here."

I rolled my eyes. "If you don't stop talking, I'm telling Caelan on you."

"He owes me a fucking medal for dealing with you," he muttered.

"Same." I closed my eyes and sent a tendril of magic deep into the earth, safe from a shifter's keen sense of smell. Thorvin's land was content, and I had to give the Lord some credit. He used no chemicals to maintain his gardens, only hard work and the occasional spell to keep things healthy during the winter.

But...the Chinese wisteria was a rookie move. I could do nothing, and the end result would be the same. Thorvin would have a very expensive problem on his hands. Wisteria, no matter what type, has fragrant flowers, but the Chinese type smells glorious. The tradeoff being the plant is invasive as hell, known to tear up foundations and pipes if left to its own devices.

That's why if you do plant the thing, you always place the bush at least fifteen feet away from any underground lines or pipes. Thorvin had not done so and was about to learn an expensive lesson, nudged along by yours truly.

Invasive roots were less than six inches from his pipes, and some had stretched even closer to the foundation. The pipes would fall first, but he might have another few years before they messed with the house's foundation. The oak on the other hand…

I kept one thread there and sent another seeking for the oak. A chuckle bubbled from my lips. Thorvin already had foundation damage from the tree. If he had tile in his house, in one to two months' time, it might sound like gunshots as the tile popped loose from the grout.

I was cooking with grease tonight. All I had to do was wait on Moira now.

Once she was back, I could let loose a little mayhem and we could get out of here.

"Target acquired?" Garrett murmured.

He stood above me, slightly to the right, his gaze locked on the house.

"I won't have to do much. Thorvin's landscapers are inexperienced.

"The oak?"

"And the wisteria. The oak has already done its work. The wisteria is close."

He glanced down at me. "Think you can do it with no one the wiser?"

I grinned. "Sure can. The earth will cover up the scent of my magic which should be faded by the time someone gets out here to start work. Not that a Lord would closely supervise the manual labor something like this requires. Should be in the clear."

"Good. Your friend on the other hand…" His voice trailed off. "She got a death wish or something?"

"Moira's always been brave."

His sharp look made me laugh.

"And a little insane," I added. "Though she's been relatively tame since she came to Joy Springs."

He pointed at the broken window Moira had disappeared into. "That's tame?"

I snickered. "You should have seen her six years ago."

Moira rarely brought up how we'd met, but we both knew one thing: we'd saved each other.

Both of us were self-destructing one action at a time, and meeting each other had brought it home how much we needed another person to rely on. But it wasn't my story to tell. Moira had been wounded in heart and soul, and I was right at the cusp of coming to terms with the divorce, the attack, and what I'd become afterward.

Looking back, maybe Moira had needed me a little more, but we'd locked onto each other and never let go. If this is what she needed to burn off some steam, I'd sit here and wait for her as long as need be.

The minutes passed by, and Garrett was getting antsy, shifting back and forth on his feet and wringing his hands. "She's been in there for too long."

"Tess hasn't reacted. If anything was about to go wrong, she'd know."

"She's a kid," he scoffed.

"She's a banshee, and arguably more powerful than all of us." In some ways, she was. Tess could travel wherever she wished, possess people, predict when someone was about to die, and more. And I had no doubt she was keeping many things hidden from us.

Garrett's brow furrowed. "No kidding?"

"Scout's honor. If she was in any mortal danger, everyone in a four-block radius would know."

"Huh. I've never been around banshees much."

A light flickered in the house. Garrett's posture straightened, eyes fixed straight ahead. A dark figure appeared from the same window and leapt off the roof in a lithe motion. Moira touched the ground and went into a roll before popping up and disappearing in a flash of light, almost invisible to the eye.

Seconds later, she appeared in front of us, grinning like a loon. "Done."

"Ready for the next act?" I asked.

She nodded. "Do your worst."

Headlights appeared in the long driveway. Tess popped out of existence.

"Hurry," Moira said, an urgent note in her voice. We were concealed by tree cover, but we couldn't linger for long.

"Cover me."

Without waiting for an answer, I closed my eyes and wrapped a tendril of magic around the wisteria roots, whispering encouragement for them to grow, to tangle, to thrive.

Ever since my Chimera magic had merged with my Floromancy, I had to be careful with my power, otherwise it might spiral out of control. After months of practice, I had the amount of pressure needed for a fine operation like this almost down to a science.

The roots responded, winding tightly around Thorvin's pipes. As they did their work, I sent my awareness to the oak, coaxing it just a little to speed up the natural process of utterly destroying Thorvin's foundation.

The moment the pressure built, and the first crack appeared, I pulled my magic back and opened my eyes. "Give it twenty-four hours, maybe less." Dusting my hands off, I stood and shivered. Regulating my temperature wasn't usually an issue, but it was cold as hell out and burrowing into the ground took a lot of energy.

Moira grinned. "Same. Ready to go?"

We looked at Garrett. He sighed. "I only came to keep you fools from dying."

"I don't want to say Thalia was wrong," Moira gloated, "but this was one of the easiest sabotages I've ever been involved in."

The vehicle came to a stop in front of the house and Thorvin stepped out, oblivious to our presence.

"See you back at the house," Moira said. With a wink, she blinked out of existence.

Damn. I needed to get my hands on some of those potions. Think of the possibilities.

A gunshot rang out into the night.

Garrett dropped like a stone.

I didn't even think or scream. There was no time. I covered Garrett's body with my own, squeezed my eyes shut, and blinked out of existence.

Moira smiled when she saw me, but the amusement dropped from her face when she saw Garrett's lifeless body underneath mine.

"He's injured. Put pressure on the wound and call Caelan," I grunted. "I'll be right back."

"Evie—"

I blinked back onto the edge of Thorvin's property, several feet away from where we'd ended up, no longer giving a shit if he sensed me. Garrett's blood had stained the snow crimson. Thorvin was still close to the house, carefully making his way toward our hiding place, the gun held up and aimed.

I crouched behind a tree and sent my power into the earth toward where Garrett fell. His blood disappeared into the soil, along with any evidence of our trespassing. Smoothing the snow over took a little more time than I expected, but there was still time left on the potion. I could make it back in time if I hurried.

I peered up at the sky. No fresh snowfall which wasn't the best news. Chewing on the side of my lips, my heart pounding like a bass drum, I slowly lifted the dirt underneath the ground a few feet away, shifting the snow up and over to cover where we'd been. If Thorvin dug around, he might scent us, but if all he did was look, this could work.

By tomorrow, all traces of our scent should be gone, especially if the weather cooperated and dropped more snow on the ground.

Once a new layer of snow covered the old, I closed my eyes and blinked away.

It had to be enough.

I'd been gone less than two minutes, but that amount of time when someone might be bleeding out could be the difference between life and death. Moira crouched over Garrett, her face pale even in the dim light, and pressed a hand against Garrett's chest.

I fell to my knees beside her. "Keep pressure on the wound. I'm going in."

Moira gave me a sharp nod. "Caelan's on his way."

I adjusted into a cross-legged position and put my hands on Garrett's body, closing my eyes as I called to the earth.

It responded so quickly the ground rumbled. Moira inhaled a sharp breath.

"Time is of the essence," I murmured. "Don't be alarmed."

She settled next to me, her breathing ragged. "He's losing too much blood."

I didn't answer, my consciousness invading Garrett's bloodstream, searching for the damage.

The answer made me swallow hard. Tears swam behind my closed eyes. First, I looked for the bullet. If it was still inside him, anything I did might not be enough.

"Exit wound?" I croaked when my search yielded no fruit.

"Not that I can tell," Moira said.

A vicious curse flew from my mouth. "How far out is Caelan?"

A flash of light from behind.

"Here." His voice was rough with fury. "What happened?"

"No time," I snapped. "Take over for Moira."

To his credit, he didn't hesitate. When his hands were over

Garrett's wound, I turned my attention to Moira, my magic still invading Garrett's body. "Go inside the house and get the sharpest knife I have, towels, and a lighter."

Moira went even paler, but she nodded and took off for the door.

"The bullet is still inside him. If we don't get it out, my magic may not help him as much as it should."

Moira was back in less than thirty seconds. Her hands trembled as she handed the towel over.

"Give me a moment. I'm still looking for the bullet." With that, I closed my eyes again and did another sweep through Garrett's body. "There." Lodged at the back of one of his ribs.

"Should we call an ambulance?" Caelan asked.

"No time. I'm going to need one of you to tilt him onto his side and the other needs to cut him open where I tell you. Once he's open, I can push the bullet out. It's too dangerous to take it out through the entrance wound."

Moira shut her eyes briefly and let out a slow breath. "Tilt or cut?" she asked Caelan.

"I'll cut." His voice was grim. "I hope you know what you're doing, Evie."

"I saved you once, and you were in similar shape."

Caelan nodded and adjusted. Moira took over the pressure.

"Ready?" I asked.

Moira's dark eyes were wide with fear. "Yes."

"Start tilting."

Moira gently pulled Garrett toward her, exposing the back of his shirt, soaked with blood. Caelan cut the material away. I lifted a hand and touched a spot on the middle of his back. "Small cut. Large enough to push out a rifle bullet."

"Rifle?" Caelan snarled. He took a deep breath and cut into his Second's skin.

"Deeper," I said. "Get through the muscle."

Moira closed her eyes and whispered a prayer.

Caelan dug deeper, blood bubbling over his hands.

"There. Stop."

He lifted the knife away. I gently extricated the bullet from his rib and worked it through his body until it surfaced through the hole. Caelan plucked it away and tucked it into his pocket, then gently wiped most of the blood away before folding the towel and setting it on the ground.

"The cut is minor. Moira, tilt him back."

With the utmost gentleness, she laid him onto his back.

"Move a few feet back," I commanded. "This will take… effort." And it would expose a secret I'd been keeping from everyone. But there was no time to worry about it.

I opened my eyes. Garrett lay still as death, covered in blood and dirt. Tears swam in my eyes, and I prayed I could help him. Closing my eyes, I sank back into the magic and sent power soaring through Garrett's cells.

He was worse off than Caelan had been the night I'd found him in the woods. Much worse, and he'd been close to death. I could not lose Garrett. He'd come for Thalia because he cared about her, and even though Garrett and I weren't exactly friends, he didn't deserve to die because he'd gone along with our shenanigans.

The bullet had torn through his body, severing veins and arteries, and nicked the edge of his heart, usually a fatal wound if he hadn't had someone like me close. I sank deep into the earth's power and got to work.

THE SMELL of jasmine jerked me awake. I blinked several times, dislodging flowers and leaves from my face, and took stock of my surroundings. I lay encased in a structure of roots and brambles, covered with vining jasmine, not unheard of after a healing like this. The odd thing was the male body lying next to me without a stitch of clothing.

I inhaled a sharp breath and reached out a hand to brush over Garrett's face.

He was breathing. Thank the gods.

A warm hand snapped up and gripped my wrist. "Who are you?"

"It's Evie." I swallowed hard. "When you open your eyes, don't freak out."

A soft sigh. "Why does that make me want to freak out?"

"You were injured. A mortal wound."

Garrett, who still hadn't dropped my hand, went still as the grave. "Then why are we talking?"

"I have healing abilities."

Garrett opened his eyes. His nostrils flared and he blinked several times. "Fuck," he said in a low voice. "Where are we?"

"On my property. Front yard."

"Caelan?"

"He was here…earlier. I don't know where he is now. Probably close."

He turned his head, a stunned gaze finding mine. "What is this thing we're in?"

"My abilities are tied to the earth. I exhausted myself last night. This is the earth's way of protecting me, though I'm surprised you're in here with me. Normally, it only covers my body. I must have burned out before I could finish healing you all the way."

He nodded slowly. "Are you going to let me out?"

I snorted. "It should release us in a bit. I've already tried, but the structure isn't quite ready to relinquish us yet."

"Is there any particular reason you're naked?"

I sucked in a breath. Shit. I'd been so focused on him being naked, I hadn't bothered to check myself. "Um. Energy, I think? This doesn't always happen, but sometimes the earth does better work when bare skin is touching the ground."

He shifted and swore. "And I had to be naked too?"

"The magic wants what the magic wants."

Garrett let out a heavy sigh. "Caelan is going to lose his shit when this thing opens and we're lying here in our birthday suits."

I had no desire to face the Shifter Lord after last night's debacle. "He's going to lose his shit regardless."

"You didn't tell him where you were going." Garrett laughed.

My silence was answer enough.

"Thorvin came home. I remember that, but nothing after."

"He shot you with a high-caliber rifle."

Garrett whistled low. "He knew we were out there."

"I have no idea how. Maybe we missed a camera."

He shook his head. "No. There was nothing else out there. I would have sensed it." His brow furrowed. "Thorvin must have another ability we're unaware of."

He cursed. "If he knows who was on the property, we're fucked."

The shelter creaked, some of the leaves beginning to recede. "I went back and got rid of the blood and our presence. As much as I could. He may not know who was there."

"You better hope," Garrett said grimly. "This could start a war with the other Lords."

Light began to pour through the shelter as the brambles and roots slowly receded into the ground. My teeth started to chatter as cold air whistled through the openings.

"By the way," Garrett said quietly. "Thank you for saving me."

I snorted. "Considering we were the reason you got shot, there's no need to thank me."

"Mm. True. Gotta say, though. Waking up next to a beautiful naked woman feeling twenty years younger isn't a bad way to start the day."

"Say that when you're out of there, and I'll punch you in the fucking face," growled a deep, furious voice.

Garrett laughed. "I knew you were there, asshole."

The top of the shelter opened enough to reveal Caelan and Moira, peering down at us.

Moira's eyebrows lifted. "Damn, Evie. Nice tits."

CHAPTER

Twelve

CAELAN

Calm down.

My brain has always been a lot more reasonable than my heart. There was a perfectly good reason why Evie was lying next to my Second naked as the day she was born.

And an even better reason why Garrett was also in the buff.

Logic told me the structure they'd been cocooned in all night wasn't large enough for them to do anything untoward.

Unless they used their hands.

Calm down, I told myself again.

Evie, seeing my look, put out a hand to stop Garrett from getting out first, but when her fingers touched his bare shoulder, my anger turned from hot to molten. My eyes cast a golden light over their bodies, Garrett lying perfectly still, his eyes lowered.

"Caelan." She jerked her fingers away and held out a hand. I knew perfectly well she could get out on her own. "You know nothing happened. Sometimes this is the way I wake up. Garrett was so close to death, even my considerable powers couldn't fully heal him. The earth takes what doesn't serve us. Our clothes are somewhere buried far beneath the ground. If you look hard enough, you might spot pieces of them if Garrett was wearing manmade fibers."

Moira took a step closer to me, her eyes tightening at the edge. She probably wouldn't be able to stop me, but she'd try, and I would hurt her.

That took me off the edge. Evie loved her. I loved Evie. I'd never hurt anyone she cared about.

I took Evie's fingers. All the fight went out of her posture. Her legs wobbled as she lifted one leg to step out of the structure. Instead of letting her struggle, I scooped her into my arms.

She kissed the tip of my nose. "I was naked in front of your entire pack, and you didn't react like this. What gives?"

"We were alone," Garrett said, slowly rising. He frowned as he looked down, his fingers gliding over his chest. He'd find no scar, only smooth, unblemished skin. The same went for the rest of his body. I'd reset his biological clock back years, but it was too late to take back now. I'd have to trust he wouldn't reveal my secret. "Nudity isn't a big deal in a Pack, but you and I spent the night together in…" He frowned.

"Whatever the hell this was."

My jaw tightened.

Evie touched my cheek. "We both just woke up, less than five minutes ago. I don't remember going under."

"You're going to need to give me a moment." I crushed her to my chest and turned, not bothering to help my Second up. He'd understand. Garrett would have the same exact reaction if I'd woken up with a woman he'd claimed.

Moira touched Evie's ankle as we passed by, relief brimming in her eyes.

I said nothing until I had Evie dressed and tucked into the couch with a steaming mug of coffee in her hands.

"Moira told you everything?"

I nodded. As much as I wanted to scream and rail, this was not the time. Garrett knew better than to get involved in shenanigans like that, but to go along with her and vandalize a Lord's house…

I gritted my teeth and dug in her fridge for breakfast fixings.

Evie expended a ton of magic last night and must be starving. "We'll talk after we eat."

"Should we check on Garrett?"

"He's fine," I said, wincing as my voice came out in a raspy growl.

"I'm sorry," Evie said quietly. "But I did the same for you when you were injured in the woods. I didn't wake up naked, but Garrett was worse off than you. I woke up in a similar structure and was able to leave before you stirred. The structure is the earth's way of keeping me safe while the magic works."

"I'm not angry at you healing Garrett. I'm so fucking thankful I could kiss the ground you walk on."

I messed with pots and pans and mixed eggs with seasonings and milk. She had heritage bacon tucked into one of the fridge drawers, so I put the pack to cook, and managed to find a bag of frozen biscuits.

"But you are mad."

How could she look so pitiful and adorable, all at the same time? Dark shadows of exhaustion hung under her azure eyes, and her hair was tangled with leaves and sticks. Her lips were puffy and pink, and her cheeks were high with color.

"We will talk," I said again, "once we've eaten."

"What about Garrett?" she said softly.

"He knows not to come any closer. The Keep will have breakfast available to him."

She let out a soft sigh. "I don't mean to come between you two—"

"Evangeline. Enough."

She clamped her lips shut and stared. Ignoring her for now, I connected my phone to the Bluetooth speaker she kept beside the stove and turned on Americana, something I knew she liked, and turned it loud enough to preclude us from having a conversation.

Her eyes narrowed. I turned before she could see my smile. Seeing her angry was far better than seeing her weak and hurt. To piss her off even more, I reached over and turned the volume up.

I heard the shoe flying through the air even over the music. With a grin, I reached up and caught it before it hit the back of my head, setting it gently off to the side.

"Keep throwing things if it makes you feel better."

Evie huffed a breath of disgust. No other shoes came flying. For now.

Caelan's furious tension had seeped away as he cooked, though he hadn't fully relaxed. We were in a different space than a few months before, and I knew he didn't think I'd done anything inappropriate, but me and Garrett waking up together like that had jostled something loose inside him, and he was struggling.

As much as I wanted to get up and snuggle against him as he cooked, I gave him the space he asked for, content to watch him so at ease in my home. Before, I thought he sucked all the air away. He was just so much.

But now, as his power lay cloaked to his skin, almost crackling in the surrounding air, I wondered what he saw when he looked at me.

"You're staring." He didn't turn around.

"Can you blame me?"

A huff of laughter as he used tongs to remove the cooked bacon.

"Is there extra bacon?" I asked hopefully.

"Eat as much as you want. Moira and I had something earlier."

He turned, his face unreadable, and set the filled plate down. I watched as he piled pancakes and bacon high on one of my old, chipped plates and drowned it with maple syrup. I started to get up, but he shook his head and carried it over to me before going back to make his own plate.

I waited to dig in until he'd settled beside me, then watched warily.

"Eat," he said with a grunt.

Not waiting to be told twice, I dug in like a starving man.

Or a Floromancer who'd tapped all her energy out trying to save an innocent man.

When my plate was clean, Caelan said nothing, only got back up, filled the dish with two more pancakes, syrup, and the rest of the bacon, and handed it to me without a word.

I stared down at the food, tears filling my eyes for no reason I could identify, and dug back in.

Magic took a lot of energy, even more than it used to when I'd hidden my Chimera side away.

When I finished, Caelan took my plate and set it on the coffee table, then pulled me across his lap and buried his nose in my hair, inhaling deeply.

"I could have lost you last night," he said softly.

"I'm sorry I didn't tell you." And I was. No longer was it me and Moira against the world. If Caelan and I stayed serious, I needed to bring him into everything I did, or at least the things which had the potential to involve him or could result in serious injury or death.

What we'd done last night had been phenomenally dumb.

Fun, but dumb.

"I understand why you didn't. I would have stopped you." I felt him smile against my hair. "Or I would have tried."

I shifted, threading my hands around his neck, and tilted my head up to press a kiss to his throat.

His chest rumbled.

I smiled and did it again.

"Stop, Evie. We're talking."

I pouted. "Spoilsport."

Caelan snorted. "Moira told me what happened, but I want to hear it again, from your point of view."

I ran through the story as best I could, straining my memory for the smallest of details.

"And when Moira left? Leave nothing out."

Moira was already gone when Garrett took the bullet. I started from that moment and what I'd done when I went back to Thorvin's property.

"I'm not sure if he'll know we were there or not."

Caelan's brow furrowed. He shifted and reached into his pocket for his phone. "Let's look at the weather from last night."

He searched for a few moments and nodded. "Snow, just like rain, clears scent molecules from the air. Weather reports are notoriously inaccurate, but there's a good chance it snowed again last night."

"He was too close when I went back to clear the evidence, and it wasn't snowing when I left. Is shifting the snow to bury everything enough?"

His jaw tightened. "Possibly. But underestimate Thorvin at your peril. He's by far the most intelligent of us."

"How soon will we know?"

"We have a meeting tomorrow. He's always been a shit liar. I'll know if he suspects anything when I see him."

I grimaced. "If he does?"

He sighed and shook his head. "He's the smartest of the Lords, but he's also the most reasonable. But we're all unpredictable. There's no way to tell what he'll do."

"Is he power hungry?"

"I've seen no evidence of it. Thorvin far prefers books to leadership."

The thought of a powerful wolf shifter preferring to bury his nose in a book rather than lead people made me chuckle. "How'd he become a Lord?"

"Again, underestimate any of the Lords at your peril. He

might prefer scholarship over war, but Thorvin takes fitness and prowess to the extreme. He won his position the old-fashioned way—through challenge."

I sighed. "Well, shit."

"Exactly."

"And Garrett?" Thorvin was a worry for another day. Garrett lived at the Keep with Caelan. The way my Lord looked at his Second when I rose from the shelter had sent shivers down my spine.

"We've been friends for many, many years. This was a blip, Evie. Do not worry about him. He's skilled enough to hold his own if I decided to take my anger out on him."

My eyes narrowed. "And will you?"

He tweaked my nose. "A couple of months ago, you would have skewered Garrett on a limb and roasted him on the barbecue. What's changed?"

I sighed. "He's still a massive pain in the ass, but he proved helpful. And Thalia really annoys him, and that's been fun to watch."

Caelan's eyes flickered at my mention of Thalia, an unreadable look on his face gone in less than a heartbeat.

"Caelan?"

"Hmm?"

"Do you not like the Seer?"

"The Seer is a chat for another day." He rose in one lithe motion, scooping me into a bride's carry. "In the meantime, you need a shower."

He buried his nose in my neck and sniffed. "You smell like dirt and my Second."

"Hmm. The shower is a little lonely. I wouldn't mind some company."

The ring of his eyes went golden. "Your energy hasn't replenished."

"I'm off today. I have all day to replenish." I wiggled my eyebrows, making him laugh.

He carried me into the bedroom and straight into the bathroom, placing me on the counter, his hands on either side of my hips. "I wouldn't want you to overexert yourself," he said huskily.

Caelan pressed a kiss to the sensitive place where my neck met my shoulder. I shivered.

"How about I wash you?"

I blinked. Images played in my mind, and I almost slid off the counter.

He grinned and slid the strap of my pajama top down. "Sounds good."

I made an unintelligible noise.

Caelan laughed and turned the shower on. "Now, Miss Quinn. Let's get you all cleaned up so you can start replenishing your energy. Once I'm finished with you."

"Yes, please," I breathed.

Fourteen

Two men stood outside the shop when I arrived the next morning.

One was an unfamiliar shifter, who did not smell like a wolf.

The other was some sort of paranormal, not fae, not shifter.

I stopped at the entrance to the shop. "Excuse me."

Neither moved. I stilled, keys in my hand. Both were handsome, but the kind of handsome that felt perfect and therefore made you suspicious. Soap opera perfect, even lines and angles, high cheekbones, perfectly crystal blue eyes. No hint of lethality, only a disturbing sense of psychopathy.

I didn't want to get caught in a dark alley with either one of these guys.

The first one, brown hair with blue eyes, smiled. His teeth were white, perfect, teen vampire drama perfect. "Hello. Are you Evie?"

"Depends on who's asking."

"I'm asking."

This guy made my skin crawl. "And you are?"

The smile widened. It didn't reach his eyes. "Your new husband if things go well."

I'd heard this term recently called "the ick." It meant when a guy did something that seemed innocent on the surface but gave you a gross feeling. Things like a dude failing to take his socks off when he's trying to seduce you or ordering for you at a restaurant on a first date.

Can you imagine a dude with his wang hanging out wearing nothing but striped athletic socks?

Or ordering you a rare prime rib when you're a vegetarian?

Basically, things that made your vagina desiccate.

Consider my vagina desiccated.

The other guy snickered. I turned my gaze to him. "You hoping to be my husband, too?"

He swallowed. I'd obviously taken him by surprise. Not used to it, his brain locked up like anti-lock brakes on a new vehicle. "Um. Well. Err. Yes."

"I bet written exams are hard for you."

It took him a few seconds for the insult to hit, but when it did, his eyes narrowed, and his cheeks flushed scarlet.

The first dude laughed. "You're clever. I like that."

This fucking guy… "Yes, I constantly seek approval from strangers in the wild. Now, please move. I need to get into my shop."

"And if I don't?" He leaned against the door and smirked.

Some women like men who smirk. I found it smug and superior, and I always wanted to punch the smirker in the kidney. I resisted letting the Chimera out to play because even my beast wanted to punch this guy. "I won't ask you again."

He laughed and held his hands up in mock surrender. "Oh, no! Look at me trembling in my boots."

I looked around. It was early. Only one other shop was open, and it was across the street, several stores over. No one lingered on the street, and there was very little traffic. Moira, Ash, and Tess weren't in yet, and Caelan was still in my bed crashed out.

The other guy laughed.

I sighed. "Last chance. Move or I'll move you."

He crossed his arms over his chest. "Do your worst."

There was a reason I kept plants outside my shop. Joy Springs had a cute downtown area, but the only trees were behind all the buildings, and there were only small patches of grass. We were, for all intents and purposes, surrounded by stone and concrete. Not exactly helpful for a Floromancer in a situation like this.

Thus, the reason for the two innocuous but large plants I kept in massive, immovable planters right outside the shop's entrance. My magic responded any time I called it, but I couldn't risk tearing up the stone or concrete to access the earth. Doing so would raise far too many questions, and as bad as I'd been about staying under the radar, even I knew it was a bad idea.

While both morons gloated, I let a sliver of magic out, both plants responding eagerly, sending thorned tendrils out to gently wrap around each male. They wore winter clothes and wouldn't sense any intrusion right away. Not until I gave the command.

That was another thing most people didn't know.

Plants might not be able to talk, but they were sentient in many ways.

And they liked these guys just about as much as I did.

I shrugged. "You've been warned."

With a flick of my hand, the vines tightened to grip each male in a close to unbreakable grasp. I smiled, letting a little of the crazy out, and watched as both realized they were trapped.

The first lurched toward me, teeth pulled back from his lips. "You *bitch*. Let go."

I snorted. "And if I don't?"

His eyes flashed with fury. And me, tired of the game, flicked my hand up and down and then away.

The plants responded accordingly and smashed both men into the pavement, once, twice, then flung them over the buildings and far out of my sight.

To my supreme satisfaction, they screamed like little bitches all the way down.

They were too far away for me to hear the impact. The shifter would have several broken bones and some internal injuries. Nothing time couldn't handle. The other…

"Fuck it," I whispered, not feeling an ounce of regret.

Once I was safe and behind locked doors, I texted Caelan and told him what happened.

My phone rang less than ten seconds later. His voice was rough with sleep.

"Where are they?"

I squinted and told him the general direction.

Caelan snorted. "I'll send some wolves out to find them." He paused.

"Are they dead?"

One could dream. "No idea."

Another pause. "Good girl." Satisfaction rang in his voice.

His approval and those words sent a shiver down my spine. Praise kinks were real. "What time is your meeting?"

"A few hours from now. I'm getting up and heading to the Keep. I'll let you know if I hear anything about your antics."

I winced. "Let's hope the snow cooperated. How's Garrett?"

Caelan grunted. "Fine, but I plan to punch his face in later."

"Ah. Too soon?"

"Wait at least two weeks before asking me about my Second."

"Done."

We hung up, and I tried to put my unease about the men at my door to the back of my mind.

Moira came in half an hour later, relief filling her when she saw me. "I wasn't sure you'd be in today."

"Healing takes it out of me, depending on the injury, but I feel fine today."

She studied me. "What's wrong?"

I told her about the men at my door. Moira frowned. "Should we make an announcement on social media?"

I blanched. "And say what? Sorry, Evie is not in the market for a husband. We'd like to discourage men from showing up at her shop?"

A shudder racked my body at the thought. "That will do nothing but encourage weirdos. I want to lie low and find the person who started this to begin with."

Moira set her bag down and started counting the drawer. "You don't think the order came from the Lords?"

"It's possible. Even likely, but until I know for sure, I don't want to react too strongly."

Moira laughed. "As in, you don't want one of us to get Garrett almost killed again?"

I rubbed a hand over my face and sighed. "That was too close. But I still can't figure out how Thorvin knew exactly where we were."

Moira tugged off her jacket and cap and hung them on the rack. "Me too. It's possible he picked up my scent around the house, but I usually move too fast for any to linger. Still doesn't explain how he fired with such unnerving accuracy."

"Caelan warned us about him. All the Lords actually. Which we already knew. But if the others can do what Thorvin can, we should refrain from trespassing on their property."

But Moira didn't look deterred. She shrugged. "This just means we need to be more careful next time. We can go in on foot and do surveillance before we move in."

I eyed her. "You sound like a military dude planning a siege."

Her eyes lit up. "Yeah? Cool."

"Err. Not cool." I poured her a cup of tea and a cup of coffee for me and carried it to the register area.

She cupped her mug and lifted it, bringing the tea up to her nose and inhaled. "Mmm."

But I wasn't finished. "Are you alright? You've been different for a while?"

Her easy smile fell away. "I'm fine."

Which told me she was anything but fine. "You haven't been the same since…"

My voice trailed off as I thought about it. "Since that night at the Keep."

The night I'd turned into the natural form of my Chimera and sent magic flooding through Caelan's lands. But I wasn't the only powerful being there flinging magic everywhere. Rhona and Finn were there, my mother, a powerful goddess in her own right, and my father, Cernunnos, the Fae King. My look turned thoughtful.

"Something happened to you."

At her silence, I knew I was on to something. "Moira. I'm your best friend. If you can't trust me, who can you trust?"

"It's nothing," she said breezily.

"If nothing happened, you would tell me that. Saying 'it's nothing' tells me it's something."

She sighed and put her mug down. "I got hit with a few stray…somethings. It's not a big deal."

The shop door opened, and Tess and Ash breezed in laughing. Moira slapped a smile on her face and gave me a warning look.

Okay then. I was the only one who suspected something was up.

"We're not finished with this," I said quietly before turning to greet the rest of my team.

Whatever was going on with Moira was not nothing, and I planned to get to the bottom of things sooner rather than later.

CHAPTER
Fifteen
CAELAN

I smelled them the moment I stepped into the woods. Fury, shock, and a touch of fear rode both men as they made their way out of the place Evie had tossed them.

A fierce grin touched my lips. I wished I would have been there to see her toss their asses through the air. Two of my top wolves followed behind, Merrick and Cole. Fierce, powerful, and utterly loyal to Pack. What transpired today would stay between us and no one else.

Both men fanned out to either side.

"They're still together," Merrick whispered, low enough to reach only our ears.

"Easier to catch them," Cole said, his grin edged with violence.

"Both injured." Merrick inhaled. "Bleeding profusely. Your woman did a number on them."

"She tossed them half a mile away from her shop," I murmured. "The landing did most of the damage."

"Good way to follow the law. Technically, *she* didn't injure them." Cole's grin widened. "The ground did all the work."

"Evie does love a technicality." I held up a hand for silence as we prowled through the woods hunting the men who dared accost my Floromancer.

We found them a few minutes later, slogging through the trees and cursing up a blue streak.

One of them spoke, a tall and handsome shifter, not mine. One more strike against him for trespassing in my territory without announcing his presence. "That *bitch*. That fucking bitch. When I get a hold of her, I'll show her exactly what a real man can do. I don't even give a shit about marrying her."

A cold rage settled over my body, the fury of the hunter seeking revenge. I motioned for my two wolves to circle around and block them from behind. They could try to run, but they'd find two more surprises if they did.

The other, slightly shorter and not as vocal, hissed between his teeth, one hand pressed against his rib cage. Blood seeped between the cracks of his fingers. "I dunno, man. Maybe we should leave her alone."

The shifter snorted. "No one treats me like this and gets away with it."

A sigh from the quieter one. "Dude. Do what you want. I'm getting the fuck out of here and finding a healer."

I stepped out from between the trees. "Hello."

The second stopped in his tracks, his eyes wide in his pale face. "Erm," he said and paused before letting out a heartfelt sigh.

And then, "Fuck."

I smiled. "It appears you know who I am."

A nod. "One of the Shifter Lords."

The first paused, a sharp tang of new scent in the air.

Terror.

I focused on the first. "Allow me to introduce myself to you. My name is Caelan, Lord of this territory. You've already met my lady."

The smell of urine saturated the air.

My eyes went gold, casting a light on the shady forest and the man who'd dared to threaten Evie.

"Hey man," the shifter said, raising his hands in the air and jerking back a step. "I don't want any trouble. I saw an opportunity and took it."

He spoke about Evie as if she were an inconvenience, not a living, breathing sentient being. The love of my life. "An opportunity," I mused. "Who gave you said opportunity?"

"I dunno. We got an email, and it became sort of a game to see who could get her."

He swallowed hard when he realized his choice of words.

"And did you?" I asked. "*Get* her?"

A flash of malice in his eyes, there and gone. "We left," he lied.

"Oh? How did you end up here of all places? Not many people go prowling through these woods. Wolves are prevalent in Joy Springs. Mine and the natural species." I let claws slip from my fingertips. "The smell of blood attracts predators, you know."

He took an involuntary step back. "Look man. Like I said, we don't want any trouble."

The second turned and took off running. I didn't even bother to look. My wolves would take care of him.

Sure enough, a single sharp scream came seconds later, followed by the metallic scent of blood.

I watched as an interplay of emotions played over the shifter's face. Shock. Fear. Fury. And resignation as he calculated the odds of walking out of here alive.

"Someone should have told you, cat shifter, to never intrude on a Lord's territory."

He took a few more steps backward, the shifter's heart pounding triple time.

"But even more important, is never threatening a Lord's woman."

This time, my smile was full of fangs, my power saturating the air.

I was on him an instant later, his scream ringing out through the still air, blood saturating the earth, a worthy sacrifice for his insult on its daughter.

• • •

I didn't bother showering or even changing my clothes for my meeting. If the Lords wanted war, I'd give it to them. Targeting Evie was the same as targeting me, and they'd know it the moment I stepped foot into the meeting room.

I'd chosen to take Simone with me. Garrett's presence made me itchy for violence. My Second understood and planned to make himself scarce for at least the next week.

Not that doing so would be an issue. Thalia took up far more time than any of us expected.

Not telling Evie who she was, was wearing on me. We'd promised honesty, and neither of us were doing a great job. Granted, Evie's secrecy wasn't as harmful as mine, though I guess I could argue almost getting Garrett killed trumped any secret I was keeping.

But that wasn't her fault. Keeping Thalia's true identity from Evie was mine and only mine. She wouldn't understand me keeping a promise to Cernunnos if it prevented honesty with her.

Once again, the goddamned fae had gotten me into a pickle I was unprepared for.

Rowan was the first to arrive, the familiar prickle of his magic reminding me of Evie. His eyes widened when he walked into the conference room and spotted me. A bark of laughter cracked through the room.

"Looks like the marriage scheme is off to a grand start." He grinned and pulled out the seat next to me. His nose wrinkled as he caught a whiff of me.

"Jesus, Caelan. Couldn't you have brought the bloody clothes with you or something?"

"It wouldn't have the same effect."

"Cat shifters?"

At my nod, Rowan snorted. "Bunch of assholes."

"Evie no longer has to worry about them."

His eyes widened a hair. "Not in the mood for a warning, I guess?"

"Nope."

He helped himself to a cup of coffee set up in the middle of the table. "How many?"

"Two today, at least one the day before. Probably a few others she hasn't told me about."

Rowan winced. "How many are still standing?"

"Depends on if I find the others." I let the violence come through in my smile.

Rowan sighed and sat back down. "I told them this was a terrible idea."

Unsurprising Rowan had nothing to do with this. He'd always been my staunchest ally and remained one of my closest friends, but even more importantly, he cared about Evie as much as I did, something that had almost ended in a fight or two between us. "You know for sure it came directly from the Lords?"

To my surprise, he shook his head. "I don't think it originated with us."

I was afraid of that.

"I can't tell you for sure where the suggestion came from, but we all know Ethan isn't smart enough to come up with something like that on his own."

We both laughed. Ethan was a Lord, so he had to be intelligent, but he'd never been crafty. Ethan controlled his territory through brute force rather than subtle manipulation or true leadership.

The man sitting beside me was the opposite. And I hoped I was too. But occasionally, I killed two people in the woods who dared hit on my woman.

Life required balance.

Footsteps came down the hall. I lowered my voice. "We need to chat once this is over."

Rowan glanced at me. "Anything I need to know before the meeting starts?"

"Keep a close eye on Thorvin and Ethan."

"You do like to keep things interesting, friend." Rowan shifted his chair to put some distance between us before the other Lords arrived.

Soren entered the room a few seconds later, an eyebrow lifting as he spotted us. "Colluding already?"

"Collusion is illegal," Rowan said, his eyes unreadable.

Soren and Rowan weren't enemies, exactly. None of us were. But neither were they friends. The other Lord and I had come to an uneasy alliance. I still didn't trust him anywhere as near as much as I did Rowan, but he hadn't stabbed me in the back yet, and he'd sided with me on a few important things.

However, I was still pissed off at all the Lords over what happened to Evie.

Minus Rowan. In fact, I owed him a great deal of thanks. He's the one who got me to pull my head out of my ass over Evie, and she and I had come to a better place because of his interference.

I had already known he was a good Lord. But after what he'd done for me, I knew without a doubt, he was a good man as well.

Soren was still an unknown player, though wouldn't life be grand if we all trusted each other?

He nodded and took a seat on the opposite side of the table. "Ethan is on the way in."

Interesting. "We're all scheduled today, as far as I know. We need to talk about replacing Donovan."

"A little birdie told me one of the shifters in the running stopped by your lady's house." Soren's eyes glittered with amusement. "They also told me he was so handsome it hurt to look at him."

Rowan snorted. "If Evie fell for every pretty face, she would have been off the market long ago."

Garrett had texted me about it the night he was shot, but only said Dario was in Joy Springs, not that he'd shown up at Evie's house. With everything going on, I hadn't thought to ask about it, and Evie never mentioned it.

Under the table, my fists clenched. "Did he say what he wanted?"

"He was asking about Donovan's territory. Dario found out Evie claimed the land."

My jaw clenched. "Curious how he found out about it. Anything we need to know, Soren?"

The Lord laughed. "I've never given a shit about Donovan's territory. You know how much I love the south. Being in the middle of a winter storm in October does not appeal to me, thank you very much. However he found out, it wasn't through me."

Thorvin came in next, his eyes darting left and right before he stepped inside. The Lord was powerful in his own right, but he preferred scholarly pursuits and leading with intellect and thoughtfulness rather than through force. It didn't mean he wouldn't remind anyone who challenged him who was in charge, but Thorvin was, overall, a peaceful Lord, probably more so than any of us.

But today, a pale sheen of sweat made his face shiny under the poor artificial light, and he was jumpier than I'd ever seen him.

"Thorvin," I said in greeting. "How goes it?"

"Fine, fine," he said, though we could all scent the lie in his words. "And you?"

"All is well in Texas." What in the hell had Evie and Moira done to him? They swore up and down, their shenanigans were limited to property and harmless magic. From the way Thorvin was jumping at shadows, I had to wonder if they'd lied.

As I watched, the sheen of his face turned…

Soren's eyes narrowed. Rowan's eyebrows went up. I stared hard at him.

Thorvin looked at us. "What?"

A horrified realization settled inside of me. If Moira had done what I thought she might have…

I asked another question. "How's the Northeast?"

Thorvin swallowed and gave us a sickly smile. "Wonderful!" he said after an awkward pause.

"Dude," Rowan said, his voice thick. "Are you…did you wear sunscreen today?"

Soren snorted.

Thorvin's brow furrowed. "I'm sorry. What?"

"Sunscreen." Rowan made a circular motion around his face with his hand. "Your face is…shiny."

Thorvin wiped his palm across his cheek and pulled it away, but there was nothing there.

Soren sighed. "It's not shiny. You're glittering like a teenage vampire."

Rowan snickered.

My lips twitched. Every time Thorvin moved, the light caught his face and shone with iridescence. And it seemed to get worse every time he told a lie. I hadn't directly asked Moira what she'd done, but I knew she'd broken into his house.

Thorvin's eyes widened in horror. "That's what they did," he murmured under his breath. "I knew someone had gotten into my house!"

Rowan carefully did not look at me. "Who?"

This was the moment of truth. If Evie's trick with the snow had worked, Thorvin would have no idea who'd sabotaged his property.

He swore vehemently. "I don't know! Whoever it was covered their tracks well."

I schooled my emotions into blankness, even though I wanted to slump with relief. She'd done it. Once again, Evie had managed to slide out of the way of trouble with no permanent consequences.

I was dating a godsdamned eel. The thought of it almost made me grin.

"They put glitter in your sunscreen?" Soren asked helpfully.

I couldn't hold my laugh in that time.

"I don't fucking wear sunscreen, you asshole!" Thorvin snarled.

Rowan lost it.

Thorvin's face didn't glitter more, so at least that was the truth.

Rowan wasn't in the mood for mercy today, either. Through

his wheezing laughter, he managed to get out, "All we need is for you to say something like, *you don't understand me, Rowan. I'll never be good enough for you*, to make the picture complete."

Even through the glitter, Thorvin's face glowed with embarrassment. "Fuck off, garden boy."

That only made Rowan laugh harder.

"Have you seen anyone about your…" Soren's voice trailed off as he fought for the right word. "Situation?"

"I didn't know I had a *situation* until this second," Thorvin growled. "And who the fuck would I see to tell them I'd suddenly turned into a Cullen?"

Rowan hooted, his hand pressed against his stomach as he cracked up.

Soren's lips twitched. "Well," he finally got out, "if that's all they did to you after breaking in your house, consider yourself fortunate."

Thorvin scrubbed a hand over his light brown hair and sighed. "That's not all they did."

I stilled. Evie wasn't the glitter type. That had to be Moira. Whatever this was had to be my eel.

"Do tell," Rowan said, his cheeks creased from laughing.

"My pipes and foundation are fucked up. Seriously fucked up. The guys I called to look said my wisteria and oak were planted too close to the house, but for both of them to do that much damage all at the same time…" He shook his head. "It doesn't seem possible."

Rowan gently nudged my shoe under the table. He knew it was Evie. From the flicker in Soren's eyes, he knew too.

"If I didn't know better, I'd swear it was your Evie, Caelan."

I snorted. "Evie was in Joy Springs yesterday. There's no way a Floromancer could make it to your territory that quickly."

Everything I said was true. She was in town yesterday. But she didn't stay there. And a mundane Floromancer couldn't travel instantaneously. Only Rowan knew of Evie's strange, mixed heritage, though he didn't know of her Chimera blood, something I'd never tell him.

Something so dangerous would have to come from her.

Thorvin slumped. "I know. That's what makes this entire thing so confusing. Unless I've managed to piss off another Floromancer."

Rowan choked and covered it with a cough. "Evie isn't known for being sneaky. You've seen her in action."

I could kiss Rowan right now.

Soren shrugged. "All the Lords have done something to piss Evie off, but I agree. She's never been sneaky when it comes to revenge. This doesn't sound like her." His gaze flicked to me and away.

"Perhaps this is merely a terrible run of luck."

Thorvin snorted.

"Minus the glitter," Soren added. "You definitely pissed someone off if they've turned you into a teenage romantic drama."

More footsteps from down the hall.

Thorvin's face was almost back to normal, only a hint of the silvery glow still showing.

I lowered my voice. "If you don't want him to know, I suggest you stick to the truth or figure out a way to talk around it."

Thorvin nodded just as Ethan came through the door. His dark eyes studied us, lingering on me. He couldn't know it was me and Evie who'd saved him the other night, and if he did, I needed to dig deeper into his capabilities.

"Lords," he said in his deep, emotionless voice.

He looked none the worse for wear after his ordeal with Donovan and Nadia, but today would tell us if he was trustworthy or if we should find a way to depose him. The last thing I wanted was an internal war, but if Nadia and Donovan were taking Lords hostage to squeeze them for information on Gianna's body, and Ethan failed to disclose what happened, he was as untrustworthy as the Lord we all thought was dead.

"Welcome, Ethan," Soren said. "The coffee is still fresh. We were just catching up."

Ethan grunted and took the chair beside Soren, reaching over to take an empty mug. He said nothing while he poured his coffee, until he took a long drink and sighed.

"This has been a shit week," he growled.

I almost laughed. "Oh? It's nice to know my territory might be the calmest this quarter."

"Speak for yourself," Rowan said. He held up his index finger. "I'm the only one who hasn't managed to make an enemy out of your Floromancer."

A second finger. "No rogues."

A third finger. "And I'm everyone's favorite."

"Fuck off, Rowan," Soren said with a groan.

"We're missing Ben." He wasn't late yet, but Ben was a stickler for being on time. I hadn't sensed him in the hotel or around the grounds when I'd arrived, but thought nothing of it because I'd gotten here so early.

Ethan shrugged. "I haven't heard from him, but he's more likely to reach out to you than me."

Rowan frowned. "You haven't heard from him?"

I shook my head, a sense of unease unfurling deep in my stomach. "Excuse me for a moment."

Without waiting for acknowledgment, I rose, already pulling my cell from my pocket.

Sixteen

Moira skipped out of work at five on the dot, moving so quickly I didn't get the chance to pin her down before she skedaddled out the door. I sent her a text bitching at her, and she left me on unread.

Once I finished sweeping up the shop, I planned to stop by her house and bang on the door until she let me in.

If she didn't let me in, she was going to get a yardful of nettles and fire ants. On that note, Ash stopped by my worktable on his way out.

"Need anything else?"

"No." I waved him away. "When are you due back?"

"Next week. I waited too long to go this time and need an extra couple of days."

Ash was a dryad who needed to return to his tree periodically to recharge his magic. If he failed to do so, his innate power would slowly drain away, eventually leading to his death. Dryads were sticklers about their time with their trees, but Ash had stuck around for longer than normal. After my own foray into a greedy fae tree, every one of my friends was worried I'd disappear again.

It made them antsy and reluctant to leave me alone.

I smiled at him when he lingered. "Statistically, the odds of me getting kidnapped and drained by a fae tree for a second time are nil."

Ash scoffed. "Don't joke about such things. With your luck, I wouldn't be surprised if a comet not seen in 10,000 years hit the shop because you somehow affected the earth's orbit."

"Funny." I shooed him away. "Go have fun in your naked grove."

If Moira were here, she'd have a field day. She was the one who assumed every time Ash went off for "tree time" that it was code for a three-day orgy in hippie territory.

Ash trying to dissuade her had only made her double down.

"Tess is still in the back. Don't forget about her."

He was only warning me because we had forgotten about her a few times over the years. Tess was so quiet and unobtrusive that if she wasn't in the front with me, it was easy to forget she still lingered about when it was closing time.

"Got it." I lowered my voice. "How are things with you two?"

He shrugged. "They'll never be back to normal, but we're figuring out how to set a new normal."

My heart warmed. "That's really good, Ash. She cares about you."

His eyes flickered. "I still feel like such an idiot over everything."

I shook my head. "You've made your amends with her. Don't keep punishing yourself."

"Easy for you to say." He sighed and straightened his shoulders. "But I'll try."

"See you next week," I said as he grabbed his tote bag from the hook.

He lifted a hand in farewell and headed out of the shop.

An hour later, Tess had left, and I was finishing the sweeping when my phone rang.

Caelan.

"Hey. I'm just finishing up. Did your meeting end early?"

"Ben is missing."

I stilled. "How long?"

"No idea. He was supposed to attend our meeting and didn't show up. We've been here for two hours trying to track him down. He's not answering his phone, and he's not at any of the places anyone thought to look."

"Can you send someone into his territory to check his home?" With all the sensitive hearing around, I didn't mention Ethan or Donovan. Was it possible the same thing had happened to Ben?

The new Lord had replaced Halvar after Finn had murdered him and took his form to infiltrate the Lord's inner sanctums. Ben and I had a tangled history, but I didn't want him dead. Or harmed.

"How can I help?"

"Is there any way you can get your hands on one of those…"

His voice trailed off, and the murmur of another voice came through.

"I'll have to ask Moira. I might be able to get one, though it's a longshot. Two is probably asking too much."

"See what you can do, please." He sighed. "I love you."

"Love you back. Give me a bit. I'll let you know."

We hung up, and I texted Moira again.

After a few minutes of her ignoring me, I snorted and yanked my coat from the rack.

She could ignore me all she wanted on a normal day. This was too important to play petty games.

The drive over was short. Her car was parked in the drive, and Moira never had wards up, claiming if anyone wanted to get to her, they'd get what was coming to them.

I marched up to the porch, banged on the door, and screamed her name.

She answered right away, her brows lifting to her hairline. "I'm not ready to discuss this."

I pushed my way inside. "Good. I'm not here for that anyway. Ben is missing."

Moira blinked in surprise. "The Lord?"

"Yes. Any chance of getting our hands on two of those transportation potions or whatever the hell those were?"

She stared at me for a long moment and sighed. "Okay. You can't get mad."

"That's a bad way to start a conversation. Why would I get mad? I figured getting more would be a long shot."

She winced. "I can make them."

I froze. That should be far outside of her capabilities. Or it used to be. Unless she'd been lying to me for the past seven or so years.

We had other things to worry about, but I had one burning question. "How long have you been able to make them?"

"Erm. About six months."

I let out a sigh of relief. "Alright. We can worry about it later. Can you spare two?"

"Can Caelan pay me for the ingredients? They're expensive, and I work at a flower shop."

"Assuming you don't want me to tell him you can make those, I'd charge more."

Relief filled her eyes. "Good. I will." She wiped her hands down the front of the yoga pants. "Do you need to get to him?"

"Shit. Yes." I sighed. "Can you spare three?"

"I can, but that's all I have on hand right now. They take two weeks to make."

I hated to take all of them.

Seeing my look, she shook her head. "Don't worry about it. As long as you don't tell anyone I can make these, I'm not worried about people bugging me for my stock." She paused.

"But if you don't mind, can you tell Caelan these are the only ones I can get my hands on? He shouldn't rely on me for these."

I nodded. "It won't be an issue. He's not pushy with that kind of stuff."

A sly look slithered over her face. "Unless you're married. Then he can raid my stock whenever he wants."

I snorted. "Straight to jail for that."

Moira laughed and headed to the back. "Follow me. One will take you to him and should last long enough to take you to Ben's territory and back." Her brow furrowed. "Maybe. Depends on how long you stay searching for him."

"No idea. We're trying to narrow down his location. They have someone trying to hack into Ben's phone right now."

"I'll start a new batch when you leave." She led me to her small library room and headed straight for the small fridge. Painted bookshelves crammed to the brim lined every wall. A brightly colored woven rug lay over the hardwood floor. A small table scattered with various herbs and tiny bottles sat beside an oversized recliner with a blanket carelessly tossed over the back. The room smelled of herbs, incense, and Moira.

A pair of slippers sat beside the chair, along with an open book lying beside a cup of still steaming tea.

I'd interrupted some R&R time. "Sorry to yank you out of your relaxation."

She waved a hand at me and didn't peek up from the fridge. "This is more important."

When she rose, she held three small bottles. "Do you remember everything from last time?"

"Two-hour time limit."

Moira nodded. "Never take more than two of these together in less than twenty-four hours."

I frowned. "Why not?"

"You'll hurl. Everywhere. All the time." She nodded, and I didn't ask her if she knew that tidbit from personal experience.

"Got it." I tucked the bottles into my purse. "Thank you for these. What can I do for you?"

She rolled her eyes. "Let me get back to my reading."

"Moira. This was a huge favor."

She shrugged. "Caelan will reimburse me. If you can hide these from the other Lords, that would be helpful. I don't need any of them coming to my door."

"Like Soren?" I teased.

She snorted. "Get out of here. Go find your hot healer."

I scooted out the door after a quick kiss on her cheek and got into my car. Before pulling out, I texted Caelan.

Got three. Where are you? I'll come to you. Don't tell the others about these.

THREE?

Yup. You're lucky to be so well connected. But it's going to cost you.

I'll pay in handcuffs and ropes.

I swallowed hard.

Sorry. Money this time. These are not cheap.

As long as the handcuffs and ropes come later.

We'll see.

The next message was an address. I drove home and hurried inside to pack the potions in a small towel to keep them from breaking in case I landed hard again when I used the first one.

Then I changed my clothes because Midwest territory had a far different climate than Joy Springs. Thermal underwear under my jeans and sweater, and a pair of thick wool socks and water-proof boots topped with a bulky jacket completed my outfit.

Send me a picture of where you are, away from everyone, preferably, I texted. *The faster we can leave, the better chance we have of finding him.*

Less than a minute later, Caelan sent a selfie of himself close to a copse of trees with an identifiable landmark. He was still around the hotel area, but no one would see me pop in.

Unless I had extremely bad luck, which was possible.

Shaking those worries off, I uncapped the first potion and drank it down, thinking of Caelan and those trees.

The world fell out from underneath my feet.

CHAPTER
Seventeen

I didn't throw up this time. Progress.

Caelan reached out and caught me as I lurched in. I swayed and pressed my hands against his lean chest to steady myself.

"Like a damsel in distress," he said with a glint in his eye.

I got myself to rights and stood on tiptoe to press a quick kiss to his lips. "Where do you want to check first?"

"His house."

I'd never been there. "What's the address?"

I pulled it up online and formed a good picture in my head, then reached in and unwrapped one of the bottles. Caelan took it and whistled.

"How in the hell has she been able to source so many of these?"

"Trade secret," I said. "You'll have to ask her."

His eyes narrowed, but he didn't press. "We should leave soon. We're on a break and there's only a few minutes left."

I held out my hand. "Mine is still active. Drink it, holding the picture of Ben's home in your mind. We'll have about two hours."

Caelan nodded and tipped the potion into his mouth. I slid my hand into his and thought of Ben's house.

A moment later we stood before a well-kept manor home, less than half the size of Caelan's. Maybe even smaller. The place had a large, wraparound porch with several empty hanging baskets. A large swing sat off to the side, the seat covered in snow.

"No one's here," Caelan said quietly. "Check the land, and I'll go inside and see if I can spot anything."

I nodded and waited as he cleverly picked the front door lock. I'd have to ask him about that later. I could break through a lock using my magic, but his skills made me wonder if he'd been a cat burglar in a past life. Once he was in, I walked off the porch and ventured further onto Ben's land.

His magic had saturated the earth, the strange yet vibrant cool magic he used when healing. I bent and tugged one of my gloves off, touching my index finger to the snowy ground. Sending a pulse of power through the earth, I searched for anything unusual. It took me a minute, but I found something toward the front of the house.

Blood. Ben's blood.

A strand of hair that didn't belong to him, and a disturbance toward the front of his driveway told me Ben didn't go willingly. I rose and put my glove back on. My teeth chattered, and I shoved my hands into the pockets of my jacket.

Midwest cold was far different from the Texas cold.

I knocked the snow off the swing seat and sat down. Caelan's sense of smell was extraordinarily keen, and I didn't want to risk messing his concentration up if I walked inside. Glad I'd chosen to change, I zipped my jacket all the way up to cover my nose and waited.

He was out a few minutes later, a grim expression on his handsome face. "Signs of a struggle inside. Ben put up a hell of a fight, but…" His voice trailed off.

"They shouldn't have been able to take him like they did. Drugs might have been involved." He sat down beside me. "Find anything?"

"Blood. Signs of a struggle toward the front of the driveway. I think they put him in a car and drove somewhere."

Caelan rose and held his hand out. "Let's check it out."

More blood dotted the area. Ben was injured, but not enough to kill him. Caelan grimaced. "I need to shift."

"In the snow?" I shuddered.

A flash of teeth as he smiled. "You forget about all the fur."

"Yeah, but you have to get naked first."

Caelan winked. "Hold onto my clothes?"

"As long as you let me ogle you for a moment."

His eyes glittered. "Ogle away, flower girl."

Time was of the essence, so Caelan didn't linger over his clothing. But he did wiggle his eyebrows and do a slow turn before a flash of light overtook him and a giant wolf stood in his place.

I laughed and ran my fingers through his fur. "Very bitable," I agreed.

He nipped at me then put his nose to the ground. I watched as he thoroughly examined the area. When he was satisfied, he'd found everything, he shifted again and dressed.

"Whatever vehicle they're in has an oil leak. That won't narrow it down much, but it could help."

His phone rang. Caelan grimaced after looking at the screen. "Thorvin is trying to get a hold of me."

I looked around at the blanket of white surrounding us. "We're on foot in rural Michigan. Pretty shortsighted on our part."

Caelan shook his head. "This isn't his Keep. I've been trying to convince him to stay with his shifters, but he's been strangely resistant. We have one more place to check, and they'll have vehicles we can use."

"How far away is the Keep?"

"A few miles." He pulled up another picture. I studied it for a bit and nodded.

We joined hands as the world fell away once more.

Wolves converged on us as soon as we popped onto the edge of Ben's property. Caelan held his hands up. "I'm here to help."

Before anyone could say anything, Caelan said the words that got everyone's attention. "Your Lord is missing."

A flash of light and a male, tall and deadly looking stood in the wolf's place. "Lord Caelan." He dipped his head before turning his attention to me. "And you must be the Floromancer."

I winced. "Evie."

"I am Christian, Ben's Second." His skin was a dusky olive tone, and his eyes were a gorgeous, green-dominant hazel. A large scar bisected his left cheek, ending at his lip. It took a lot of damage to disfigure a wolf to the point where their innate healing abilities didn't override any scarring. Instead of taking away from his allure, it only served to heighten his good looks.

"Ben didn't show up to the Lord's meeting," Caelan said. "We went by his house—"

A flicker of something in Christian's eyes. He disapproved of Ben's residence choice, too. "Someone took him."

Caelan nodded. "I'm afraid so. We'd like to borrow a vehicle if you've one to spare."

"Of course. We can provide an escort."

Caelan shook his head. "I'm happy to take a couple of you, but I want to have the element of surprise."

Christian's eyes narrowed. "Who do you believe is behind this?"

"I don't want to say yet. Not until we find them."

Christian looked like he wanted to argue, but kept his mouth shut. "Very well." He jerked his head back. "Pax! With me!"

A massive white wolf stepped forward and shifted. I'd never been around this many naked dudes since I accidentally walked into the wrong gym bathroom when I was in college.

Correction. This many hot dudes. I kept my eyes firmly on the collarbone and above and tried not to fidget. Shifters were used to nudity all the time. Floromancers, especially this one, were not. Not that we were prudes about it, usually, but shifter packs had very few women, and I was a woman in my prime.

Caelan stepped closer, almost like he'd seen my internal

struggle not to ogle and slid his fingers over my arm. Proprietary and steadying.

Christian's eyes glimmered with amusement, but he turned. "Follow. The garage is toward the back of the keep. There's a private road out. Pax and I will lead, if you allow it, Lord. We've become familiar with some of the places Lord Ben frequents."

Caelan inclined his head. "Of course. I'm here to assist only."

They led us to a large, multiple car garage. A large, dark SUV already waited for us, the engine running. Two bags sat by the driver's side door. Christian and Pax each grabbed one.

"Excuse us for a moment," Christian said.

He and Pax disappeared into the house.

"Do you think we'll find him?" I asked in a low voice.

"With his wolves helping, there's a much better chance than before."

The two wolves stepped back outside dressed in t-shirts, joggers, and slip-on tennis shoes, the uniform every shifter adopted once they got tired of shredding clothes every time they shifted to animal form and back.

The quiet, blond wolf opened the back passenger door, gesturing for me to get inside.

"Thank you," I murmured.

Pax said nothing, closing the door gently behind me. Once we were all inside, the vehicle roared out of the Keep.

Everywhere I looked there was white. The ground was a sheet of ivory, the trees skeletal, limbs bowing with the weight of snow. "I wonder if there are other Floromancers living here," I said mostly to myself, but Christian met my eyes in the mirror.

"The weather proves challenging," he admitted. "We had one several years ago, but she didn't stay long. We've been unable to lure one here since."

Caelan's eyes narrowed, making the other wolf laugh. "I have no designs on your woman, Lord Caelan, but Floromancers are good for a wolf's land." He snorted softly. "Shit, they're good for the world."

I nudged Caelan. "I like him."

Caelan snapped his teeth at me.

"For serious magic, I have to be connected to the earth," I told Christian. "I can imagine it might be a challenge to do so with so much snow on the ground."

"Do you require bare skin?"

I thought Caelan was going to lose it. "Yes, when I'm deep into my magic, at minimum, my feet are against bare earth. I usually try bare legs too, but sometimes, I lie down all the way. But there are other times, when the earth requires me to be completely bare, and I will wake up unclothed." I chuckled. "I've lost some good pieces of clothing that way, though it doesn't happen often."

"If you know of any other Floromancers who seek a good home, Ben has proven to be a good Lord, and we would welcome one. Though, if I'm not mistaken, you and our Lord are familiar with each other?"

Caelan snorted.

"Yes," I said slowly. "We've had our ups and downs," I admitted, "though things are growing easier between us."

Christian looked over at Caelan, his eyes lingering for a moment too long. "Ah," he said finally. "I see."

"You see nothing," Caelan said softly. "Evie and Ben are acquaintances, that's all."

I sighed. "So dramatic." Shaking my head, I met Christian's eyes in the mirror once more. "I like your Lord, and if things would have been different, who knows what might have happened."

Caelan let out a loud sigh. I grinned at him. "You know it's true."

"Yes, yes, now can you quit twisting the knife in? Otherwise, I might abandon this search and take you back home."

I rolled my eyes. "Fine. Let's focus on finding him so we can get back home. It's cold as hell here."

Pax had stayed silent the entire time. He flipped his visor

down and opened his mirror, his eyes trained on me. "You are the Floromancer who took on the gods, Miss Quinn?"

"Evie, please," I said with a slight grimace. "And, yes, I suppose I did in a way."

Pax had an unnerving intensity about him. Under his attention, I felt like he and I were the only people in the vehicle. "Is it true you were trapped inside of a tree?"

"Pax," Christian hissed.

I held up a hand. "No. It's okay. Really. The fae are tricky, and the more knowledge you have, the better, especially since they're finding our plane of existence far more interesting than before."

Christian's eyes narrowed. "You're seeing more fae in Joy Springs?"

Caelan nodded. "Far too many for my liking."

"We are, though I'm afraid part of it is my fault. I am of mixed heritage, which adds some unique flavor to my magic. My Floromancy is…strange among my own kind. And, to answer your question, yes, I was trapped in a tree for…a month, I think." I shook my head. "Time was fuzzy inside. I was incorporeal in a way, and my thoughts weren't always coherent."

Pax studied me. "How did you get out?"

I shifted in my seat and tugged my jacket closer. This question required treading carefully. I'd escaped that tree because of my Chimera magic. If I'd gone in as a simple Floromancer, I don't think I would have survived. "A witch cast a spell focused on my…" I frowned. "My soul, I guess? I'm not sure, but it was a beacon back to her and the people who loved me. Once I had a direction, it was a matter of channeling every bit of power I had left to find my way home. My mixed magic came in handy."

Pax's eyes lit up with gold around his irises. Caelan stilled beside me. He'd noticed it, too. One day this young wolf might be a Lord. The promise of power glimmered in his eyes. "You believe other species can find peace and sometimes love with each other?"

I blinked in surprise. That was not where I expected this

conversation to go. "Absolutely. I never expected to be involved with a Lord, yet here I am, tracking another one down."

Pax's eyes flicked to Caelan and back to me. "Has it been complicated?"

At that, Caelan let out a belly laugh, surprising all of us.

I laughed too. "Extremely," I admitted. "Forces worked together to keep us apart, but I'm still here. With Caelan. And with all of you. I think paranormals should be able to love and mate with whomever they want to. Though I understand purity in bloodlines and know it's necessary in some cases where mating outside of the line might be harmful, intermingling bloodlines allows for new veins of magic, and interesting opportunities to solve problems."

"Problems?" Pax's brow furrowed. "What do you mean?"

I thought about how much information to divulge. "Well, some bloodlines are volatile and breed magic that is harmful both to the user and to those around them. Intermingling might help tame those abilities to something more manageable. Take seers for example. Many of them can't drive or hold normal jobs. What if having children with a shifter could tamper their line just enough to allow them to live normally?"

I shrugged. "I'm no geneticist, but if you continue to breed within your kind, you can't breed out any problems."

"We don't have illnesses," Christian said.

"Sure, but I'm sure there have been cases where certain genetic factors might pop up in families. Let's take cystic fibrosis as an example. One parent has the gene, and one does not. That child will not be born with cystic fibrosis because only one gene passes down; however, there's a fifty percent chance of them being a carrier of the gene, so the cycle continues. If both parents have the gene, there's a 25% percent chance of their child having cystic fibrosis, and a 25% chance of not being a carrier of the gene. Right?"

Everyone nodded, though Caelan was giving me an odd look. "Same thing with shifters or witches or Floromancers, any paranormal really. There's always a chance of something odd in the gene pool. So why wouldn't you want outside blood and genetic material to see if you can eventually breed those out?"

Caelan's lips twitched. "That is both a coldly analytical and surprisingly scientific take."

I shrugged. "The fae cling to their bloodlines like a tick on a thigh."

Pax's look lingered before he turned his attention to Caelan. "Your Floromancer is both intelligent and beautiful. I look forward to seeing the future of your Keep and your shifters if you two marry."

For the first time since I'd known him, Caelan looked nonplussed. "Err. Thank you?"

I hid my smile. "Why are you so interested in interspecies relations?"

Pax's eyes flickered. "My parents dealt with their own genetic issues."

I waited for him to elaborate, but when he didn't, I nodded. Maybe this was an extremely personal matter, and Pax only wanted the opinion of an outsider. "I hope one day they will find a resolution."

The shifter inclined his head before snapping the mirror shut and raising his visor.

"We're almost to town," Christian said. "Pax, roll down the window and see if you can catch his scent."

"I have the vehicle's scent," Caelan said. "It had an oil leak and at least two people inside, minus Ben."

Christian nodded. "We'll stop at his apartment first."

"How many places does Ben have?" I murmured.

"He stays in the apartment when he has business in town and then with us a few days of the week. Most of the time he resides at the home you just left."

Curious. I didn't like leaving my home much and couldn't imagine splitting my residences between three places. Ben didn't seem like a typical Lord, and I wondered if that had something to do with his reticence to live at the Keep full time. He wasn't a wolf, nor was he a bear…maybe the difference made him uncomfortable?

Shaking my head, I tugged my jacket closer and looked outside the window. Caelan and Pax both had their faces out the window sniffing like German Shepherds. The sight of it amused me, and I wished we were here on something much more mundane than finding a lost Lord.

Ethan had escaped with our intervention, though he didn't know we were the reason for his reprieve. But Ben could be anywhere. I interlaced my fingers together and sent a whisper of power out the window as Christian slowed the vehicle. Plants and trees couldn't talk, not in the sense we could, but they could send back images and feelings.

I projected an image of Ben to the landscaping and waited for it to respond. Seconds later, a faint sigh came through my senses. They'd seen nothing of importance.

I touched them with thanks and waited as we moved on.

Christian pulled into the parking lot of a small apartment complex a few minutes later. Nondescript, taupe apartments with black doors, all the units identical. "Come," the shifter said as he pulled into a parking spot and slid from the vehicle.

We followed, Caelan coming up beside me. His body heat beat at my skin, and I squashed the urge to burrow into him.

Christian went upstairs and knocked a few times, but no one answered. He pulled out a keychain loaded with multiple keys and, after a moment of searching for the right one, opened the door.

I knew the moment we walked in Ben wasn't present. Christian and Pax searched every room before shaking their heads. "There's a warehouse under Keep ownership where we conduct business sometimes. Let's check there."

Without a word, we loaded up and got on the road again.

This place was fifteen minutes away, and there wasn't much around to hide our presence.

"We'll need to park somewhere and walk in if we want any hope of stealth," Christian said.

Caelan nodded. "How far?"

The shifter pointed to a large gray building maybe half a mile away.

"Do you want to stay in the car?" Caelan said.

I snorted. "Not particularly. I can help once we get closer. I see one large tree, but there may be more. I can try to calculate how many people are in the building before you approach."

Christian's eyebrows rose. "Can you really?"

I shrugged. "Trees and plants can communicate in their own way. If there's any greenery inside, that's even better.

His brow furrowed. "We don't use the place to meet that often, so I don't think so. Anything inside would have died."

I chewed on the side of my lips. "No admin people with plants on their desks or anything like that?"

Pax spoke up. "We do have a female wolf in charge of operations. It's very possible she has something. Should I call her?"

"Text," Caelan ordered. "We need to get moving." He looked at me. "Do you need to know what it is?"

I shook my head. "Approximate location would be nice to prevent anyone from sensing my magic, but if they don't have it, I'll make it work."

Pax bent his head over his phone and typed rapidly as we headed over.

"Let's get within a block. We may need someone to go to higher ground and see if anything stands out." Caelan moved to the front, leaving me walking next to Pax.

"Pothos," Pax said. "That's all she has. And she said it wasn't in the best shape. Some shit about the lighting."

My look was disapproving. "Just like people, plants have needs that must be met, too."

To his credit, he looked chagrined. "Sorry. I'm not used to plants being of assistance in something like that."

I nodded. "That's because they're too busy keeping you breathing."

From ahead, Christian barked a laugh. "She's got you there."

Pax grinned. "That's why we need a Floromancer around."

We fell silent as we approached a two-story building. Christian examined it with a critical eye. "It's higher than most buildings, but I'm not sure how much advantage going up there will give us."

"Try anyway," Caelan said. "You never know if there'll be a clear path to a window in your eyesight. If they left one open, we might be able to see what's going on from a distance instead of going in blind. If not, we'll keep moving and let Evie do her thing."

Christian said nothing, taking hold of a drainpipe and shimmying to the top of the building. He gave us a thumbs up before disappearing up and over the side.

"The building isn't that large, so it's possible he'll be able to see something," Caelan said.

"Who are we potentially dealing with?" Pax asked.

"I'll tell you when I know for sure," Caelan said.

If it were Donovan and Nadia, which it had to be, I wondered how far they would go to get answers. The problem was, no one they took had any answers. But there was an even bigger problem. Donovan knew what happened to Gianna, so he was playing Nadia, allowing her to question the other Lords without divulging he knew where Gianna was buried.

Or used to be buried.

I'd discarded her bones to the elements and hidden her DNA so deep into the earth, no one would ever find it. Unfortunate, but I wasn't the one who'd killed her. Finn and Rhona had done those honors, involving Donovan as well, in an effort to frame me.

While I felt for Nadia and thought her mission to find out what happened was honorable, if she found out, it could cause a war with the other Lords and potentially with the fae as well.

There was no way to return Gianna's body, which might have appeased her, because it simply no longer existed.

My brow furrowed. Could we rebuild her a new body? Was there a fae who might be able to create something that might serve as Gianna's body so they could hold a funeral for her?

Or was there another reason Nadia was searching so hard to find her cousin? Was it possible Gianna had something on her that Nadia needed? Something I'd missed when I sent her remains to the earth?

Paranoia was occasionally one of my specialties. While my theory seemed a little outlandish, I grew up with a fae mother and nothing about them surprised me anymore, except for their most recent revelation which I was still trying to process. They'd go to the ends of the earth for revenge and never let a slight go. But, at least in the case of my mother, they had an endless capacity for love and would go to extreme lengths to keep their loved ones safe.

Shifters also had some of the same mentality, especially if it had to do with Pack. I knew jack shit about swans, though. Everything I knew came from those funny video shows where swans would harass the shit out of someone. Maybe the swan shifters hated each other.

Or maybe I was making shit up just to try to make sense out of this mess.

A soft thump revealed Christian crouching. "Those idiots left the windows uncovered. We're too far away for a facial I.D., but there's two men and one woman." His expression was grim. "One of them is in a chair and covered with blood."

Caelan swore. "Let's go. Evie, as soon as we get close enough, see if you can find anything else out."

Christian gave us an odd look but shrugged.

We took off running, careful to avoid the icy spots, but hurrying as fast we could.

Ben's life depended on our expedience.

Eighteen

Hiding in winter was difficult as hell. Caelan and I hadn't thought of our attire when we'd barreled into Michigan on a rescue mission. We stuck out like sore thumbs.

"We should shift," Caelan murmured. He looked over at me. "How long will it take you?"

"A few minutes. The snow makes things a little more difficult, but not impossible."

"We're having odd weather this year," Christian remarked. "It's colder than usual and snowed far sooner than it normally does."

I stripped off my gloves and sat onto the freezing ground, wiping snow away until I hit the frozen ground. Caelan moved closer. When Pax and Christian noticed what he was doing, they moved as well, trapping me in a protective circle.

I closed my eyes and centered myself, shifting the Chimera magic away to focus only on my Floromancy. Concentrating twice as hard to prevent any of that other magic coming to the forefront because of the mixed company, focusing took me twice as long.

Once I felt completely in control, I placed my fingers on top of the soil and gently sent my magic forth, seeking anything I could find out about Ben.

Natural magic roared through my veins as I gently cracked through the frozen ground and down where the soil was softer. A shiver rolled over me, and I felt the heavy weight of something… another jacket or blanket, settling over my shoulders, already warm from someone's body.

It didn't take long for the ground to tell me a story. The land closer to the building was shaken at the violence. Blood lay at the surface close to the door. Not enough to be worrisome and probably from the same wound he'd sustained back at his home.

I examined the soil around the entire building, but the brunt of the information stayed by the front door. Easing a vine through the soil, I crept up the wall, searching for any vulnerabilities to allow me in.

The building was old, so there were several. Something to keep in mind if things went really sideways. Holding the vine there at the first tiny opening, I withdrew and searched for the supposed pothos inside.

It took far too long, and when I finally found it, it was so close to death, it was almost useless. Resisting the urge to boost nutrients in the soil and perk it up, I gently touched one of the leaves to read the plant's emotions. I gasped in horror. Blood. So much blood. Violence. Anger. Despair.

I jerked away, coming out of my magic with a gasp. "Ben is seriously injured." I swallowed hard. "That's all I know."

Caelan's eyes glowed with power. "We go in. Right now."

"We only have half an hour before the potion wears off," I warned.

"If things go well, everyone will be dead in five," Christian growled.

Three flashes of light revealed three wildly different wolves, Caelan looming over the other two. He nudged me once with his head. When I went to follow, he pushed me back and yipped softly.

"Stay?"

He nodded.

I scoffed. "I can help."

He shook his head and nudged me again.

I crouched and looked him in the eye. "We talked about this. I'm going. I'll stay outside, but I'm going with you."

Caelan's upper lip curled, showing off impressive fangs.

I patted his head. "Yes, you're so impressive."

A soft huff of air from the other wolves. Caelan bumped me again and turned.

When I followed this time, he didn't react.

We crept silently closer to the building, sticking to areas of thicker brush as best we could, though the entire area was thin with plant life, even in the densest of areas. When we were a few feet away, Caelan nudged his head, and Pax and Christian veered off to the right.

Caelan speared me with a look and veered left. I sank to the ground and waited. All three wolves had their noses to the ground, carefully investigating. They disappeared around the corners, but it wasn't long before they were back.

Caelan loped over to me and shifted in a flash of light. "Ben's missing an arm. We'll need your healing abilities, and I don't think we'll have time to get him home."

I blinked. "An arm?" I swallowed. "Can a shifter regrow a limb?"

"Maybe." He bent and pressed a firm kiss against my lips. "Stay ready."

I nodded. He ran back over and waited by the door. Pax and Christian crouched, their lips pulled away from their teeth. Caelan braced himself and ripped the door off the hinges.

A high-pitched feminine scream rang into the quiet winter air. Savage satisfaction flooded my bloodstream. The back door banged open and two huge wolves barreled out, tangled together and tearing each other apart.

Caelan and another who had to be Donovan. Pax and Christian came out the front in human form, the younger wolf holding Ben in a bridal carry. Blood pumped from his severed arm. I sucked in a shocked breath and rushed toward them, gathering my magic as I ran.

"We have to get him back to the Keep," Christian said as I struggled to keep up.

Ben's face was white, his head lolling with Pax's movement.

"I'm not sure he'll make it." My mind spun at the thought of losing him. "Is there a garden center around?"

Christian stumbled. "What?" He looked at me like I'd lost my mind.

"Indoors. Warmth. Dirt, plants. It's too dangerous to heal him right here, and I might freeze my ass off. Or die. Shit, I don't know. I live in Texas, and it rarely gets below freezing for more than a few days at a time. The ground is frozen, and my magic feels more sluggish than normal."

"There's a hardware store with a garden center a couple of miles down the road," Pax said.

I looked at Christian. His nostrils flared, but after a long moment, he gave a sharp nod.

We reached the vehicle. "Lord Caelan?"

Caelan would be furious if I waited on him when his best friend was near death. "He'll be fine."

Christian blinked.

"I'm serious. Let's go."

Pax took off at a furious run, but Christian scooped me in his arms, ignoring my undignified squawk, and chased after him.

"Apologies, Miss Quinn. Wolves run much faster, and if Ben doesn't have much time, we can't wait."

I wrapped my arms around his neck to keep from bouncing everywhere. "No problem. I never was much of a runner."

He bared his teeth in a smile. "No one expects that of Floromancers."

We reached the vehicle in what felt like record time, and soon we were racing down the road while Pax and Christian dressed in extra joggers and t-shirts. I held Ben's head in my lap, magic pulsing from the hand I held pressed to the stump of his right arm. With my other, I stroked his hair away from his face.

"I'm here, Ben," I said quietly. "Probably not the one you were hoping would swoop in and help, but I'm what you got. So, maybe don't die, okay? Because I'm going to be super pissed if we went through all we've gone through, and I can't save you. And before you say, 'Evie, this is not about you', yes, it is, because it's my turn to save you. Also, we might wake up in a cage, and we might be naked—"

A choked laugh from the front.

"And that's going to make Caelan really mad, but I can't help it, and neither can you, okay? The earth wants what the earth wants."

I couldn't stop babbling. "Oh, and we might wake up in a hardware store, which will be really awkward if we're naked, so maybe your nice wolves can bring us some extra clothing."

The vehicle stopped. Pax and Christian barreled out. Someone opened the passenger door and helped me out. Pax scooped Ben up.

"Around back," Christian said. "I'll call the owner and let him know what we're doing so we don't get interrupted by the police."

We ran around to the back. Christian unceremoniously broke the glass and forced his way in. My boots crunched over broken glass, and I winced as I thought about the costs involved in what we were about to do, but Ben wasn't just a shifter. He was a Lord, and once upon a time, he'd been something more to me. Now, I consider him a friend. Whether he considered me one was up in the air, but I don't think he hated me anymore.

Even if he did, I wasn't going to let him die.

"By the potting soil is the easiest place," I said, following Christian as he ran through the store. Pax followed close behind.

When we got there, I looked around. It would do. There was room enough for the cage that formed over me when I performed healings like this. I pulled my cell out of my pocket and shared my location with Caelan. He'd come when he was finished. However, it ended.

"Lay him down," I instructed as I stripped off my jacket, sweater, and undershirt.

Christian swore and looked away. "Is that necessary, Miss Quinn?"

"That's good Merino wool and cashmere, and I don't want the earth to eat it. If one of you doesn't mind sharing a shirt, I'm happy to wear it, but even so, I'm thinking about stripping my bra off, too. It was expensive."

Without a word, Pax shrugged his jacket off and pulled the t-shirt over his head, handing it to me. Once I had it on, he stripped off his pants, too. Christian sighed as he pulled several bags of potting soil down.

"Organic is best. Nothing with chemical fertilizers, please."

I put Pax's joggers on and lay beside Ben, scooting until I was spooning him. "Cover every inch of us, except for our faces."

The shifters worked quickly. Moments later, my teeth were chattering like crazy. It was cold as hell inside the building, and the dirt was moist. But we weren't outside, and there was no longer a real danger of getting hypothermia.

"You might want to stand back. Once I go deep enough, I can no longer control how the magic works."

"We'll be close, Evie," Pax said, his eyes burning as he watched.

I closed my eyes and sank into my Floromancy.

Ben was in agonizing pain. Bruises and broken bones lit the inside of his body up like a Christmas tree. So much damage it took my breath away. I started at the most crucial point first—his arm, sending power directly to the arteries and veins, tendons, and muscles, willing them to repair. I'd never grown any body parts back and had no idea whether that was even possible, but I followed my intuition and the magic, allowing it to wrap Ben tightly in the power of the Mother.

I'm not sure how long I worked on the missing appendage, but finally, the blood flow stopped, his arm glowing with green and pink magic. Keeping my senses open for any regression, I swept through his body searching for other pain points, slowly knitting bone and easing bruises and other damage. Nadia and Donovan, if that's who hurt him, had done a thorough job.

Ben was a Healer, a powerful one, and if even he couldn't keep up with the damage, he was lucky to be alive. I only hoped this was enough.

As I worked, knitting and soothing his hurts, my magic waned, my thoughts turning away from coherency into feelings and emotion, and the Mother swept in, taking over my watch and helping keep Ben tethered to this world, safe in her arms.

Nineteen

CAELAN

Donovan was a sonofabitch, and I was going to kill him. Again.

Walking into that building and seeing my friend unconscious and slowly bleeding to death had set off a dangerous rage, the likes of which I hadn't felt since I was a young wolf coming into my power.

We circled each other, Donovan bleeding from multiple bites and claw marks. He was starting to limp, but I wasn't in the mood to finish things. He'd gone after Evie and tried to kill her. He'd unsettled the Council, pitting us against each other. I'd watched him slowly and meticulously undermine every Lord, sometimes taking years to dismantle their authority so he could pass something on his still confusing agenda. I'd always hated the sonofabitch, and I didn't mourn him when I'd killed him.

Or so I thought.

Donovan sat on his haunches and bowed, his body language asking for a break. As pissed as I was, even I didn't have the heart to kill a weak man. I stepped back, keeping a careful eye on him.

He shifted in a flash of light and crouched in the darkness, weak moonlight reflecting off his pale skin. I did the same, carefully watching him.

"So it's come to this," he rasped.

"It's come to nothing since you were supposed to be dead," I said mildly. "I'm only trying to finish the job."

He bared his teeth in a semblance of a smile. "You always were too clever for your own good. How'd you figure it out?"

"I didn't. Evie did."

At the mention of her name, Donovan's eyes flashed with fury. For some reason, he hated Evie with a passion I'd rarely seen the man show. "And how did the Floromancer find out?"

I shrugged. "What can I say? She's a very clever girl."

And gone, which was the reason I was continuing to bait him. It was only he and I, Nadia was long gone. Well, maybe not long gone. A swan could never outrun a wolf, and I still had a good bead on her location. When I finished here, I'd go after her next.

"Still protecting your Floromancer?" Donovan snorted and rose to his full height. "She will be the death of you."

"And what a death it will be. To be led by a woman firm in her convictions and immune to the political bullshit we deal with on a day-to-day basis, most of it our damn fault." I smiled. "I'd gladly die next to her if I meant I finally stood for something."

Donovan snorted. "When did you become such a sap?"

I lifted a shoulder in a careless shrug. "You've never been in love. Once you know the pain of your heart when it struggles to grasp the one who's taken it, you will know why I speak the way I do."

"Now you spout flowery poetry?" He scoffed. "You are nothing like the man I knew a few years ago."

"You're right." I was better. Less prone to pick fights, more likely to listen before I reacted, and more invested in the people around me. While Evie was mostly responsible for the changes in me, I had to credit Rowan as well. He was the reason Evie stood by my side.

I didn't give a shit what Donovan or any of the other Lords thought about me. "What's this about? Why target Ben? And why involve Nadia?"

"If you're expecting a villain monologue, I'm afraid I'll have to disappoint you."

"Then there's nothing left to say."

Donovan held a hand up. "If you kill me in cold blood, you will bring war down upon the Lords."

If the other Lords turned out like him, maybe it's time we went to war. "The kill is justified. The Lords have already decided so."

"And Ethan?" Donovan said, wearing a too satisfied smirk.

"Ethan won't care if you live or die. I'm sure he'd prefer you in the ground. Just like the rest of us."

"He didn't tell the other Lords about me." A crafty look slid over his face.

"I wonder why."

When I stepped toward him, Donovan took a step back. "Wait. I have information you'll want to hear."

"Then spit it out." My patience wore thin. Evie had taken off with Ben's wolves, and the Lord himself had looked close to death. I wanted Donovan out of the picture, so I could track down Nadia and shake some sense into her. Then I needed to find Evie.

Relief filled me the moment I spotted them deciding to take off with Ben. She'd trusted me and trusted herself. This felt like…

I don't know. I felt like we were winning. With each other. And wasn't that a big leap from where we were a few short months ago?

Donovan swallowed hard at my expression. My patience was running extremely thin, and I was sick of looking at his sniveling face. "Nadia is looking for something."

He licked his lips and shifted his eyes to the left.

Donovan wasn't telling me something.

"You've got five seconds to come clean. I'm freezing my fucking balls off and have no interest in continuing this."

Maybe he was delaying so Nadia could get away…

"She needs it for something." He shook his head. "Won't tell me what it is, but Gianna had it on her when she died, and it's making her fucking crazy she can't find the body."

Explained why they were kidnapping the other Lords. "And you decided to go along for the ride, even though you know damn well where Gianna is buried?"

His eyes glittered with greed. "She didn't need to know that. Not yet, at least. And I wanted to know what it was that she needed so badly."

"What's she looking for?"

Donovan licked his lips again. "She won't tell me."

I took another step forward, my claws sliding from my fingers.

"I'm serious, Caelan!" He held his hands up. "Whatever it is, it's big."

Evie might not have noticed anything when she sent Gianna's remains to the earth. She would have been focused on only biological material. We needed to look at her property when we got back.

"Tell me why we need you to find it."

Donovan blinked. For a Lord, sometimes he was a dumbass. "I'm the one who has the in with her! She trusts me!"

I snorted. "You can't be that stupid. She thinks we're the ones responsible. Have you thought maybe she trusts you just as much as you trust her?"

Donovan stared at me for a long moment. In a flash of light, he shifted and took off running through the snow.

A heavy sigh came from deep within my chest.

I hated running in the cold.

CHAPTER
Twenty

Something was wrong. I came to in complete darkness, lying next to a warm, familiar body. No light streamed in anywhere, and my power felt…off.

Off in a good way, but still off. Magic leached through my veins and bones, Mother Earth's power flowing through my body, into Ben by the hand I had on his chest, and back into the dirt. The cycle of life.

But the normal cage that formed around my body wasn't there, and if I didn't know better, I'd say we were buried in the earth, far below ground. We had a small pocket of air surrounding us, I think. I couldn't see a damn thing.

"Ben?"

The shifter stirred.

"Don't panic," I murmured. "But I think we're below ground. There's air. For how long, I can't say."

His chest rumbled. "Evie."

"Try not to move. I'm not sure how stable this place is. I don't think the Mother would kill us after all she did to heal you, but we shouldn't risk it."

"You saved me." His voice was rough and tired.

"I had help. Caelan is still out there. And two of your wolves are waiting above."

He laced his fingers through mine. "Thank you."

I scoffed. "I'd never let you die. I have lots to make up for."

Ben slowly turned until he lay on his side facing me, our fingers still interlocked. His face was lined with exhaustion. "I was an asshole to you."

I said nothing because this was not a lie.

The edge of his lips tipped up. "You didn't know me enough to share your secrets, and I pushed much too fast and was too aggressive." He sighed. "And Caelan swooped in and got you."

"He did," I agreed.

"Evie?"

"Hmm?"

"Is there a reason we're both naked?"

I laughed. "The Mother likes to eat my clothing when I go into extreme healing mode, and, by extension, the ones I'm healing. Sorry about that."

He shook his head. "Caelan's going to be pissed if he sees us."

"It already happened once. He's going to have to get used to it if his shifters keep getting wounded."

His brows drew together. "Who was it?"

"Garrett."

At his wide eyes, I shook my head. "He's okay."

"I didn't know you could heal like this." He sucked in a breath. "My arm."

I smiled. "Is back and whole again. I wasn't sure about that one, though I'm glad to know it's possible to regrow a limb."

"Shifter healing allows for regrowth depending on the wound." His mouth tightened. "I'm not sure mine would have. The wound was…extreme."

"You almost died." I blinked tears away.

He brushed wetness from my cheek. "You mourn for me even when being treated so poorly."

Ben sighed. "I did not deserve you. Caelan is the better man."

They're both good men. I shifted, soil and roots digging into my back. "I should start looking for a way to get us out of here. You're being far calmer about this than I expected."

Ben chuckled. "If I were here with anyone other than the most powerful Floromancer in the country, I might be a little more flustered."

"Don't get too relaxed," I muttered. "This is the first time I've ever been underground. I'm scared I'll collapse the entire thing down on us."

He squeezed my hand. "I have faith in you."

"That makes one of us." My cell was in the clothes I'd left above ground, and there was no way Nadia and Donovan had left Ben with his, but I had to ask.

"No chance of a phone on you? A flashlight would come in handy right now."

"No need," Ben said. His eyes began to glow ice blue mixed with a ring of gold.

Just as I suspected. We were buried in the dirt on all sides. I shifted my body and investigated, reaching out to touch the barrier. Thick, dark dirt and roots on all sides.

"Alright, I'm going to send up some vines to gauge the depth. Try not to move."

Ben nodded.

I sent a thin vine from my fingertips up through the dirt, thickening it as needed to break through the thick, moist soil. We had to be under the surface of the store, and if we were down here, then we must have broken through the concrete and foundation.

I winced. That would be an expensive bill.

Ben shifted closer, his hand snagging around my waist. I stilled. "Ben?"

"It's cold in here."

I huffed a breath. "Liar. We're in a cocoon. It's plain toasty."

His large, calloused hand splayed over my bare stomach.

"Ben."

Lips pressed to the side of my neck, and God bless America, it took everything I had to keep my thoughts somewhat coherent.

"Hmm?"

I cleared my throat. "This would have been welcome a few months ago. But I'm with Caelan. If we break through the dirt, and Caelan is there, you might lose another arm."

His lips stopped moving. He chuckled, warm air shuffling through my hair. "You're right."

A heavy sigh and then, "I'm sorry."

"Maybe move your hand back over to your side. We're at least six feet deep here and still going up."

Ben stilled. "What the hell happened?"

"No idea." I turned my head to study him. "Are you okay? Does everything feel normal?"

Ben laughed. "I feel twenty years younger."

He froze. "*Evie.*"

Ben was a Healer. He knew what I'd done, what I could do. If he told anyone, I'd be in danger from all sides.

His eyes were wide and frigidly blue. "How long have you been able to do this?"

I shrugged. "I'm not really sure. Maybe always. I never had the chance to fully test until recently."

"Do you know how much danger you'd be in if anyone knew about this?"

"Yes," I said quietly. "I do. Are you going to tell anyone, Ben?"

His nostrils flared. "Evie. How little you must think of me." He shook his head. "And I deserve it. I have not been on my best behavior with you." He interlocked our fingers once more and squeezed my hand. "The answer is no, I would never betray your confidence."

A pregnant pause. "Does Caelan know?"

I nodded. Good possibility Garrett knew, too. Or suspected, at least. Did I regret it? No. I'd never let someone die if I had the ability to help him.

"You healed him the first night you saw him. I'd forgotten about that." He let out a soft laugh.

"I should have known from that moment when he spoke about you with such awe without even knowing who you were, you'd become special to him. To me. To all of us, really."

My heart warmed. "You make it sound so cozy when it was anything but rosy for the first few months."

We both laughed at the disaster that was our courtship. He'd never trusted me, and I never trusted him. We were doomed from the start, even if I had wanted more. Yet, Caelan, for all his pushiness and the ferocity of his pursuit, he was the one who never gave up on me. Even if he went about it the wrong way for a long time.

As we talked, I kept sending my magic up, up, up. I was at twelve feet, then thirteen, then fifteen until finally, there was no resistance.

"Sixteen feet," I murmured. "Holy shit." How is that even possible?

"Wow. Any idea how we're going to get back up there without a ton of dirt collapsing on us?"

I sat there for a long moment, my thoughts whirling with the possibility and odds of keeping both of us alive. "How long can you hold your breath?"

Ben's brows flicked up. "I'm not much of a swimmer, so I couldn't tell you."

Could I breathe for him?

Something tugged gently on the end of my vine. A familiar sense washed over me.

"Caelan is up there." No way to be 100% sure, but I'd bet money on it. I thickened my vine and sent more up. Two gentle tugs before a firmer tug that moved me up several inches.

"Ben. Wrap your arms around me. Now."

He blinked. "But—"

"I don't care that we're naked. Caelan or someone is up there pulling me up. Hitch on for the ride. I'll speed it up as fast as I can, but you may need to hold your breath."

Another firm tug, pulling me away from him. Ben rolled into me. I shifted, wrapping my legs around his waist. My breasts pressed into his chest, as I embraced him tightly.

"Caelan is not going to like this."

"Caelan is not trapped fifteen feet underground."

"Fair enough." Ben's arms tightened around me. I pressed my face against his chest and shot multiple vines up toward the surface.

A few seconds later, I was flying through roots and dirt, wrapped around a Shifter Lord.

CHAPTER
Twenty-One

CAELAN

en appeared first, followed by Evie, both wrapped around each other.

Both nude.

I had to close my eyes for a long moment and get myself together. This was the second time in less than a week that the woman I loved more than life ended up trapped with one of my shifters.

In Ben's case, former shifter.

It wasn't her fault. Evie's nature was something I had to work with and not against. But seeing the way she and Ben were entangled…it took everything I had not to swipe his pretty face with a fistful of claws.

Both of their eyes were closed, their heads lolling against each other. And even though they were tangled together, neither was conscious. They looked as if their last act was to make sure neither was lost in the dark as they sought the light.

Evie's vines went limp. I swore and reached for Ben, jerking him out of the ground, Evie still holding on. I tried to separate them, but neither would let go, almost as if they were glued together.

Gritting my teeth, I rolled Ben onto his back, forcing Evie right on top, and hit her in the middle of her back twice.

Just enough for her lungs to restart. She coughed once, twice, three times, and gagged, expelling an alarming amount of dirt.

Evie probably wouldn't have died, not from inhaling dirt. Her nature, after all, was inherently tied to the earth. But seeing her prone, unconscious body stirred something dark and dangerous inside me.

Her eyes dragged open, unfocused and filled with dirt. She blinked away the worst of it, realized who she was on top of, gasped, gagged again, and threw herself to the side, her back thumping to the ground.

"Caelan?" she croaked, not seeing me yet.

I crouched beside her. "I'm right here."

Her lips pulled back from her teeth in a grimace before dirty tears slid from her eyes. "Is he okay?"

In answer, I flipped Ben over none too gently and whacked him on the back, far more forcefully than I did Evie.

But nothing happened.

I shook his shoulder. "Ben?"

Evie scooted closer to him. She lay a hand on his shoulder. Seeing her touch him made my jaw tighten, but I kept my burning jealousy inside. "Ben?"

No movement.

Evie sat up abruptly. "Roll him over."

I didn't ask why, simply did as she asked.

She shook him again. "Ben!"

No response once more. She called her magic to her fingers and pressed her hand against his chest. Magic the color of watermelon tourmaline rose to the surface and covered his body from head to toe. As I watched, Evie snaked a vine into Ben's body.

The Lord jerked, his back bowed.

"Turn him to the side," Evie commanded.

I tilted Ben seconds before a torrent of dirt and gravel poured from his mouth.

Evie rubbed his back, withdrawing her magic. "Get all of it out."

We watched as Ben shuddered and gagged, vomiting up black soil. When he finally finished, Ben sagged against the ground and groaned.

Evie winced. "I'm so sorry." She looked up at me.

"I don't know how it happened. I've never gone underground like that, not that far. If I do, I usually stay mostly above the surface." Her voice trailed off as she got a good look around her.

Eyes wide, her mouth opened in a surprised oh. "I'd ask if I did that, but I know I did."

She closed her eyes and exhaled. "Shit. That's going to cost an arm and a leg."

I couldn't wait anymore and went to my knees, yanking Evie into my arms. She smelled like dirt and leaves and undeniably Evie. My fist tangled in her hair.

"I'm so fucking glad you're alive. You scared the hell out of me."

"I'm so sorry." Her arms tightened around me. She pulled away and put her dirty hands on either side of my face. "But did you see Ben's arm?"

I nodded, feeling so proud of her my chest was close to bursting. "You've got a Lord in your debt."

Ben let out a raspy laugh and came to a seated position. Christian hurried forward with an extra set of clothing. Pax came over with Evie's.

"I'm sorry the earth keeps stealing my clothing."

"Let's try to get through a week where you don't have to heal anyone, okay? If you wake up naked with another one of my shifters, I'll get a complex."

She smiled and pressed her cheek against mine. "Deal."

I helped her up and walked her over to a spot where she could get dressed in private. She'd never be as comfortable with nudity as a shifter, and I thought enough people had seen her naked for the rest of my lifetime.

When she was dressed and wearing a grimace, she stepped out. "I need a shower," she said with a shudder. "I have dirt in places I didn't know I had cracks."

I grinned and reached for her hand. "There's only one potion left. Why don't you use it, and I'll get a flight home?"

She frowned. "How long were we in there?"

"Eight hours." The longest eight hours of my life.

"You could take the potion, and I can fly home. Moira and Ash can run the shop. You have an entire Keep who needs you."

"She can stay with us," Pax said, his eyes lingering a little too long on Evie.

Ben, dressed but still filthy, came over. "Evie will be safe with us if you need to get back."

The sound of a door opening made all the shifters tense. "No one should be here," Christian said.

"Considering there's a tree growing through the roof of the garden center, I can only guess the commotion alerted the authorities," Ben said, rubbing his head as he stared up at the gaping hole in the roof and the massive tree growing through it.

After Evie melded with the World Tree, I had a difficult relationship with large trees, but this one didn't feel like the other. This one had the look of a birch and pine but with bright red berries on the limbs.

But it wasn't the authorities who stepped through the door.

The Shifter Lords had arrived and looked none too happy.

Twenty~Two

Ugh. The Lords were here. While I was thankful I was dressed, I was less thankful I had to deal with them before a hot shower and a week of sleep.

Thorvin stepped forward, looking none the worse for the wear after Moira and I destroyed his foundation. "Caelan!"

Relief filled his eyes. "Thank the gods, man." His eyes found Ben.

"They've found you." Thorvin exhaled. "Mission successful, then."

The Lord's eyes found mine. "And Evie. I'm glad to see you are unscathed."

A strange glitter came over his skin, a sheen that made him look like…

Ben burst out laughing. "The fuck, man? Why do you look like a regular in a teenage vampire movie?"

Thorvin flushed.

Caelan cleared his throat. "Good to know how you feel about Evie," he murmured in a low voice.

All of a sudden, it clicked. "Oh gods." I burst out laughing.

Whatever Moira had done to him triggered when he lied. "It's good to see you, too," I said before laughing again.

"Oh wait. That's a lie." I held up my arm and twisted it to and fro before clicking my tongue. "That's a shame. I look good in glitter." With a wink, I stepped closer to Caelan.

Ethan's eyes found mine. "Evie." He tilted his head in greeting. "I'm unsurprised to find you here."

"Where Caelan goes, I go," I said simply.

His eyes flickered before moving to Ben. "I'm glad you are unharmed."

Ben stepped up. "Let's take this back to the Keep. We have coffee and food there, and after everything, I'm starving, and I know Evie must be, too."

I nodded. I'd burned off so much energy healing him, my fingers were starting to shake.

The Lords agreed, and we piled out of the store. Before we got into the vehicle, I pulled on Caelan's arm to hold him back while everyone else loaded up.

"Donovan and Nadia?" I whispered.

"The Lord is dead. For good this time. Nadia…" His voice trailed off. "I'm not sure how she managed to hightail it out of here like she did, but she's gone. When I return to the Keep, I'll tap my contacts."

I leaned in and whispered in his ear. "I think Gianna had something on her when she died. Something Nadia needs."

Caelan squeezed my hip. "I agree." His gaze flicked over my shoulder.

"We have an audience." After pressing a firm kiss to my lips, he pulled open the passenger door. "Let's get some food into you."

BEN'S HOME at the Keep was tasteful and understated, but Ben didn't look like he fit in. He wore flannel, blue jeans, and work boots, and this was a place for wealthy family dinners on Sunday where everyone wore slacks and mock turtlenecks and talked about their stock portfolio.

But his chef was excellent. He was a jovial man named Boudreaux and had a thick accent that dripped south Louisiana. The man slapped a large bowl of something dark brown with large chunks of meat and okra, and a little rice. It smelled absolutely heavenly.

After the first two bowls, Boudreaux had given me a long, appraising look and nodded. "You want another bowl, *cher*?"

The word sounded like *shah* when he said it, and it made me feel special, like a favorite grandpa had told me he was proud of me.

"Yes, please. May I have some more of that bread, too?"

"You can have whatever you want, little flower."

The third bowl he set in front of me was twice as large as the one before. I smiled with delight and picked up my spoon before he added a large plate of bread and a small bowl filled with chilled butter.

"You're no wolf, but you're something," he said more to himself than me. "You got the look of the fae about you, but that's not it is it?"

My spoon stilled. How much did this man see and did she have to worry about it?

He touched the back of my hair, gently pressing my scalp with firm fingers. "Don't you worry, *cher*. You're safe here."

My fingers trembled, but for some odd reason, I believed him.

The other Lords were at the table, too, but they were engaged in animated discussion.

Animated, meaning everyone was yelling a lot. Everyone except Ben, who kept looking over at me with a peculiar expression on his face. Finally, he got up and sat next to me. Caelan's brows drew together when he noticed, but he said nothing, only tightening his grip on my knee for a brief second before returning to the fray of circular conversation.

"Your chef is amazing," I said, caring little for manners as I dug into the bowl for another bite.

"Boudreaux always makes chicken and sausage gumbo during

the winter. I can't imagine the meat he goes through trying to fill a Keep of hungry wolves."

My brow furrowed at that. "You're some kind of bird, aren't you?" I mused, my voice so low only he and I could hear each other. Possibly Caelan, but he was currently yelling something about nosy Lords and taxes. It made sense. He wasn't a wolf or a bear or anything too predatory. Ben liked open spaces and nature, and I used to catch him staring up at the sky sometimes with a shimmer in his eye.

"I will neither confirm nor deny," he said with a grin. "And no, you can't take Boudreaux with you. Mostly because I'm convinced he'd go if you asked him to."

I snorted. "No, he wouldn't. Feeding one starving woman is far different than feeding all the shifters around here. He'd grow bored in a week."

Ben laughed, the sound free and wild. I'd never heard him laugh like that. He wiped his eyes. "No one is ever bored around you. Boudreaux would be in love in a week."

"If he cooked like this every night, I might do the same."

Caelan's grip tightened, and I hid my smile. So he was listening.

"We've been friends for years now, but Caelan had his own chef, so he took work a couple of hours away from Joy Springs. When I became a Lord, it seemed like the perfect opportunity to bring him with me."

"How do you like Michigan?"

"All the nature suits me. The Keep has several hundred acres, and there are parks and lakes everywhere."

"But you don't like the Keep." His shoulders were tense, and he hadn't relaxed since he'd walked into the building.

Ben gave me a sharp look. "Why do you say that?"

I lifted a shoulder in a shrug. "You don't seem happy here, and you have another home a few miles down the road. A home with only a single house. I smelled you outside. You spend a lot of time there."

His jaw tightened. "I forgot how observant you are."

Ben sighed and took a hunk of bread. I had to stifle the urge to smack him with the back of my spoon and hoard all the bread. "I'm not used to being a Lord. Coveting power never sat right with me. I'd rather be free, but my power levels preclude me from ever being a lone wolf."

"You aren't allowed to?"

Damn this gumbo was amazing. I was slowing down, but if Boudreaux came back, I would not turn down another bowl.

"I could, I suppose, but someone like me, as much as I want to be alone, I crave being with other shifters."

"What about a…mate? Isn't that what the shifters call them? Have you ever looked for one of those?"

Caelan's fingers tightened again.

Ben grinned. "It's not quite so simple. Mating is complex and animalistic in a way."

"Would you know your mate if you saw her?"

Ben speared me with a look so intense, I stopped chewing. Power rose in the air, tingling the back of my neck and making the hair rise on my arms. "Ben?"

Caelan's hand slipped from my knee. He turned toward us and leaned forward. "Ben," he said slowly. "Don't you even think about it."

I blinked. I had no idea what was going on.

At that moment, Pax stepped forward. "Miss Evie?"

"Just Evie," I said to the shifter.

Pax's gaze shifted first to Ben, then to Caelan before his strange eyes rested on me once more. "Are you currently mated?"

I snorted. "I'm sorry?"

"Mated. I do not see a mating bond between you and the Texas Lord."

Caelan went still. I put a hand on his forearm.

"I'm not sure it's possible for a shifter to formally mate with someone who's not another shifter," I mused.

"It's possible," Ben said, an emotion in his voice I'd never heard from him.

"To answer your very forward question," I said, a note of reproof in my voice, "no, I am not formally mated, but I'm also not a shifter. I do not need to be mated to commit myself to someone."

Caelan's muscles relaxed under my fingers.

"You are committed to Lord Caelan?" Pax asked.

"I am."

Pax bowed his head. "Then he is a lucky man indeed." When he lifted his head, his eyes held a golden spark—a promise of power glimmering in his eyes. "If you find yourself uncommitted, I hope you will find me again."

I blinked in surprise. "Err. Umm. Thank you, Pax. I am very flattered."

"You are a tempest of power, Evie. Any man would be fortunate to bask in the adoration of your gaze."

And with that, Pax turned and went back to the corner he stood in, watching and waiting.

"What the hell is going on?" I whispered. "Is there something in the air?"

"Pax is right," Ben said. "It is possible to mate outside of our species. Perhaps your lack of mating bond is more telling than you realize."

"You overstep," Caelan snarled in a low, dangerous voice. "You had your chance, Ben. Do not make me teach you a lesson about trying to take what is mine."

I held up a hand, glaring at the flash of triumph in Ben's eyes. "First, I am not your possession. I thought we'd worked through all that. Second, I don't think Ben is making a claim on me."

But when Ben smiled, the words died in my throat.

"Are you?" I croaked.

"I'm the Lord of a large territory, Evie. The natural world here is bursting with power, and we've lacked a Floromancer for years."

"The winter is horrific. My power is sluggish here."

"Then I suggest you visit during spring and see how glorious your magic may bloom."

"You cannot be serious," I murmured. "Ben, you all but threw me away. What in the world brought this on now?"

Caelan sat rigid with fury, but he had learned something. He hadn't gone immediately for Ben's throat, and that was progress.

"I've seen the error of my ways."

"Yes, you've also seen me very naked. Does this have anything to do with this? I mean, I'm not a supermodel or anything, but maybe it's been a while for you and—"

Ben shook his head. "I've seen my fair share of women, Evie. And no, I'm not itching for female company unless you'd like to ditch—"

"Ben, stop antagonizing Caelan." I pinched the space between my brows. "I'm not sure what's going on here, but we should probably leave."

The sound of throats clearing got my attention.

"So sorry to interrupt your lover's spat," Ethan drawled. "But we do have other business to discuss. The others will be here soon."

As if summoned, the doorbell rang, revealing Soren and Rowan. They stomped the snow from their boots on the front mat and walked toward the dining room. Rowan grinned when he spotted me, that smile widening when he saw the two men I was sandwiched between.

Soren looked bored as usual. He was dressed like he'd walked off the runway, in black slacks and an azure-blue pullover sweater my fingers itched to touch. I had an eye for cashmere, and the sweater he was wearing looked like the highest quality.

Rowan took the seat on the opposite end of the table and wiggled his eyebrows at me. "You smell like dirt and Ben," he said gleefully. "Something I should know?"

I sighed. "You suck."

Rowan laughed.

Caelan relaxed a little in the new Lord's presence. "Rowan. Nice of you to finally show up."

Rowan rolled his eyes and jerked his thumb at Thorvin. "Those dicks wouldn't wait on us. And Soren had to pack an overnight bag but had to pick up his damn dry cleaning before we left."

Soren winked. "If you aren't going to look sharp all the time, what is the point of life?"

I pointed my spoon at my empty bowl. "This gumbo for one. The bread is excellent, too."

Soren grunted. "I prefer meat and vegetables. Rice is too simple of a carb."

I stared at him. "Okay, weirdo."

Ben chuckled.

Rowan plopped his chin on his hand. "So, what did we interrupt?"

"Absolutely nothing. Ben and I were having a conversation."

"About mating," Ben said helpfully.

Rowan's eyebrows rose. "Oh?" His eyes flicked to Caelan.

"So that's why Caelan is so pissed off." He chewed on his lip. "Brave to poke that bear," he mused.

"A Lord needs a mate to come to his full strength," Soren said, his eyes glittering when they landed on me.

My stomach jolted, Soren's words souring the gumbo I'd inhaled. Was it true? Was there some sort of power imbalance with us not being mated?

Caelan stiffened. "Let's drop this conversation."

But Ethan stepped in. "No, this is a good subject and one we should have talked about a long time ago."

Thorvin stayed silent, like usual, but Rowan surprised me. "Why do you guys have to act like such dicks all the time? They're not mated, so fucking what? If I recall, Gianna and Caelan weren't mated either—"

"Gianna came from a powerful family of shifters. It was only a matter of time—"

"The hell it was," Caelan snarled.

"A mate brings with it an unbreakable bond. A mate cannot betray her mate without death following," Soren added. "Evie is an unknown with an unheard-of amount of knowledge of our internal systems. It's only natural for the Lords to be concerned about the lack of a formal bond."

Rowan scoffed. "You guys are such dicks. Not a single one of you are mated, and you're giving Caelan—the only one of us in a committed relationship—shit about not having a mating bond?"

Only Thorvin winced.

Soren grinned. "I'm having far too much fun to settle down. Nor do I need to."

I watched this conversation like a ping pong match. But I was the ball.

Ben finally spoke up. "Perhaps Evie is not with the right Lord."

You could have heard a pin drop. I leaned over and hissed in his ear. "What are you doing?"

"Oh?" Ethan said. "I believe she dislikes everyone but Rowan. Do you perhaps think it's him Evie should be with?"

Rowan wiggled his eyebrows at me.

I sighed. "Please stop."

But as most men did when they had a point to make, they spoke right over me.

"Moving Evie to Rowan's territory would solve a few problems," Ethan mused.

Caelan bristled with fury. I put my hand on his knee. "Don't listen to them," I said quietly. "Rowan and I are friends."

"Ben is not talking about Rowan," Caelan snarled, his eyes ringed with molten gold.

"Or she could stay here with me," Ben said. "The Joy Springs area has at least two Floromancers who can maintain the land."

Righteous anger filled my veins. "Excuse me?"

Ben turned those beautiful eyes to me. "I screwed up. I know it. I want to make amends for it."

"So you strongarm me and try to force me into a new territory without asking me? I have a shop in Joy Springs. Friends. A life."

"You can make that here with me."

My fists clenched. "I love Caelan."

"You aren't mated to him. A true mating is indescribable. It's… glorious. A true melding of hearts and souls."

"Humans don't mate. Their love is no less than a shifter's or of someone like me."

"The lady said no," Caelan said. He leaned over. "I'm trying very hard to respect your autonomy, but as soon as you say the word, I will rip his head off."

His words made me smile. "No violence on my behalf, please. I thought I handled this nonsense the last time, but apparently, I'm just a wee lassie who needs to be shuffled off to the biggest, strongest man there is."

"No one is trying to cage you, Evie," Ben said.

"If I hit you, I'm not going to stop," I said with a growl in my voice.

"Ben's territory is ideal," Ethan said. "But so is Rowan's. Since she and Rowan have a friendly relationship, he makes the most sense."

"She and Rowan are friends. A mating bond won't form."

Rowan smirked, the picture of ease. "My parents weren't a love match initially. They have a true mating now."

"You are not helping," I hissed.

Rowan winked at me. "Would you rather it be me or Ben?"

A helpless laugh escaped me. "I'd rather it be no one if it isn't Caelan."

But they kept on, refusing to heed my warnings, and finally I had enough. I rose and slammed my hands on the dining table. Silverware jerked into the air and rattled, and a glass carafe of salad dressing tipped onto its side, spilling creamy Caesar from the spout.

"Shut up!" I screamed.

All the Lords blinked owlishly at me, but they stopped talking.

"I've told you multiple times that I am not a pawn in whatever shitty game you keep trying to play with me. I'm not a chess piece to be moved to an advantageous spot at your whims. I'm not in love with Ben or Rowan—"

"Time will tell," Rowan sang.

I almost laughed. Instead, I shot him a withering glare. "My home is in Joy Springs. My life is there. And the man I've chosen is there, too. I don't give a shit if you like it. I don't care if you think Caelan is gaining too much power. I don't even care if we have a mating bond. That's something Caelan and I will discuss later. Away from you ignorant fuckers. All I wanted was some food and some coffee—"

I turned my withering glare to Ben. "Which I have not had yet. What does a girl gotta do to get a good cup of coffee, especially after she saved your ass from almost certain death?"

A few sucked in gasps.

"Yes, you assholes, I healed your precious Lord, who has promptly thanked me by turning into a pompous pig and still hasn't given me any coffee." I slashed a hand through the air.

"But beside that point is my autonomy. If I wanted to, I could take all of you out and not bat an eye."

Ethan scoffed. "I hardly think—"

"She had you strung up by your feet screaming like a little bitch," Rowan drawled. "The woman has a point."

Thorvin ducked his head to hide a smile.

Ben's brow furrowed. "Evie, there's no need for you to decide now—"

"There's nothing to decide!" I screeched, and I hated it because it made me sound hysterical. "I will not marry any of you unless I want to! And If there's ever a day that Caelan and I sunder, I can assure you, I'd rather give myself a lobotomy than ever get involved with another Lord."

Rowan grinned.

A crack of thunder sounded in the room. Every Lord snapped to his feet, eyes and head on a swivel, searching for the unseen threat. I closed my eyes and stifled a groan. Of all the times to make an appearance…

The Fae King appeared in a flash of emerald light, in complete regalia. My father, Cernunnos, stood seven feet tall, eyes burning with magic, wearing a crown of antlers so high they came close to scraping the ceiling. Bioluminescent moss hung from the tines, and mushrooms clung to his body. He wore the face I didn't often see, one of ancient cruelty and malice. Fae power soaked the room as Cernunnos' glowing eyes took the measure of each one of the Lords.

If they were not very careful, someone might die tonight.

Caelan was the first to overcome his surprise. He dipped his head in a greeting.

"Welcome, Cernunnos, King of the Fae."

"Well met, Caelan."

Ethan's eyebrows inched up on his forehead like bushy caterpillars.

Rowan was slack-jawed as he stared at my father, his eyes scanning Cernunnos, taking in everything that he was. He was the second to acknowledge him.

"Cernunnos." He placed a hand over his heart. "Welcome."

"Lord of the Land," Cernunnos said. "Well met."

Thorvin's mouth gaped like a fish. "Cernunnos," he breathed. "There are so many questions I want to ask you."

Soren shot him a sharp look, but my father smiled. He had a soft spot for scholars. "Perhaps another time," he said to Thorvin. "I will offer some of my time for something in exchange. We will barter later."

Thorvin dipped his head. "Your generosity is immense."

Oh brother.

Soren dipped his head. "Cernunnos. Welcome."

Cernunnos studied him for a long moment. "You are heart-sore, young Lord. Perhaps there is a dark-haired woman who would soothe your ache?"

My lips twitched. So he was pining after Moira. I *knew* it.

Soren's eyes flashed with horror, but he remained silent.

Ethan was the last to speak. "Cernunnos."

The Lord looked furious at the Fae King's presence, which was highly amusing, and also disturbing because did Ethan not realize my father could crush him like a bug if he wanted to?

Instead of greeting Ethan, my father tilted his head and studied the Lord. "I couldn't help but overhear some of your conversation about your Floromancer."

I braced myself. Cernunnos never randomly showed up just to show up—unless he was coming over for tacos. He didn't show up in a room full of Lords after I'd had a shit day and had just lost my temper over the idiocy of shifters.

The Fae King was here for a reason, and I was pretty sure I wasn't going to like it.

"Your Majesty," I said, placing my hand over my heart and bowing my head.

When I lifted my eyes, amusement sparkled in the swirling depths of his gaze. "One woman has graced me with my formal title instead of my given name. She has shown deference where the rest of you have shown familiarity despite not being given permission."

The temperature in the room dropped by about twenty degrees.

"You are no king of ours," Ethan said.

I wanted to sigh. Ethan could be such a dumbass sometimes.

"Perhaps not," my father said, "but you forget I could be, and that each of you stand here by my grace."

Ethan's eyes glittered with anger. Cords of fury stood out on his neck, but he could not refuse Cernunnos' statement. If the fae ever tired of existing side by side with us, it would not be a difficult thing to take over our world if Cernunnos stepped in to assist.

"Evie," my father said. "It is nice to see you again."

"And you."

"Is there something we can do for you?" Rowan asked after a long silence.

"There is," Cernunnos said. "But it's not for me. It's for Evie."

I stilled. Oh shit. Here it comes…

What in the world could he possibly ask or demand of them, and, the more important question, how much worse would it make my life?

"You ask for a favor for a Floromancer?" Ethan said, derision dripping from his voice.

Cernunnos laughed, the sound wickedly amused. "I do not ask for favors, Lord. You seem to have forgotten who she is, and what her capabilities are."

"We know of her magic and abilities," Ethan snapped. "We are merely trying to find a place for her…uniqueness within our world."

"Oh?" Cernunnos said, far too much curiosity in his voice. "What have you decided?"

Rowan blinked, his eyes narrowing on my father. He knew of our relationship, and based on everyone else's lack of reaction, he hadn't said a word to the others, which only made me like him more.

Ethan looked at Thorvin, who gave him one sharp shake of his head. He wanted Ethan to shut the fuck up, just like everyone else in the room. No matter what Ethan said, things would not go well for him. The absolute last thing Caelan needed was one less Lord. Ethan's absence would complicate everything, and I'm not even sure it would stop them from trying to find "a place" for me and my "uniqueness."

To his credit, the first signs of nervousness showed in Ethan's frame. His fingers tapped against his thigh. "Err. We believe Evie would be more suited to Rowan. Perhaps even Ben."

One of Cernunnos' eyebrows flicked up. "Interesting. Why Rowan?"

"Their powers are similar, and they seem to like each other."

Amusement flashed over my father's face, there and gone in a heartbeat. "And Ben?"

"He obviously wants her, and he owes her a boon."

My father focused on me. "A boon from a Lord is no small thing. What great achievement or feat did you perform to win his approval?"

The way he said it made it sound like I was a Victorian lady who'd shown her ankle in a bar. "It wasn't much, and I don't need a boon. I just want to go home."

"She saved my life," Ben said.

I closed my eyes for a brief moment.

"And what was so wrong you couldn't save yourself?"

The edges of Ben's eyes tightened. "I was overwhelmed and taken hostage. After a serious injury that almost resulted in my death, Caelan and two of my wolves came for me. Evie managed to heal me before I succumbed to my injuries."

"Evie. Is this true?"

I nodded. "The Lord had lost an arm. Blood loss from the injury was significant."

My father looked at Ben. "She regrew your missing limb. Impressive."

The other Lords weren't aware of the circumstances in which we'd found him. Everyone trained their eyes on me, and a couple of their gazes flickered with interest.

Again, being a thing of interest for a Shifter Lord was never a good thing.

"Would he have regrown the limb on his own?" Cernunnos asked.

More than likely he already knew the answer, but he waited for one of the Lords to answer. To my surprise, Thorvin stepped up.

"Maybe," the reticent Lord spoke. "It depends on the injury, the weapon used to cause it, and how long ago the injury took place. Even a fresh injury is no guarantee. Others who have more minor injuries might not always grow a limb back. We don't know the parameters of why or why not, but we throw everything we have at an amputation and hope for the best."

"It sounds like you owe Evie more than a small boon," the pot stirrer said.

That was Cernunnos. Him and his big ol' giant stirring spoon.

"I've already offered my Keep to her," Ben said.

"Did you now?" Cernunnos' voice was flat. "You wish for her to be your mate?"

"I do."

"And what do you think, Evie?" My father was having a blast.

"A few months ago, we couldn't stand each other. Today, he almost died. I think it's…pheromones or something. He had a near death experience and he's imprinting on me like a… duckling."

Caelan snorted. Rowan choked and coughed lightly into his hand.

"A duck," Ben said flatly. "You're comparing an offer of marriage from a Lord to an imprinting duck?"

I shrugged. "You didn't even like me a few months ago. I can't help but think this was caused by something, other than just my presence. We've been around each other many times and never have you acted like this." I rolled my eyes. "Swear to the gods, there must be something in the air."

Ben opened his mouth, then shut it. "Can't a man just want to marry you, Evie? Does there have to be some big reason behind it?"

I stared at him flatly. "Yes. Love is a great start. You don't love me. I don't love you. The end."

"And you, Rowan?" My father said, "Would you want to carry Evie off and make her your Lady?"

Rowan grinned. "Evie is a catch for whoever finally manages to tame her. I would gladly accept Evie if she wanted to come, but I cannot guarantee a mating. Our magic is too similar, and I wonder if even I would find Evie difficult to handle."

"Ass," I muttered.

Rowan winked at me.

"But you like her," Cernunnos pushed.

"Of course."

"And you find her attractive?"

"I'd have to be dead not to," Rowan said.

A hysterical laugh bubbled from me.

"And you would stand idly by while someone else tried to win your woman?" he asked Caelan.

"Never," Caelan said. "If Evie wished to leave me, I would let her go. But if someone tried to take her, I would raze their world to the ground."

I reached over and interlocked our fingers. Caelan had changed. In a fundamental way. And he'd done it because he loved me. My throat thickened with tears, and I blinked them away, refusing to cry in front of these damned Lords.

Cernunnos inclined his head in approval. "Most of you assume you know who Evie is. You think she's a simple Floromancer, powerful, yes, but nothing you can't overcome if you all work together. Would you say this is correct?"

He'd directed his words toward Ethan who merely shrugged.

Soren had remained deathly quiet the entire time, and I'd almost forgotten he was standing there. "I've seen Evie in action. She's unpredictable, which always makes for a difficult battle. I would not idly take her on without backup."

"That might be the nicest thing you've ever said to me," I said.

Soren shrugged. "Don't get used to it."

There he was. He might be pretty, but I still couldn't see what Moira saw in him.

"Even so, you believe you can actually force her to do something she doesn't want to do, yes?"

No one dared agree to that statement. The room fell into a tense silence.

Where was my father going with this?

"Why are you so concerned with her?" Ethan asked. "She's a citizen of the Lords."

Cernunnos smiled, and it was terrifying. He lifted a finger and gestured toward me. A soft gust of wind and an emerald and gold wash of magic flowed over me. I knew what he'd done even before the gasps of shock in the room.

"Evangeline is a citizen of Faerie. She is also a princess of our realm and is to be respected in all your dealings with her. *Furthermore*," he emphasized, when Ethan opened his mouth to object or say something stupid. Who knew with him?

"She is my daughter, and she will marry whomever she chooses, whenever she chooses, without interference from you or any of the other Lords."

I lifted my hand and felt the edges of the fae crown on my head. That was Cernunnos. Things were secret until he didn't want them to be anymore.

"Your daughter," Ethan said weakly.

I wiggled my fingers at him in a wave.

Soren let out a vicious curse. Thorvin stared at me owl-eyed, and Rowan, that smug sonofabitch, was still grinning from ear to ear.

"Did you have to announce it like that?" I grumbled to my father from the couch.

He was in my kitchen messing with the new coffee pot he'd brought. "You should have killed at least one of them long before now."

"Killed?" I coughed. "Why would I kill a Lord?"

"Because they've grown far too arrogant." He scoffed. "Not to mention their behavior toward you."

Disgust laced his tone as he stirred some cream into the coffee he was making for me. "Trying to strongarm a fae princess."

He grumbled something else I couldn't make out. "That Ethan Lord is a real piece of work, isn't he?"

My father sounded more human tonight than he ever had.

"He has been a thorn in my side for a long time now," I admitted.

He handed me a steaming mug. "Try this. The coffee I make in this machine is world's better than other machines."

I took a sip and closed my eyes. "Mmm. That is good."

Happiness shone on his face, and I wondered how often he'd experienced true bliss. When he was here, he could take his crown off and relax. He could bring his daughter coffee, and his daughter could make him tacos. There was no artifice between us, but as much as I wanted to relax and hang out with my father, there were still a couple of large issues between us.

"I haven't seen Mom around much."

Cernunnos settled into his favorite chair and blew on the top of his mug. "She's trying to give you space."

"She never tried before," I grumbled.

"Things are different now. May I make a suggestion?"

"Yes, but I reserve the right to ignore it."

He sipped his coffee and studied me. "Have you tried making the first move?"

The suggestion made anger flood my system. I took a beat to calm down and carefully set my mug down. "I was a child. Mom was a goddess. Even though I see things differently now and know she made the best decision of all the bad choices she had, it doesn't change how I felt then. I can't just throw those feelings away and pretend everything is butterflies and roses now."

He nodded. "I had a feeling you'd say that. Your mother is a complicated woman. She will reach out. Eventually. Keep in mind, Evie, she has feelings of her own. To protect you, she had to go against her nature for years. You were a weapon that could be used against her, and so she had to pretend the child of her heart was nothing more than an inconvenience, something she had to keep alive to avoid violating fae law."

"I will talk to her when she comes to see me. That's all I can promise."

My father nodded. "Now, let's talk about why you were in Michigan and what happened when you were buried in the dirt with that other handsome Lord." He wiggled his eyebrows.

"Absolutely not," but I laughed just like he wanted me to.

"Now that they know who you are, they will approach you in a different way. Do not be surprised if you receive several marriage proposals."

"Nothing new about that."

Cernunnos' brow furrowed. "What happened?"

I told him about the strange men showing up and the flyers and internet posts about my "single" status.

"Someone is playing a joke on you?" He sounded confused, just like I'd been when the first two showed up.

"No, I don't think it's a joke. I think it's a way to manipulate me. Or tear Caelan and me apart."

But even that theory didn't quite fit. Why would someone do something that had no guarantee of working? To annoy me? It felt more sinister than simple.

"What happened to those men who showed up?"

"I flung them out of town using magic. They're probably still alive."

He let out a hearty laugh. "Good. They're lucky that's all they got."

I picked up my coffee and took a sip, grimacing at the luke-warm temperature. My father rose and took my mug, refilling my coffee.

"Now," he said as he sat back down, "I want to talk about my retirement."

My father stayed another few hours, and I learned how to dodge giving answers to a fae king. The crown was still on the table, though I still had a ton of trauma thanks to the one Titania shoved on my head right before the magic shoved me into a magic tree to die.

I had zero desire to take over my father's reign, and even though I was his only heir, taking his crown and becoming queen seemed so farfetched I had a difficult time wrapping my head around it.

As far as I was concerned, this was a problem for another day. We were all immortals, and there was time to push this to the back of my list.

I changed into pajamas, washed my face, and was about to slide into bed with a good book when my cell phone pinged with a message from Moira.

I may or may not have done a thing while you were gone.

I frowned at the screen. *Is it more I changed my hair color or more I destroyed some property and broke multiple laws?*

The second.

Do I want to know?

Nope! Plausible deniability. I'll tell you when you come into work.

Will it get us killed?

You? No. Me? Shrug emoji.

I sighed out loud and fell back onto the pillow. *I'll be there tomorrow morning. You opening?*

I am. Ash and Tess are off.

Stay out of trouble tonight. See you first thing.

I'll do my best.

Shaking my head, I plugged my charger in and put my cell on the nightstand. Her reticence to tell me was telling in itself. Whatever she'd done had something to do with the Lords.

Thorvin was one of the better Lords, so if she'd glittered him and destroyed property, I couldn't imagine what she might have done to the others.

In spite of my misgivings, I chuckled before pulling the blankets over my head.

Moira was a good friend to have.

CHAPTER
Twenty-Five

Caelan sat on my couch early the next morning, chowing down on an enormous plate of pancakes. He'd gotten in sometime in the middle of the night and woken me up enthusiastically.

He had so much enthusiasm, I was late to work the next morning.

"Are you free tonight?" I asked.

"I have a meeting at five, but it shouldn't go longer than an hour. Are you digging for whatever Gianna might have had on her?"

I nodded. "Whatever it is must be important if Nadia resorted to taking the Lords. With Donovan gone, she won't be able to overpower any of you."

"Nadia is clever and vengeful. I wouldn't put anything past her."

"Are all swans mean as hell?"

Caelan laughed. "I've only known a few. With my limited experience, I can say definitely, yes. They are."

We grinned at each other. "I have to get to work. Moira is there by herself. Meet me here at 6:30?"

"Done."

I pressed a kiss to his lips and was about to head out when he tugged my hand. "Hey. Are you okay after your father announced your heritage?"

I shrugged. "I knew I wouldn't be able to keep it hidden forever. Now that it's out, maybe they'll think twice about screwing with me."

From Caelan's grim expression, he did not agree. He grunted. "I think you'll receive more attention than you want. But they won't try to marry you off anymore."

"That's a bonus."

Caelan snorted. "Not so fast. They won't try to marry you off to each other anymore. They'll try to claim you for themselves."

I groaned. "This is dumb. They know I don't want anyone else."

Satisfaction gleamed in his eyes. "Good."

"My father suggested I start killing them." I smiled at him and dropped a kiss on his nose. "Maybe I'll do that next time."

Caelan blinked, opened his mouth, then snapped it shut.

I winked and grabbed my purse before heading outside.

Maybe Cernunnos had a point. Killing a Lord might put the fear of the gods in them and stop them from making my life hell.

The thought stuck with me all the way until I got to the store.

Moira wore a cute Norwegian sweater and a smile when I walked in. "Have a little too much fun last night?"

I breezed past her. "Wouldn't you like to know?"

"Well, duh. It's as dry as the Sahara in my house. Of course I want to know."

"Eww." I waved her away. "I don't kiss and tell."

"One day I'll get Hazel to send some more of that good booze, and we can see what happens."

I fixed myself a cup of coffee and brought it over to the register desk. "Spill. Tell me what you did while I was gone."

Moira's eyes twinkled. "Those potions came in handy. Seriously."

"They did. Caelan is sending a wire transfer to pay for your supplies later today."

"Good, because I need to make a few more. I visited Ethan's Keep last night." She rolled her eyes.

"It looks just as stuffy as the man himself. Gold everywhere. And marble." Moira shuddered.

"Did you set his house on fire?"

Moira flashed a grin. "Nothing so obvious. I want them to wonder if someone sabotaged them and then bam, they're glittering in the sun like a Cullen."

The sight of Thorvin glittering every time he lied brought a smile to my face. "Clever and unexpected. How long will it take to wear off?"

"If he hired a witch worth her salt, he could break the spell immediately."

"He's rich, so I assume that will happen soon."

"He still has to write a big fat check to repair his foundation."

"Care to share what happened?"

Moira untangled her long legs and took a sip of her tea. "Ethan has staff. Butler, kitchen and dinner staff, people who run the stables, everything."

I stared at her, a terrible feeling unfurling in my stomach. "Is everyone okay?"

Moira gasped. "Evie! I don't hurt innocent people."

I pressed my hand against my stomach. "I know that, but there was a terrible moment where I wondered."

She clicked her tongue. "I know you're worried about me, but my personality has not changed. I am still the same Moira I ever was. And, yes, everyone is fine. I simply made everyone tell the truth for a period of forty-eight hours."

My hand crept up to cover my mouth. I wanted to laugh, but that felt like encouraging her. "How's it going?"

"I waited inside a closet for Ethan to return home last night. One of the maids told him she was sick of him throwing his jackets everywhere and that he was completely insufferable."

A terrible thought occurred to me. "What if he fires them?"

Moira let out a throaty chuckle. "Rowan has already agreed to take them on."

"But they'll have to move territories. Moira! What if they have families?"

"Ethan is smart enough to realize they're under a spell. He'll figure it out."

"And if they say something that angers him? Ethan isn't like the other Lords. He's vindictive."

Moira waved my concerns away. "They're all shifters in his Pack. He doesn't hire humans."

I pushed my chair away and stared. "That's better, I guess." Ethan wouldn't put out Pack.

No Lord or true Alpha would, but this still felt meaner than usual. And not toward Ethan, but toward his people.

"Oh, come on. These are his people. And Ethan isn't the same Lord to his people as he is to the public."

"Is he better?" For some reason, that would surprise me. He was totally insufferable any time I spoke to him.

She nodded. "Surprisingly. And built like an Olympic swimmer."

"Moira! Did you hide in his bedroom closet?"

She looked away, a wicked smile playing over her lips.

"Oh my gods." I cackled.

"He seems like a hard nut to crack, but I think what you see from him is not what you get if you had a different relationship with him."

"But you still sabotaged his crew."

Moira shrugged. "He's a shithead to you. Of course I did."

We high-fived each other. "Thanks, friend."

No matter how far she had to take it, Moira would always have my back.

. . .

Moira was on one corner of my land, Ash on another, and Caelan and I would take the other two. Armed with flashlights and metal detectors, everyone was doing a thorough search for anything Gianna might have dropped.

"I think we should bring in some wolves," Caelan said. "They'll be able to sense Gianna's presence and find anything she may have dropped far faster than Moira or Ash."

"We don't know who we can trust," I argued. "If Nadia has anyone on the inside, and she gets wind of our search, she'll know we're on to her."

"Garrett and Simone, then. You know they're beyond reproach."

I thought about it. We could use more than one delicate nose tonight. "We should have done this during the daytime."

"I disagree," Caelan said. "Searching now might make things more difficult, but we won't be so obvious. Moira and Ash are equipped with stealth flashlights and know not to use them until they're sure they've found something. Both have impressive night vision. The quieter we keep this, the better."

"Alright. Just them. No one else. Got it?"

Caelan smiled. "Got it." He pulled out his cell and fired off a text.

"Should we start?"

"They can both get in the wards?"

I nodded. "I thought about keeping him out, but Garrett proved himself when he took a bullet for us."

"He's softened toward you as well. And Moira, though he has concerns about her impulse control." At my look, he laughed and held up his hands.

"His words, not mine."

I couldn't tell him what Moira had done to Ethan. He wouldn't tell on us, but it would put him in a difficult position if he was ever questioned about our potential involvement. Bad enough he knew about Thorvin. "Well, he didn't try too hard to stop any shenanigans, so he wasn't too hard to like. At least the other night."

Caelan tugged me close to him and pressed a kiss against my temple. "Garrett isn't used to females like you. Wolves are different from you two."

"Simone seems pretty stubborn herself. She can't be too different from us."

"My Omega is much sneakier. You have trouble lying when asked a direct question. Simone can snap on a guileless expression in an instant."

"Well, maybe she should come with us next time."

"Hell no," Caelan growled.

I snickered and sat on the ground. "Just wait. We're already working on her. Soon we'll drive you all into an early grave."

Caelan sighed. "I'm going to look around, but I won't stray too far. Anything in particular I should be looking for?"

I shook my head. "No idea. I can't fathom what she might have had on her. Maybe a flash drive? Maybe a spell?"

"I'll search for anything that seems out of place. You don't get many trespassers, so that narrows things down."

"Not anymore. The wards keep people out, but I didn't always have them. I walked through a few times and cleaned things up. Humans are total litterbugs."

"Ten minutes?" Caelan asked.

"Make it fifteen. I'm going to search as far as I can. It's been a few months, but I don't think anything she dropped would become too buried."

He touched my hair and shifted in a flash of light. A massive dark wolf stood in his place. I reached up and ran my fingers through his soft fur, tugging a little at his ear. Caelan bumped me with his nose and trotted away.

A smile tugged my lips up. Magic rose to the surface the moment I stuck my fingers in the dirt next to the spot they buried Gianna. There was no lingering magic here, nothing to tell the story of how violently she'd died, but I didn't like sitting here, knowing what had happened to her.

Every trace of Gianna was gone, her body decomposed and her bones scattered to ash, swept through the earth and faded to nothing. Even so, I still felt a trace of her in the dirt. Nothing physical, no, only her essence. And maybe it was because I knew she'd been there that I felt her presence, but grief filled me all the same.

For all her faults, she didn't deserve what happened to her. No one deserved such a violent end.

I steadied myself and pulled my magic closer to where she had lain, searching for anything in the soil I may have missed. When Cernunnos had shown me she was here, I'd panicked and swept every trace of her away, but I only had power with organic material—at least back then. I could do a lot more these days, if I practiced my magic.

After the tree, all my training with my father had stopped. The trauma was too fresh, and I needed a substantial amount of time to recover.

Even now, the thought of it made my teeth clench. The fae would always remind me of what I had gone through and what I'd almost lost thanks to them.

But even so, I had a moment of regret that I couldn't do more to speed this search along. I swept through the soil and went several feet out on either side, carefully investigating anything that wasn't biological or organic material.

I grimaced at the amount of plastic I found swimming through the soil—plastic soda lids, pieces of water bottles, nails and screws, and other miscellaneous things that didn't belong in the dirt.

But no trace of anything linked to Gianna.

Frustration filled me as I pulled my magic back to the surface. Caelan lay a few feet away, his head on his enormous paws, the gold of his eyes focused on my face.

"Nothing," I said with a sigh. I rose and wiped my hands on

the thighs of my jeans, swooping down to pick up the go bag I'd brought filled with extra clothes for Caelan.

The temperature had dropped into the low forties this evening. Tolerable but still chilly.

Better than a few feet of snow, I thought. Caelan bumped his head into my hip as we walked. "Nothing on your end, either?"

He shook his head.

"Damn. How far did you go?"

He trotted ahead and looked back. Smiling, I broke into a jog to follow.

Garrett and Simone showed up ten minutes later, a sullen young woman following behind them.

"Hey, Thalia." I shot Caelan a wtf look.

He huffed and rolled his eyes, the sight of the huge wolf's annoyance bringing a smile to my face.

"She won't say a word," Garrett assured me.

Thalia stuck her tongue out at Garrett's back. When I stared her down, she sighed. "Garrett rarely lets me out of his sight, so here I am."

Simone turned her head to hide a smile. The Omega was dressed in dark clothing, her light hair tucked under a black beanie.

At my silence, Thalia huffed. "I won't say a word." Thalia mimed a zipper motion.

I let a flash of red roll over my eyes. "You better not."

She blinked and took a step back, fear flashing over her face.

"Evie. That's unnecessary." Garrett watched me carefully.

"Is it? She's still a stranger."

Thalia smirked. "Am I?"

My brow furrowed. "Err. Yes? This cannot get out to anyone, Thalia. If it does, I'll know who to come visit."

She waved a hand. "I don't plan to help. I've got a game on my phone. Go play in the woods or whatever you're doing tonight."

"Helpful as always, Thalia," Garrett said dryly.

The seer rolled her eyes and plopped down to rest her back against a tree trunk. "It's dark and I don't have wolf eyes."

Something about this bothered me.

"What?" Thalia snapped when she caught me staring at her.

"How did you get through my wards?"

Her expression turned guileless, though a spot of color touched the tops of her cheekbones. "I have some fae blood. Maybe that's how?" She shrugged.

Garrett didn't look at me. "She was holding onto my arm when we passed through. Maybe that's it?"

"Shouldn't be." How the hell had she gotten through? I was diligent when building my wards. If Cliona couldn't get through, a seer shouldn't be able to either. I studied her thoroughly but could sense no other magic around her. She was fae, I could tell, and there was something extremely familiar about her. I'd noticed it the first day we met, and the feeling I knew her had never left.

But I know we'd never met. I would have remembered.

Simone stared at Thalia, too, before she turned to meet my eyes. An unfamiliar emotion flickered over her face before she dropped her gaze. "I'm ready to start when you are."

Caelan nudged me with his nose. I ran my hand over his head and nodded. The Thalia problem could wait until later.

We had to find whatever Nadia was looking for before she came for the rest of us.

Twenty-Six

During the third hour of the search, a mournful howl rolled through my land. Garrett had found something. Caelan shifted in a flash of light and reached for the bag of clothes I carried. "He's to the west. Do you want to wait here with Thalia or come with me?"

Thalia was engrossed in her brightly lit, flashing cellphone.

"We can't leave her here?" I asked.

"Garrett would lose it. When Simone gets back, you can follow."

His tone sounded hesitant almost, which was unusual for him, and he kept giving Thalia side-eyed glances.

"I can hear you," Thalia said, a note of exasperation in her voice.

"Why are you under such a tight guard?" I asked.

She lifted a slender shoulder in a careless shrug. "I'm a seer. A really good one, apparently. I can't be left unattended lest I faint and hurt myself. Or something."

Not once had she looked up from her cell phone.

"Is that the only reason?" I murmured to Caelan.

He pressed a kiss to my cheek just as Garrett howled again. "Gotta run. Follow when Simone gets back."

Without waiting for a response or answering my question, Caelan took off at a jog.

I sat down close to Thalia. "What are you playing?"

"Tetris. They monitor my phone and won't let me have anything with messaging capability."

My jaw dropped. "What? Why?"

"My father doesn't want me to get involved with the wrong crowd." A small smile played on her face.

"You aren't a prisoner." Was she?

Thalia laughed. "I can't drive or hold down a normal job. I've been in prison since the first time I had a vision."

I rested chin on my hand. "I'm sorry. I don't understand why Garrett monitors your cell like that. You don't think that's weird?"

"Garrett isn't the one monitoring it."

I waited for her to elaborate, but when she didn't, I nudged her with my foot. "Not a big talker? You seem different from when we went shopping."

"Because that was fun and this is lame."

Thalia wasn't a teenager, so her word choice was odd. "How old are you?"

"Not sure anymore. Twenty-something, I think." She still hadn't looked up from her phone.

"You don't know how old you are?"

"It doesn't really matter. My lifespan will be quite long."

"You don't celebrate your birthday?"

"No one is usually around to celebrate it with me."

Thalia was difficult, but she was also stunted in a way. Cliona had her faults, but when she couldn't or didn't want to take care of me, she'd dropped me with loving parents. Human parents who celebrated a child's birthday every single year.

"You don't know what month it is?"

"July, I think. No idea what day." She finally looked up.

"Why are you so interested?"

"Everyone should celebrate their birthday. If they want to. What's your favorite kind of cake?"

"Lemon." She frowned. "No. Italian Creme."

"How about next July, you and I celebrate your birthday?"

Thalia studied me for a long moment. "Why are you being nice to me?"

"I was nice to you the first day I met you. Maybe I'm just a nice person."

Thalia laughed. "Garrett can't stand you."

Ouch. This girl had a way of barbed speaking. Her words peppered against me like stones almost every time she opened her mouth. "He and I have a complicated relationship."

She snorted. "If that's what you want to call it."

Alright. I'd had enough. "Is there a reason you're being such a bitch right now?"

Thalia's eyes widened. "Well, I—I—?"

One of my eyebrows rose. "You what?"

Her shoulders slumped. "I'm sorry," she finally said. "Moving around a lot makes it hard to make friends."

"So you push anyone who's nice to you away so you don't get hurt when you leave again?"

Her behavior made a lot more sense now.

"I guess," she muttered under her breath.

Simone stepped into the clearing, dressed in joggers and a sweatshirt. "Nothing unusual in my area."

Noting our body language, she stopped. "Everything okay here?"

"It's fine. Evie likes to ask a lot of questions."

I rolled my eyes and came to standing. "Thalia is like a cactus. One of those inedible ones that has no use other than to poke you and piss you off."

"Hey!" She picked up a stick and threw it at me.

Simone grinned and plopped onto the ground beside the seer. "I'll take over babysitting. I heard Garrett howling, so he must have found something."

I waved and took off through the woods.

• • •

My land pulsed with harmony, even through the cold weather. As I ran, I touched leaves and limbs, my feet squishing through damp leaves and loam.

Caelan met me when I was almost there, stepping into my path, his eyes glowing.

Shit. That was never good. I slowed down and approached. "What happened?"

He held out his hand. "You'll want to see it for yourself."

Caelan tugged me through a dense area of trees and brush, holding up limbs to allow me to duck through. When I reached Garrett, he was in human form, holding a flashlight in his teeth and flipping through a small, damaged notebook.

He looked up at me, his expression somber. Without a word, he stood and handed me the flashlight and notebook. Garrett never voluntarily touched me, but he placed a hand on my shoulder and gave it a gentle squeeze.

I glanced back at Caelan who watched me with an unnerving intensity. "What is it?"

"Gianna's blood was on the notebook. I can only assume she was still alive when they carried her in and she either dropped this on purpose, or it fell out of her pocket. Nadia must not have realized what Gianna had until it was too late."

"I don't understand why a notebook would make you two look like my life is over." I didn't know Gianna before Caelan, and I had only seen her a few times before a Chimera took over and tried to marry him to wrest power of his region away and put it under Chimera control. What could she have written in this tiny thing to make Caelan look at me like this?

"Just..." He sighed and ran his hand through his hair. "Take a look, please."

I found an open spot and sat cross-legged on the cold ground, my hands trembling as I opened the bloodstained cover. The feeling of holding belongings from someone whose existence had been so thoroughly erased as if she'd never existed made something clench tight inside me. The first page had bloody fingerprints smeared down the cream color of the paper. Several pages had been torn out, half the contents gone as if someone had done so in a hurry. My heart sped up as I flipped to the first legible page.

There is evidence there is still one left—a male, somewhere in Europe. He is elusive and rarely seen, and when we get close, he disappears as if he'd never been there. It's maddening.

We need to open discourse if we hope to save our kind.

Frowning, I looked up at Garrett and Caelan, still not understanding what was going on. Swallowing hard, I bent my head to keep reading.

Odd power pulses are being reported all over Europe which leads us to hope there may be more than one still operating. We still can't find the male. He might be onto us. If so, hope dwindles for a conversation. Their kind are known to respond with violence first and are not known for peaceable relations with any other form of paranormal.

A horrible feeling began to churn in my gut.

One of our shifters spotted him in a bar with a dark-haired woman. Human, possibly. Though he seems quite taken with her.

My fingers shook. I tried to turn the page a few times before my fingers cooperated.

We lost him. Again. He knows we're following him.

The next entry had a date coinciding with the time I was in Scotland. Hot, angry tears pricked the backs of my eyes.

We tracked him to a field. There are signs of a struggle and blood that is decidedly not human. No signs of a body, though it's doubtful the woman with him survived such a horrific attack.

"Gods," I whispered.

I kept reading, dread growing in my body until it was rooted there permanently.

The last couple of entries were the most chilling of all.

We must find the Chimera if we are to save our fertility and our way of life. A normal shifter won't introduce the power we need to survive into our bloodline. There's a woman in Joy Springs who looks strangely like the one our brother swan spotted in Scotland, but she shows no signs of the Chimera curse. Her presence could be a coincidence, but it is unlikely.

We will monitor the situation. If we cannot find the male, the woman is an even better choice. We're testing the blood for traces of the Chimera curse.

And the last entry.

Evie Quinn is the last living Chimera. Approach with extreme caution.

CHAPTER
Twenty-Seven

The notebook slid from my fingers. I stared blankly at nothing, my mind whirring with the knowledge that there was an entire faction of shifters who knew exactly what I was.

Numbness set in. I couldn't speak or move, but I was desperate to speak or move or cry, something other than this horrible maw of a pit opening inside of me.

Caelan came to his knees beside me. "We'll fix it. We'll figure out who knows and take them out."

"It's possible the knowledge is only with a small number of people," Garrett said. "And one of them is dead."

"How?" I croaked. "How did this happen?"

Caelan brought me into the circle of his arms. "Terrible luck, Evie. They weren't after you. They were after Finn. Perhaps that's what drew him here."

"That must be how he found me." I raised a trembling hand to my cheek. "Why he and Rhona killed Gianna. Maybe they weren't trying to stab me in the back after all. Maybe…"

I shook my head just as a thought occurred to me. I'd forgotten about him. "Barrett. He's here. Maybe he can tell me. Maybe he's here to help."

"You cannot trust any of the other Chimeras, Evie. Not now. Not when you don't know who they're working with or what their goals are."

"I can't trust the shifters, either."

Caelan stilled. "You can trust me. Always." But there was an odd tremble in his voice. Maybe he would keep my secret. Maybe he would even protect me when others might try to take me. But I knew in my heart that he was keeping a secret that somehow involved me. Had I been the biggest fool of all by trusting him? Even after everything, would trusting him finally lead to my downfall?

Garrett stood a few feet away, his eyes trained on Caelan. A gold ring outlined his eyes, and his jaw was taut with tension.

"You're hiding something from me," I said when the silence became unbearable. "Both of you."

Garrett looked away. Caelan's arms tightened. "No," he said quietly. "I'd never hide anything like this from you."

"But you *are* hiding something."

Caelan sighed, and I waited for him to come clean, but he shook his head. "No, Evie. I'm not hiding anything."

A frigid wind swept through the area, the same temperature as my heart. He was lying. I knew it as sure as I knew that my heart was breaking. It had taken me years to trust someone again, and just when I had opened my heart and finally let Caelan in, let myself love again, he lied right to my face.

I swallowed my pride down, forced my emotions into the same box I used that night while I lay dying in that field of heather, and forced a smile. "Right. Of course. I'm sorry for doubting you. It's just...that notebook. Others know about me now, and I'm not sure how to handle that, or what I should do about it."

Garrett's glowing gaze rested on my face, but I saw no judgment in his eyes. Only resignation. He and I both knew that I knew, but he would not call me out on it. At least not right now. I would get up, dust myself off, take this notebook with me and call Moira. Then we would call Barrett and feel him out. Regardless, Moira and I would come up with a plan.

I was a survivor. If the shifters came for me, I would respond in kind.

It was time to take the gloves off and show them what a Chimera could do.

Caelan wanted to stay, but I pled a headache.

We both knew I was lying, but even though his jaw was tight, he brushed a kiss over my cheek and left. Garrett gave me a long look before he followed his Lord out, but Thalia hesitated at the door.

She looked back. "I'm sorry," she whispered.

Before I could ask for what, Thalia hurried after Garrett. Moments later, the sound of a vehicle started up, and lights flared in my window as they pulled out of the driveway.

They were gone.

I collapsed onto the couch and buried my head in my hands. What a night.

Moira didn't bother knocking. She burst through the door, holding two large bags in one hand and a tray of drinks in the other.

"Who do I need to kill? It's been a while since I drew blood. Screwing with the Lords is fun, but your insistence that I don't take it too far is super annoying."

She dropped the bags on the coffee table and shoved a large cup of something at me.

I cracked open the lid and almost choked at the smell of alcohol.

"Drive through daiquiri place just opened up down the road."

"In Texas?" I blurted.

"Not Texas. Or at least not completely. This is Joy Springs." She wiggled her eyebrows. "We have magic. And no respect for proper laws."

I took a sip of the frozen fluorescent concoction. "Mmm."

"Blue raspberry with enough booze to tranquilize an elephant."

"Awesome." I took a long drink.

Moira took hers from the tray, red and swirled with something yellow. "Raspberry mango." She took a large draw from the straw and shuffled through the bags.

"Boneless and regular wings, three different flavors, curly fries and tots."

"You're the best friend a girl could ever have."

"I know," Moira said with a sigh. "Let's eat. Then you can tell me who I get to murder."

MOIRA'S EYES FLASHED A BRIGHT, jagged green sometime later. "The swans? I don't know whether to laugh or cry."

"Swans are assholes." My words were on the slurry side, but I still had twenty percent of my daiquiri left.

Moira nodded. "Have you seen the memes where the ducks are running around with knives in their mouths?" She shuddered.

"It's what I imagine the swan shifters must do when they shift. How do you fight with wings and a pretty yellow beak?"

"They don't have arms. How would they stab anyone?"

Moira's brow furrowed. "Maybe they have fangs. Like vampires."

"Vampire swans?" I shook my head. "Maybe they have retractable claws on their feet. And blades in their wings."

"Like a swan ninja." Moira nodded. "Makes sense."

I laughed. "It makes zero sense."

She leaned forward, her eyes intense. "There's one thing I

don't understand. Why are you afraid of swan shifters? Even if they do have fangs and blade wings."

"I'm not."

"You're afraid of something. If it's not the swans, what is it?"

Moira started to giggle and slapped her hands over her mouth, but she couldn't stop. "This is the dumbest conversation we've ever had," she wheezed. "Swan shifters? Were the gods high that day?"

I snorted. "It's not the swans. It's…" What was it? Worrying about shifters who communicated through honks made me want to scream.

"They know about me," I finally admitted. "If Gianna knew that means Nadia knows, too. Who else did they tell? Have they shared the info with other shifters, or has it stayed with them? If I retaliate or try to wipe them out and they haven't told anyone, I'd be shooting myself in the foot. If they have told other people, maybe it's just a matter of time before they come for me."

I stared down at the daiquiri. "Why the hell is this so good? What kind of alcohol are they using in this magical drink?"

Moira wiggled her eyebrows. "The witches in town got together a few years ago because everyone was tired of drinking without being able to get tipsy. From what I understand, Hazel met with them when she was here. Looks like they were successful."

I blinked. "Oh shit."

"Yeah. Joy Springs is about to get lit!"

She kicked off her shoes and curled up on the couch. "I do my best thinking when I'm buzzed. Now, let's talk this out. You're a Chimera. The swans found out after they found you with Finn. May he burn in a fiery pit of awfulness forever. They want to bring more power into their bloodline, which might negate the wings with blades theory, and since Finn is dead, they set their sights on you." She took another sip of her daiquiri.

"Obviously, you don't want to be a broodmare, and killing them all, while fun and deserved, is illegal."

"If they knew it was me."

Moira gasped. Her eyes lit up. "Now we're cooking! If they didn't tell anyone else, which is likely considering they want your power for their own, we could find out where their Keep is and take them all out."

Maybe it was the alcohol. Maybe it was the fear. Maybe it was the bone-deep exhaustion. Whatever it was, swan mass murder was sounding better and better.

"They only have one Keep in the entire world," Moira said. "A good indicator of fertility issues or an iron-fisted control on breeding within the race. Since we have proof it's fertility, there's a good chance they don't have any secret populations of swans who might swear a blood oath and take out your entire genetic line once those left behind grow to adulthood."

A hoarse laugh bubbled from my throat.

"I'm serious." Moira took a sloppy sip from her cup. "Blood oaths are serious things."

"Let's assume there are no future warrior swans with a vendetta in our future."

"Okay. Good. The only thing is, swans can fly, and they're bound to do routine sky sweeps around the Keep. How do we take out their entire Pack without alerting those in the sky?"

"At night?"

"Easier to sneak in, but swans fly at night."

"Snipers?" It was a joke, but Moira was super into planning the total annihilation of all swan kind.

She snapped her fingers. "Excellent. Think we can get Garrett to do it?"

I hadn't told her my theory about Caelan yet. My long pause clued her in.

"Evie?"

"We can't ask Garrett because I don't want to ask Caelan. Plus, we can't involve them in something like this. Too complicated politically."

She tilted her head, her eyes narrowing. "You never cared about politics before. What happened?"

I looked at my empty cup and sighed. "Maybe we should have gotten two more of these."

"What. Is. It."

Before I could say a word, I started to cry.

Twenty-Eight

CAELAN

My enforcer was furious. He sat on the chair opposite my desk, eyes glittering with a ring of gold. "You need to tell her."

"I'm aware. You know I can't."

Garrett scoffed. "Since when have you cared about the whims of the gods?"

"This particular god happens to not only be the Fae King, he's Evie's father."

"Which makes it four times worse."

Where was this coming from? "You hate Evie."

His jaw tightened. "I don't."

"What changed? A while ago, you most certainly did."

Garrett looked away. A staccato thumping noise came from the shelf above. Seymour, resident vicious, sentient flytrap sailed through the air, his traps waving as he headed right at him.

Garrett's hand shot out, carefully catching him by the bottom of his pot. "You are a nightmare." But his voice was touched with fondness. The flytrap had become a permanent fixture inside the Keep, but it took a while for the other shifters to get used to his antics.

He'd become part of the family, in an odd way, and now I couldn't imagine my life without him.

Seymour snuggled up to Garrett, and the shifter gently stroked him on top of his main trap. "She's good for you," he muttered. "As much as I hate admitting that I don't hate her. She's unhinged and sometimes volatile, but once you have her loyalty, it's yours forever."

His lips thinned. "Unless you deceive her, which you have been doing since the moment you brought Thalia under your protection."

"Evie is one thing. Cernunnos can crush us if we violate his oath."

Garrett sighed. "Do you think he would harm us when his daughter loves you? The king is playing you. I don't know the rules or the goal of the game, but mark my words, this is a test. And it's one I think you're failing."

I always listened to Garrett when he spoke because he never said a lot, but whatever he said was worth listening to. But this? I wasn't sure he was right, and testing the fae king's threat could end with him decimating the Keep.

"I can't risk Pack lives over this agreement."

"But you'd risk a potential mate?"

Claws threatened to slip from my fingers. I bit back a harsh response. "What do you suggest I do?"

"You come clean and throw yourself on the altar of Evie, consequences with Cernunnos be damned."

A bark of laughter escaped me. "Since when did my stringent rule follower become someone who'd throw all the rules out for a woman?"

When Garrett stayed silent, I smiled. "You care about Thalia, and it's scaring the shit out of you."

His cheeks turned ruddy. "Doesn't matter. She can't stand me."

"Evie hated me for months and threatened to kill me every chance she got. Now look at us."

"She knows you're lying to her," Garrett said. "You're fooling yourself if you think she doesn't."

I leaned back in my chair. "I'll talk to Cernunnos."

"You never should have agreed to this in the first place."

"If I hadn't, you wouldn't be smitten over Evie's sister."

"Yeah, but don't you think this is going to fuck up Thanksgiving dinner if Evie sends assassins after you once she realizes what you're lying about?"

"Assassins?" I shook my head. "Not her style. She'd do it herself. Probably while I was in my garden or something."

"You joke," Garrett said in a somber voice, "but that girl has been betrayed more than anyone I've ever known. Myself included. If I were you, I wouldn't be sitting here debating with me. I'd be at her house throwing myself on her mercy."

"I'm not you," I growled.

Garrett rose, carefully setting Seymour down on top of my desk. "If I ever had the chance with a woman like Evie, I wouldn't squander it. The gods be damned." He headed toward the door, turning one more time to look at me. "You keep fucking up, Caelan. She won't wait forever for you to get your shit together. There is at least one pretty Lord waiting in the wings who wouldn't mind shooting his shot."

Fucking Rowan. And now I had to worry about Ben. Literal wolves were circling around the love of my life just waiting for me to screw this up. "Heard and noted," I said mildly, trying not to show how pissed off I was at the thought of Rowan or anyone else swooping in to claim her. He had no designs on her, I kept telling myself. Otherwise, why would he give me the necessary advice to finally right things between us?

Because he knew I'd fuck it up again by doing something stupid like keeping her sister a secret?

"Fuck," I muttered.

Seymour hopped over and jumped into my lap, but even he wasn't enough to lift my dark mood.

I needed to get into contact with Cernunnos and end this once and for all.

CHAPTER
Twenty~Nine

Ash and Tess opened the shop today while Moira and I paid Thalia a visit.

The seer opened the door and gestured for us to come in. I wondered if her powers had clued her in to the reason for our visit.

Garrett, thankfully, was nowhere to be found. "Slipped your jailer for a little while?"

"He's on a coffee run."

Moira laughed with delight. "You sent Caelan's Second out for iced coffee?"

"No," Thalia said. "I sent him out for a caramel drizzle, white chocolate, whirled latte."

She gestured for us to sit. Thalia's apartment was a riot of color. Her couch was a modern shape in a pretty teal fabric. Burgundy throw pillows were haphazardly tossed on each side, and the couch rested on a teal and burgundy rug in an abstract pattern. On the other side was a squat burgundy chair with a book lying face down on the seat and a blanket across the back. A scarred round wooden coffee table scattered with magazines sat in the middle.

Two large bookshelves were crammed with beat-up paperbacks, a mix of fantasy, romance, and modern literature. Her kitchen was small but neat, clean dishes still dripping on the rack.

"Cute place," Moira said. "How are you liking Joy Springs?"

Thalia shrugged. "The place is cute and quirky, but there's not much of a nightlife around here." Her lips turned down. "Not that my jailer would let me go out after eight."

Moira's lips twitched. "Evie mentioned you don't know how old you are?"

Thalia shook her head.

"How old do you think you are?"

"Twenty something, I think. I remember low-waisted jeans being all the rage when I was in primary school."

"Maybe born in the late 90s?" Moira mused aloud. "You don't remember any years?"

Thalia shrugged. "Not really."

Something about this girl was way off. Who didn't remember the years they spent in school or events that happened in the world? Was she under some type of spell or charm? If she was, and we could figure out how to break it, would she remember everything?

Or was Thalia just being herself and maybe this was just the way seers were? Their brains were under constant attack from psychic visions, and maybe that affected their memory.

"Does your magic cause memory loss?"

Thalia flopped onto her couch and put her feet up on the arm rest. "Lots," she said with a wry grin. "Every time I have a vision, I only remember bits and pieces, and eventually I lose most of those, too. Sometimes I lose pieces of the day, even if I don't have any visions." She sighed and stared up at the ceiling.

"I always wonder if I'm going to wake up one day and not remember who or what I am."

"Sounds lonely," Moira said.

Thalia grunted. "Most seers are lonely. I don't know anyone who's happily married or one who's had kids. How could they without constant supervision? What if they were walking through the house holding a newborn and dropped them?"

Horror rolled down my spine. I had intuition, sometimes strong intuition, but I'd never know what it was to be a seer like Thalia, to fear my own body sometimes. "I'm sorry," I said quietly. "I never thought about it like that."

She waved a hand. "I'm too young to have kids anyway. Not like I want them, either."

"You're still young. Maybe you'll change your mind one day."

"Even if I did, who would marry someone who's constantly losing pieces of herself?"

I tamped my smile down. "You'd be surprised," was all I said. Garrett's expression every time he looked at Thalia when she thought she wasn't looking told me he'd pick up those pieces every time she lost one and keep them safe for her.

"Yeah, well, I have sex sometimes," she said grumpily.

Moira burst out laughing. "Good for you!"

A small smile appeared on Thalia's lips. "I got curious a few years ago and wondered why people were so obsessed with it, but I don't know what the big deal is."

Moira blinked like an owl, eyes wide and stunned. "Umm."

"Oh, Thalia. Gracious." I rubbed my hand over my face. "What that means is you haven't had the right partner yet."

She slid a look my way. "Oh yeah? Things are good with that walking sex stick you're dating?"

Moira snickered.

"Things are fine," I emphasized, giving Moira a look to cool it. "But we're committed and we have been for a while. I'm not the kind of person to...play around. I never have been. There's nothing wrong with that, but I like knowing the person and being willing to commit."

"Again," Thalia said, "I'm trapped in an apartment and at work for the vast majority of my time. "Not exactly conducive to having a boyfriend."

Moira and I exchanged a look. This poor girl was clueless.

Thalia turned her head and speared us with a look. "I can't answer the question you want to know."

Should have seen that coming. "Oh? What question is that?"

Thalia rolled her eyes. "You want to know what Caelan is lying to you about."

"So he is lying?" Moira asked.

"Can't answer that either."

"Can't or won't?" I asked.

"Can't." She mimed a zipper against her lips. "I'm magically bound. I can't discuss my origins, my reasons for being here, any targeted questions about specific details concerning my magic, or speak about the person currently obligated to act as my caretaker."

Moira's eyebrows lifted. "Your caretaker. Is that Garrett?"

"It's Caelan," I said. He'd never come right out and said anything, but he was way too involved with Thalia not to be responsible for her. He'd assigned his Second to her, which was telling.

Thalia didn't respond, but I saw the look on Moira's face. The vampire loved a puzzle, and this one required a lot of thought and maneuvering.

"How long are you here for?" Moira kicked off her shoes and tucked her feet under her thighs.

Thalia grinned. "Eighteen months, give or take a few."

"What happens after that?"

Thalia lifted a shoulder in a shrug. "No idea. I'll either go back to where I came from, or I'll move somewhere else."

"Why do you keep moving?"

Damn. Moira was good at this.

"Clever girl," Thalia said. "People get tired of handling me and want me out of their hair."

"People? As in more than one?"

"What can I say? I'm popular."

"Do you know who your parents are?"

"I know who my dad is." A flicker in her eyes. Moira was close to hitting a nerve.

"Is he a paranormal?"

Thalia pretended to yawn and sat up. "Garrett will be back in a little while. He's not going to be happy that I answered the door."

"A paranormal, then," Moira pressed. "You have the look of the fae about you, but I also suspect that's not completely it. And there's something about you I can't put my finger on. Something familiar."

Same thing I thought.

"Do you sell your visions?" I asked.

Thalia stiffened. "Are you calling me a whore, Evie?"

I froze. "What? No! Why would I do that?"

"I dunno. You seem a little judgmental."

"I just wanted to know if you're taking advantage of your magic. If you have all those negative sides of your power, one would hope you'd use it to get rich."

Thalia's look morphed from annoyance to thoughtful. "I've never tried forcing a vision before. Not to the specifics it would take to work with clients." She tapped a finger on her chin.

"Damn, Evie. I could be an entrepreneur." The smile she bestowed upon me lit up her entire face and turned her face from interesting to devastatingly beautiful.

A key turned in the door. Garrett walked in carrying a tray with two coffees, one of them piled high with whipped cream, sprinkles, and what I hoped was edible glitter on top.

My lips twitched, but I couldn't laugh. Garrett was just now looking at me like he didn't want to murder me, and I wanted to keep the peace.

"You aren't supposed to answer the door," he growled.

Thalia rolled her eyes. "She's your Lord's girlfriend. Why wouldn't I open the door for her?"

"Because glamours aren't that hard to make," he said, kicking the door shut with his foot. "Are you sure that's actually Evie and Moira?"

"Well, we haven't tried to murder her yet," I drawled.

Garrett rolled his eyes. "I know it's you because of your scents, but Thalia doesn't have a good nose."

"I'm not an idiot," she snapped.

"Never said you were." He set the tray down on the table and pulled her frozen concoction out with a grimace of distaste.

Thalia grinned and took it, popping the straw in and pressing it against her chest like it was a precious diamond.

"I do not know how you drink that crap."

"That's because you have no joy in your life," she said as she took a drink and sighed.

Garrett's eyes flashed with hurt, but he played it off. "Ladies, did you need something from Thalia?"

"They're trying to figure out why your Lord is lying to her."

Moira choked.

"Gods, Thalia!" I glared at her.

Garrett let out a heavy sigh. "Alright."

"That's all you have to say?" I demanded.

He sat on the edge of the couch, a defeated look on his face. "You and I both know I couldn't help you even if I wanted to."

I didn't want to feel bad for him, but the expression he wore coupled with the slump of his shoulders made my stomach twist with empathy. "You aren't denying he's lying to me."

He held up his hands. "I'm not getting involved in this at all. I can't."

Garrett hesitated, his mouth opening and shutting before he scraped a hand through his hair. "I know we've had our differences, but I think you're good for Caelan. And I would hate for anything to come between you. He needs someone powerful who doesn't put up with his bullshit."

"Of which there is a lot," Moira interjected. "So. Much. Bullshit."

Thalia laughed.

Garrett took a long drag of his coffee. "I think you should speak to Caelan directly."

"Oh, don't worry," I said. "'I plan to."

"Good." He rose and went to the kitchen where he promptly dumped out his coffee.

"You wanted the glittery one?" Moira asked with a smirk.

"They added sugar," he clarified with a glare. "The devil's spice."

I stood and tucked my purse strap over my shoulder. "Thanks for being candid and not lying to me."

Garrett shrugged. "Good luck."

"Evie isn't the one who needs luck," Moira said cryptically as she followed me out.

We didn't speak until we were back in the car.

"There's something familiar about her," Moira said. "Did you notice that?"

"I did, and it's bothering the hell out of me."

"Are you going to Caelan's?"

I shook my head. "Not yet. How do you feel about paying Barrett a visit?"

Moira smiled. "Great idea. I've got a good internal lie detector. Maybe he can tell us what he knows about the swans. And whether it's worth wiping them all out."

I couldn't believe I was thinking about wiping out an entire species to save myself, but they were thinking about enslaving me to use me as a brood mare, so maybe I could think of it as tit for tat.

We'd know more in a little while, provided Barrett was honest with us.

HE OPENED the door on the first knock, seemingly unsurprised to see us standing on the porch. Barrett held open the door.

"I was about to take a cup of coffee on the outdoor patio. Would you like to join me?"

"Sure. We have some questions," I said.

Barrett inclined his head. "I figured you'd want more information." He poured us both a cup, offering us cream and sugar, before leading us outdoors to a beautiful, covered patio area.

"This is a nice place," I remarked. The patio backed up to a densely wooded pocket of land.

"Not as private as I'd like, but with quick access to the woods, it was acceptable."

Barrett was rumpled this morning, blond hair unkempt and a five o'clock shadow gracing his strong jaw. He wore a pair of loose pants and a long-sleeved sweatshirt with a pair of what had to be wool socks.

"Have you given any more thought to my proposal?" He picked up his coffee mug and took a sip, and I had an odd thought that he had nice hands, strong and scarred.

"I thought your timing was unusual," I said. "You came when things had finally settled down for me, disrupting everything once more."

Barrett's lip curled in a one-sided smile. "I'm afraid I'm not psychic, Miss Quinn. My timing was irrelevant. I came when I could and when it was most advantageous to me."

"Some concerning information has come to light. I'm here to see if you knew about it in advance."

His eyes tightened at the edges. Barrett set his mug down and faced me. "You know about the swans."

It was not a question. "Yes. They were after Finn initially."

"They were. Your involvement was a complete, unfortunate accident."

"They have my blood."

Barrett blinked in surprise. A sharp inhale and a nod. "That explains how they knew what you were other than a mere Floromancer."

"Do you know what they want from me?" The coffee had soured in my stomach.

To his credit, his expression turned grim. "There are only a couple of reasons someone might want one of our kind."

"My next question is, are you here to help or hinder me?"

Barrett's eyes crinkled at the edges. "Our people are scattered across the world. I believe there are less than ten of us left, including you and me. If we hope to replenish our numbers, we will have to intermarry or find peace with each other."

I opened my mouth to object, but Barrett held up a hand. "I am not suggesting you do either. Our people have been driven to near extinction due to the hatred and prejudice of others. I do not plan to continue down that road. If you find a willing Chimera partner, we will all bless the union. If you find another outside of our kind, I will do the same. Or, if you choose to stay single and produce no children, you will have no argument from me."

Moira had stayed suspiciously silent. I glanced at her, but she was still and silent, long fingers wrapped around her mug as she watched Barrett.

"My hope is for us to make such a commotion the Lords have no choice other than to sit down at the table with us and bring us into the fold. We deserve to have a say. We are too powerful not to."

I agreed with what he was saying, but I wanted no part of the Lords. He smiled when he saw my face.

"You underestimate yourself. I'd like you to think about stepping up as our representative."

Moira finally spoke. "You don't want the job?"

Barrett shook his head. "No, though I will have to step in if Evie refuses. She is what our race is meant to be. Smart, powerful, beautiful… she would bring our race into the forefront of the world."

I grimaced. "You are all of those things, too."

He laughed. "But I am not a female."

My brow furrowed.

Barrett's eyes widened a hair. "You don't know."

I hated admitting being out of the loop, but I had no clue what he was talking about.

"Female Chimeras are far more powerful than males. Not everyone can access their true forms, but seventy-five percent of our females can." His eyes flickered. "Or they used to."

Something in his tone piqued my attention. "How many females are left?"

A sad smile. "Rhona's death left only one."

I sucked in a breath. "No."

"I'm afraid so. You are the last living female Chimera, Evie Quinn. And our last hope to keep our bloodline true."

Moira swore viciously. "Is that why you wanted her?" She looked like she was about to come out of her chair and claw his face off.

He shook his head, watching her warily. "Not at all. But Evie must know how important she is to our kind and the good she could do if she wanted to. Her bloodline is unique and must be protected at all costs. If anything, consider me a form of protection."

A thin smile before adding, "Though I do not believe she needs any protection. She's more than proven her capability of protecting herself."

"True that," Moira said proudly.

"In saying this, I have to add a caveat."

"You better not say a word about my ovaries," I growled, fed up with every single man on the planet at that moment.

"You need a teacher," he said bluntly. "Chimeras are masters of magic, and you have relied on blunt force instead of stealth. This is the second reason I came here. Allow me to show you who you can become. Then decide on your path forward. With or without us."

I didn't sense any subterfuge, which made me nervous.

Nothing he proposed was simple. Not being taught how to master my magic or stepping up to act as the Chimera representative, an act that would paint a big fat target on my back.

I looked at Moira who simply shrugged. "This one's on you. I think you should go for it, though."

"Doing so will change everything. You, me, Ash and Tess, the shop. Where I fit in with Caelan."

"Yes," she agreed. "You need to ask yourself if you want to keep living in fear or if you want to be able to finally exist as you are."

Barret wisely stayed quiet, allowing us to debate.

Finally, I squared my shoulders. "I want to meet the other Chimeras."

He didn't say no right away. "Why?"

"I want to see who I'd represent if I chose to step up."

"We can't gather everyone in one spot. Are you amenable to video meetings?"

"With some, yes."

Barrett nodded. "I'll see what I can do."

"Fine." I crossed my arms and stared him down. "In the meantime, what are we going to do about the swans?"

A vicious smile touched Barrett's mouth, and a sheen of crimson rolled across his iris. "Give them exactly what they deserve, of course."

"I'M PROUD OF YOU," Moira said on the drive back.

I glanced at her. "I didn't say yes."

"True. But you didn't say no, either. A year ago, you would have laughed Barrett out of town."

"I would have," I said with a sigh. "Many things have changed, haven't they?"

"Especially you." She reached over and squeezed my knee. "All good. Moments of temporary insanity and general brattiness—"

"Hey!"

"But you always seem to level out, which is a good thing. We can chalk those moments up to temporary insanity or wild hormone fluctuations based on the gravitation pull of the moon."

I rolled my eyes. "Don't you talk about my golden goose ovaries like that."

Moira reached over and touched my lower belly. "The preciousssss must be protected at all costs. You are the Chimera's only hope, Evie wan Quinnobi."

My lips twitched. "You are such an ass."

"Running through all those male Chimeras might be fun. If only pregnancy didn't last nine months and ruin everything good."

I cackled. "You don't want kids?"

She shuddered. "Gods no. A lifetime of handing out money like candy and praying they're smart enough not to ruin their lives? And the social media. So much social media. Eww."

"Good thing I have no plans to engage in a Chimera harem then."

"Honestly, you can still have the harem without the babies. I'm sure none of them would mind."

"They could all be hideous. And, just, no. You saw how long it took me with Caelan."

She speared me with a droll look. "None of them will be hideous. That goes against the gods' ancient laws of making powerful, pretty things they can torture with their wicked whims."

"Doesn't matter. We see pretty people every day. I do not have a weakness for a pretty face."

"Yes," Moira said deadpan. "They have to be pretty and have a death wish."

Thinking about Caelan hurt. Whatever secret he was keeping from me had to be big, otherwise, why would he damage everything we'd built together? I'd spent a lot of time racking my brain, trying to figure out what kind of leverage someone might have on him to force him to keep something from me and…

I straightened, my hands clenching on the steering wheel. "It's Cernunnos. That's why Caelan is keeping the secret."

Moira's expression turned contemplative. "Then two people in your life are keeping a secret. But why? What's so important about Thalia they'd both risk screwing things up with you?"

We pulled into the driveway to see a stunning woman with dark hair and familiar eyes waiting for me.

"Uh oh," Moira whispered. "I'll call you later."

I hadn't seen my mother in a long time. My fists clenched. Anger wasn't the right emotion I was feeling. There was some fury there, but how I felt was a lot more complicated than simple anger.

"Thanks for toting me around today," I said, surprised at how normal my voice sounded.

Moira nodded and put the car in park. Once I was out, she waved and pulled away.

I turned to Cliona, ancient fae goddess and my mother. "Long time no see."

Mom was dressed far differently than usual. She wore a pair of what looked like wool slacks with smart boots on her feet, a crisp white, satin shirt tucked in, and a leather belt with a gold buckle. Her hair fell in loose curls almost to her waist, and she wore makeup today—a shiny berry gloss, blush, and mascara.

She looked like an executive for a Fortune 500 company.

"Has the economy taken a downturn in Faerie?"

Mom rolled her eyes. "Honestly, Evie."

"You look like you're going in for a job interview."

"Do you think I spend my days floating around my mounds with a magical wand spreading glitter everywhere?"

I shrugged, a grin tugging on my lips. "Glitter? You? Never. Mayhem and terror? Absolutely."

Mom huffed. "Contrary to popular belief, I do regular business in the human world. Now, I would like a cup of tea. Have you gotten past your fear that I will wreck your life so you will lower your wards for me and invite me in, or do we need to have this conversation outside?"

Old habits died hard. I wanted to lower the wards. She deserved for me to lower them. But all those years of living in fear of her had changed something inside me, and I couldn't seem to let go of that deep seated terror that if I let her in, she'd use my secrets against me.

To her credit, she waited, her face a blank mask, and allowed me to decide.

The silence went on, the wind swirling her dark hair around her face.

I was slowly finding out I couldn't trust people as much as I once had. But Caelan, as important as he was to me, wasn't family. Cliona was.

I swallowed hard and nodded once. "Earl Grey?"

We both pretended not to notice how hoarse my voice was.

"Please," Mom said a little breathlessly.

I lowered the wards and allowed an ancient goddess to come onto my land.

Thirty~One

om was in my living room. Sitting on my couch. Drinking from one of my teacups.

The sky had fallen.

She'd even kicked off her boots and curled her feet under her. I'd lit the fireplace, turning my living room into a cozy, quiet space.

"So…" Mom stirred cream into her tea. "We have much to talk about."

We did, but I wasn't sure I wanted to do it right now. There were more pressing questions I needed to ask before we dove into our sordid family history. "Mom?"

"Yes?"

"Do you know someone named Thalia?"

Mom didn't hesitate. No flicker of recognition on her face. "No. Why?"

Dead end there. "No reason. She's become something of a puzzle, and I can't find the right pieces."

"Does she live here?"

"She's new to town. Thalia is a powerful seer but seems pretty normal."

Mom tilted her head in that peculiar way she had. "Then why are you so interested in her?"

I squirmed in my seat. Trusting my mother was much harder than I expected. When I hesitated, Mom sighed. "I understand you do not trust me. I would not trust me, either. Not after everything that has transpired between us. Even if you never trust me again, even if we can't repair what's happened through the years, I want you to know every step I took. I did it in the hopes you would get one more day, one more week, one more year without being thrust into danger."

She took a sip of her tea and sighed. "Excellent and fresh. Thank you."

I always kept a fresh tin of her favorite tea. Even when I hated her. "You're welcome."

"This woman. Is she a friend?"

"No. I don't like her all that much."

Mom's lips twitched. "Okay. An acquaintance, then?"

"Yes. She says she's trapped here and not allowed to leave without an escort."

Mom frowned. "Who is holding her here?"

"I don't know, but Caelan is the one overseeing her protection."

"You're curious as to why?"

"Yes," I admitted, "but there's something familiar about her. It's bugging me to death. I know I've never met her before now."

Mom frowned. "Is it possible Caelan is keeping her for…other reasons?"

I snorted, not even offended. The fae were a bunch of dirty birds, and many of them banged anything that moved. "No. He seems to tolerate her. That's all."

"You think he's keeping her for someone else?"

I nodded. "Thalia claims she has an overprotective father, but I've never seen him. Her power prevents her from driving or holding down a normal job, but she also can't do normal things like shopping or going to get a coffee by herself. She claims not to remember her birthday but doesn't know if it's because her powers are stealing her memory or if something else is going on."

"A spell."

At my nod, a thoughtful look appeared on her face. "You have a theory. Tell me."

"I think Cernunnos stashed her here."

Mom blinked. "A young girl?"

"Not a girl, although she acts like one sometimes. She's in her mid-twenties, I think. But why would he stash her here and keep it a secret from me? We're in a small town. He knew I'd find out eventually."

"You're right. Has Caelan said anything about her?"

"No. He's been silent since he's had her and claims he's doing someone a favor."

"The Shifter Lord does not take on favors of that magnitude without a great boon in return, or it's not a favor at all, and he owes someone something. Has your father done something for Caelan?"

I thought back and came up with nothing. "Not that I know of."

"Something else is bothering you."

I swallowed hard. "I think he's lying about something concerning her, but I can't put my finger on what."

Mom set her cup down. "And you have built your life with him on trust because so many people have betrayed you." Her eyes softened. "I am sorry for my role in that." She dropped her eyes. "More than you could ever know."

Tears pricked the backs of my eyes. The seeds of a reconciliation and new relationship were there, but they would take years and years to grow. "Thank you."

Mom let out a soft breath. "You believe Cernunnos and your Caelan are…conspiring on something concerning this Thalia woman. But you don't believe there is a sexual relationship between any of them."

I nodded. "Right. No funny business in that regard, I don't think."

"Could it be as simple as power? You said she was a powerful seer. Maybe either one of them is using her for her sight?"

Her nose wrinkled. "That doesn't sound right, either. Cernunnos has access to the most powerful seers in creation."

"I wouldn't think Caelan would do that either, even without access to the same."

Mom took a sip of her tea. "Right. Have you thought of asking your father what's going on?"

"I'm not sure he would tell me."

"Has he ever lied to you?"

"No, but he does avoid questions."

Mom smiled, but this time there was no artifice in the gesture. She looked genuinely amused. "True. Your father has quite the talent for avoidance."

The oddness of hearing her speak fondly of my father would unsettle me for a while.

"I would start there, Evangeline. Ask your father first before your thoughts spin out of control and you take implausible leaps."

"And Caelan?"

Her look held an uncomfortable amount of sympathy. "I would not advise you on how to approach him. You know him best. But be sure before you throw out accusations."

Soon after, we finished our tea, and the silence grew awkward rather than comfortable. Mom stood and carried her teacup and saucer to the sink, rinsing both off before placing them on the drying rack.

"Thank you for allowing me inside. You have a beautiful home."

"Thank you for coming."

I walked her to the door, but before she left, she reached out and brushed my cheek with the back of her knuckles. "I hope to visit again."

I nodded, my breath catching. Cliona rarely touched me, and when she had before, it was only to direct or correct. Her magic reminded me a little of Tess's and a little of mine.

"Goodbye, Evangeline."

"Bye, Mom."

She stepped outside and disappeared in a shimmer of light. I thought about altering the wards to allow her to come and go at will, but I wasn't there yet. We weren't there yet.

But today was a good start in the right direction.

Thirty-Two

Cernunnos sat on my back porch, rocking in one of the old wooden chairs. I walked outside when I sensed his presence, carrying two blankets, one of which I handed to him.

He situated it over his lap, even though we both knew he didn't need it.

Silence stretched between us until he finally broke the stalemate. "You have questions."

"Who is Thalia?" I blurted.

"I'm not ready to answer the question."

I let out an impatient huff. "Why is Caelan taking care of her?"

"Your Lord and I came to an agreement."

Which wasn't really an answer, but I was glad I was right. "For how long?"

"Eighteen months."

I choked. "He's responsible for her care for a year and a half? Is she a princess or something?"

Cernunnos's eyes flashed. "Again, I am not ready to answer your question."

"She's important."

"Would it matter?"

"The answer would explain some things." Cernunnos was maddening when he got cryptic—an annoying trait all fae had because information was king in their realm.

Arguably, the same could be said for our realm, so getting mad felt pointless.

"She's important to me."

"And to everyone else?"

"Evie," Cernunnos warned.

"Why did you involve Caelan?"

His eyes narrowed. "Do you truly love the Shifter Lord?"

"What kind of question is that? Of course I do."

"And if he kept a secret from you? A big one?"

My eyes narrowed. Was my father trying to stir the pot? Or was he trying to help me? "I suppose it depends on what the secret was and why he kept the information from me."

"And if it affected your future? Your family? Your potential rule?"

"Why would Caelan do something like that?"

Cernunnos's eyes whirled with power. "Why indeed?"

Something about this wasn't sitting right with me. "Unless he was forced to by an extremely powerful king who had leverage on him."

My father's teeth flashed. "Would you keep a secret like that from him?"

"I did. For months."

"But you weren't in love with him while you kept that secret. Would you do it now?"

I thought about it. My Chimera blood was the reason I was so hesitant to get involved with Caelan in the first place. I knew it wasn't something I could hide from him if we became seriously involved. I wouldn't even sleep with him before he knew. The truth made me uncomfortable, and I struggled with the word.

"No," I admitted. "I wouldn't. Though I'm no saint. I've kept small things from him." Though they never stayed hidden for long.

"You told him a secret that could ruin your life and potentially get you killed because you love him. Ask yourself if he's willing to do the same."

I stared at my father for a long moment. "I thought you liked Caelan."

"Daughter, I am the Fae King. I do not merely *like* anyone. There are too many factions out there trying to destabilize my rule. Trusting anyone is a delicate dance, one I am still trying to perfect all these years later."

"So you don't like him?"

Cernunnos smiled. "I wish for you to be with someone who bares his soul to you. Who does not keep things from you. Who supports you in your endeavors and doesn't hesitate to lift you up when you are down. You are destined to be queen, Evangeline. I wish for you to be with a king."

I swallowed hard. "And you don't think Caelan is king material."

His smile was sad. "My dear, you are also my daughter. No one who keeps secrets from his lover, especially my daughter, is king material."

With those telling words, he disappeared.

I stared at the place he'd been sitting and let out a frustrated sigh. I couldn't tell if he was trying to get me to break up with Caelan, get me to force him to tell me the truth, or get me to whip Caelan into shape to one day become a king. And that last one…I was trying not to think about that, especially now that my father had announced my heritage to all the Lords.

If my father wanted me to be queen, the man I eventually chose would be king. That opened up an entirely new can of worms I would never be prepared for. If I chose a Lord, the new title would make him a fae king and a king over his own territory. Their power would be unparalleled.

The first sense of unease rolled over my shoulders. Caelan had no idea who or what I was when we met, right? I believed that was true.

But did he know later? Was that why he pursued me so relentlessly?

Surely not. Caelan had never done anything to violate the boundaries of the other Lords' territories. He'd never reached out and grasped for my power or tried to influence me in any way.

Except...he hadn't batted an eye when I turned into my Chimera form and killed some people. Was that he wanted?

I let out a groan. Fucking Cernunnos. His cryptic words were sending me into a self-induced tailspin I couldn't find my way out of.

Moira showed up later than evening with another round of takeout and two guests—Ash and Tess.

They barreled in with grins and hugs, all three kicking off their shoes and plopping onto the couch, sprawling together in a friend pile. Warmth filled my heart.

Maybe I'd be a spinster forever. Friends were better than boys anyway.

I shut the door and went over to the couch, climbing onto Moira's lap.

She chuckled, her breath ruffling my hair, and put her arms around me. "Love you, weirdo."

"Love you, too."

Ash and Tess got into the hug. "We love you, too!"

After a couple of quick squeezes, Moira let me go, so I could dive into the takeout bags.

Mexican food? Nice.

"I brought more daiquiris," Moira said, reaching down into another bag to pull out two large trays.

"More than two this time, I see."

She cackled. "Thought we could use them."

This right here...this was what kept me sane. Unconditional love, tacos, daiquiris, and laughter.

Thirty-Three

ROWAN

A shimmer of magic in the greenhouse alerted me to his presence.

I stiffened. "I've told you a dozen times I'm not going to participate in your schemes."

Goddamned fairies.

Evie's father appeared in a flash of emerald and golden light. He'd foregone the horns this time and appeared as human as one like him could appear. His eyes swirled with his ever-present magic, but he wore a pair of jeans and a long-sleeved t-shirt. But his feet were bare in twenty-degree weather.

I shook my trowel at him. "Go away."

Cernunnos hopped onto one of the potting benches. "Evie loves her greenhouse. She spends most of her time there."

"When she's not trying to overcome yours or the other Lord's schemes?" I drawled.

His laugh sent my hackles up. "I've always played the long game, Nature Lord."

"Yes, well, I prefer coming in from the front so I don't have to keep my lies written down."

Cernunnos grinned, and the sight sent my hackles up. "You

have a refreshing sort of honesty about you, something I rarely see in someone of your kind."

"Fuck off, Cernunnos." Speaking such to the Fae King was dangerous, but this fucking guy had been visiting me at least once a week trying to get me involved in another goddamned scheme concerning his daughter or the Lords or…anything, really.

The king was a walking MLM scheme. Or at least it felt that way. Granted, he always had a plan, but I was either too stupid or too honest to see it. Every time he started talking it felt like I was a crazy person standing in front of one of those police string boards trying to explain how aliens were going to invade New York City in two days' time.

I adored Evie. Her father was a completely different matter.

"Why are you not afraid of me?" Cernunnos asked, but this time he was genuinely curious.

I set the trowel down. "I've never been afraid of dying, but I am afraid of losing myself. The moment I allowed you to manipulate me, I would lose a piece of myself. That is a road I am not willing to start walking. The first request is always small, right?"

Cernunnos smiled.

"The second one is a little bit bigger. The third, a little more. I start getting nervous, wondering what I'm doing. Then you come in with a fourth and a fifth, and soon enough I'm running for my life and being chased by the paranormal mob. No thank you. I'm content with my territory, my life, and my plants."

"There's one lie in that statement," he said.

I picked my trowel back up and stabbed it in the pot of dirt I was filling. "Oh?"

"You never wanted this territory."

"True, but now that it's running well, I don't have to do much except ensure order."

"That's not quite true either, is it?"

"It's a job, Cernunnos. That's all. We all need one, unless we're fae royalty, right?"

He tilted his head and studied me. "Would you like to be royalty?"

I laughed. "I'd like nothing less." The thought of that much power sent a cold shiver of fear rolling down my spine.

Cernunnos smiled. "Heavy is the head that wears the crown. Isn't that the statement?"

"Something like that. I don't want a crown. Even this territory is too much some days. I'm content where I am, so stop trying to manipulate me. There's nothing you can offer me that would make me take you up on any of your harebrained schemes."

"Harebrained?" Cernnunos placed a hand over his heart. "How you wound me."

"Cut the shit. What do you want?"

"Do you have some coffee?"

I eyed him. "I do."

When I didn't offer him anything, Cernunnos laughed. "You're a hard nut to crack."

"There's no cracking happening now or ever."

"I believe some changes are about to occur. Serious changes with the potential to upend the current power structure."

I set my trowel down and turned to fully face him. "Spurred on by you?"

An enigmatic smile but no answer.

"What did you do?"

"I've done nothing that didn't need to be done. But my actions have not caused anything to happen, only begun the process."

"Does this involve Evie?" The poor girl needed a break. She finally had one after her near death by tree experience and she and Caelan had finally achieved some sort of balance together. Long overdue balance.

"Everything I do involves Evie."

"Can't you leave her alone? Let her go back to a life of relative peace?"

Cernunnos's lips thinned. "She is the heir to my kingdom, Nature Lord. The second she discovered who I was to her, Evie's life as she knew it was over. I've given her time and freedom, but it is time she steps up and accepts her destiny."

"Evie doesn't want this."

"No one worthy of a crown wants to wear one. But I am not here to discuss Evie's peace of mind. I am here to discuss you and Evie."

I went very still. "Whatever scheme you're cooking up, I want nothing to do with it."

"You don't need to do a thing."

"That's even worse. Leave me out of whatever this is."

Cernunnos smiled and hopped off the table. "You and my daughter have a genuine friendship, yes?"

I sighed. "You already know the answer."

"You would do anything for her, yes?"

"Spill it," I growled, power rising in my veins.

But Cernunnos surprised me. "She will need a friend soon. One who will not use her or take advantage of her position. She is more than she seems, Rowan. More than the Fae Queen. More than this world is ready for."

I'd always known Evie was keeping big secrets from the world at large, and her power was off just enough to make me wonder if she was more than a Floromancer and more than a demi-fae. Even with the revelation of who her father was, I always wondered if there was something strange swimming in her blood.

"Why are you telling me this?"

"She trusts you."

I snorted. "Not enough if she's keeping a secret that big from me."

Cernunnos smirked. "You are not her lover, and you are still a Lord. One day she will trust you enough, but until then all I ask is you pick up the pieces when they shatter. And they will."

"You're asking me to step into a position of…" My voice trailed off. Of what? A lover? A mate? "We are friends. That is all."

Despite the insistent voice in my head that screamed at me we were more than that, more than simply friends, more than people who asked the other how their day went and occasionally showed up with takeout, I wouldn't push that boundary. Not while she was involved with Caelan. My friend. And a powerful Lord I did not want to alienate.

"She has friends, Lord. But she does not have friends with the power to protect her from what's coming."

"I'll do as you ask," I said against my better judgment. "If she comes to me, I will protect her. But not for you. I'll do it for Evie. If she's the one to ask."

Cernunnos held his hands out at his sides, palms up, and smiled. "I wouldn't have it any other way. Good luck, Lord Rowan. You will need it."

The Fae King disappeared in a splash of magic, leaving me alone in the greenhouse contemplating his words and the potential fallout coming Evie's way.

What could possibly be so bad that she would have to ask for the protection of another Lord?

And why was anticipation unfurling in my stomach?

Thirty~Four

I was neck deep in dahlias the next morning, humming a happy little tune. I'd been too distracted by everything to keep up with orders, and Moira and the others had to take up the slack. This morning, I arrived two hours before opening to get set up and make some seasonal bouquets.

My Floromancy hummed in my veins, happy to be used in the way it felt natural. The flower heads stretched toward me, and I stroked the tips of their petals, sending a nutrient boost all the way down to the roots. I'd been remiss in communing with my land, remiss in shifting, and remiss in everything but my own self-pity.

So what if Caelan was lying to me? Maybe I was overreacting. Maybe the lie was small. Or maybe he really was after Thalia's power. Would it be so bad to be selfish for a little while and stay with him because I wanted him? Because I loved him?

I set the handful of dahlias down and groaned.

Yes, it would be bad because I'd be going against my own morals, everything I stood against, everything I'd fought so hard for in a partner. If he was lying to me, I deserved to know why and I deserved to know the truth.

Then I could make my decision on what I wanted to do.

Until then, I'd do my best to give him the benefit of the doubt. He deserved that much from me.

Moira and Tess came in not too long later and joined me at the table after they fixed their drinks.

"Is Ash coming in today?" I asked.

"You used to know the schedule like the back of your hand," Moira said with a laugh.

"Everything has skidded off the rails," I agreed.

"He's coming in at eleven today. I think his uncle is coming in for a visit or something." Tess wore several sparkly barrettes in her hair today, and a cute pink dress with matching shoes.

"You look adorable today," I said.

Her cheeks colored. "Thanks. I met someone at the coffee shop the other day. He's taking me to lunch."

Moira gasped. "You have a date?"

"Not a date," Tess corrected. "Lunch."

"Ah. Okay." Moira grinned. "I hope you enjoy your not date."

"Thank you."

We worked for a couple of hours, catching up on all the new bouquets and a few of the standing orders before the first customers came in. Tess excused herself and went to help them.

Moira leaned over. "How are you doing?"

"I'm fine. But I'm stalled on the swans."

"No trace of Nadia?"

"Not a one."

"Have you asked Caelan?"

I sighed. "He's been texting like crazy, but I've fobbed him off by claiming we were swamped at the shop."

Moira snorted. "We are, but it's nothing we can't handle. He won't wait too much longer."

"I expect him on my porch when I get home this evening." I wanted to see him, but I didn't want to fight. And I knew we would when I started pressing him for answers.

"Dad showed up and made everything worse," I grumbled.

"He is fae," Moira said as if that explained everything.

"I don't think he likes Caelan."

Moira's eyebrows rose. "I don't think he actively hates him."

"Right, but I'm getting a major vibe from him that says he may not hate him, but he doesn't think the Lord is appropriate for me."

Moira waved her hand in dismissal. "Meh. That's what fathers do. No one is ever good enough for their little girl."

I shook my head. "There's something coming. Something bad."

Moira's amusement faded. "Evie?"

I pressed a hand to my stomach. "I can't explain it, but I can feel it."

"Then I believe you." Moira reached for my hand. "Whatever it is, we'll face it together."

"How about we do a little spying this weekend on the swans?"

"Already done. I've gone out there to check things out."

"Wait. When?"

She fluttered a hand at herself. "You forget what I am. I go zoom zoom, very fast. No need for a car or plane."

"See anything interesting?"

Moira snorted. "Lots of bird shit, but nothing concrete."

"Damn. How are we supposed to find out who knows about me?"

"Simple. We break in."

I started laughing, but Moira's expression didn't change. "You can't be serious. Break into a *shifter* Keep?"

Moira grinned. "Why not? Their sense of smell is shit. Swans rely on hearing and vision. It will be dark and they'll be sleeping. We're both quiet as mice. They'll never expect a vampire and someone like you to show up. We'll be in and out before they realize a thing."

I thought about it. "You're done screwing with the Lords?"

"We've got better things to do now. There will always be time left to screw with them, but you're more important." She wiggled her eyebrows. "What do you say? You want to go swan hunting?"

Hmm. "Why the hell not?"

"I'll meet you at your house at ten p.m. Good?"

"As long as Caelan isn't there."

"Text me if he is."

"I'll bring coffee. You bring snacks."

Moira grinned. "Done."

"Fine." I tossed a bunch of flowers at her. "In the meantime, we have work to do."

Just as I expected, Caelan was sitting on my porch when I got home.

The moment I shut the car off, his eyes glowed the golden glow of his magic. He rose, his lean form filled with power and grace.

"You're avoiding me," he said.

Alright. He went for the throat. My turn.

"You're lying to me."

His eyes flashed with anger. "And you think the way to solve this issue is to stay away?"

"I needed time to think."

"And?"

I fished my keys out of my purse and walked up the steps. "And I haven't made up my mind yet."

He held the door open for me and followed me inside. Once the door shut, I felt like all the air was sucked out of the room. Caelan had presence. He was a storm in human form, and I was a piece of debris caught in the rain. Every time he was around, I felt like this, like I was swept up in him.

And I wondered if I was losing a little bit of myself in the process.

"You haven't denied it," I said.

"You seemed pretty sure." He made no move toward me, only stood there like a stone, watching me with those burnished golden eyes.

I crossed my arms over my chest. "Since you're still not denying it, I must be right."

"And if I am?"

My throat went dry. He sounded so callous. "I'd ask why? I thought we were moving past all of that."

"I can't tell you."

I snorted, but I was not amused. "You won't tell me."

"I can't tell you."

"Caelan, even if I was sworn to a blood oath or a binding, I would find a way to tell you what was going on so I didn't have to lie to you. We promised each other no more lies."

His eyes faded to their normal stormy gray blue. "Evie." He took a step toward me and reached his hand out. "I'm hopelessly in love with you, and I can't tell you because I am sworn to secrecy."

"By my father."

He blinked, which was answer enough.

"And it has to do with Thalia."

He gripped me by my upper arms and swept his lips over mine, the heat of his kiss wiping away all my hesitations and reservations. I lost my mind when he touched me, became a wanton female. All I wanted was him and me, together against the world.

Caelan pressed his forehead against mine. "Marry me, Evie. Marry me and I'll be able to tell you everything."

I blinked up at him. A tiny voice in the back of my head wondered if he was being manipulative, wondered if this was his way of worming his way deeper into my soul, then I admonished myself for the thought. This was Caelan. He'd always been honest with me about how he felt, and this wasn't the first time he'd asked me to marry him.

He'd asked multiple times before he knew who I was and before I figured out the Fae King was my father. Caelan wanted me. He didn't want the crown.

The words bubbled from my throat before I could stop them. "Yes."

Caelan stilled. "What?"

"Yes. I'll marry you."

He sucked in a shocked breath, his hands sliding down my body to grip my hips. "Yes." A little laugh escaped him. "You finally said yes."

I swallowed hard. I had. I'd accepted his proposal. I should be thrilled, but there was a stone in my throat, preventing me from saying anything.

"There's so much we need to discuss, so much we have to do." He stepped away, a brilliant smile lighting his face up. "We need to tell the Pack, get them ready to formally accept you. Let's do it soon, Evie. In the next few weeks, okay?"

I nodded dumbly.

He kissed me again, so thoroughly my knees went out from under me. Caelan gripped me around the waist, devouring my mouth.

"We need to tell your father," he murmured against my lips.

"Can you tell me about Thalia now?"

"Not until we're married. We can do it sooner if you really want to know. Maybe even tomorrow. How do you feel about that?"

I shook my head. "No. Not that soon. I need time to get some things together."

He kissed me again. "I hate to do this, but I need to run back to the Keep." His nostrils flared.

"This—this is going to be great, Evie. I've wanted this for so long. I know there's a lot to work out, but we'll figure it out, okay?"

I nodded, unable to form any words.

"I'll be back later tonight."

"No," I said hoarsely. "I'm supposed to go to dinner with Moira, and we plan on having a few drinks."

Forcing a smile, I pressed a quick kiss to his lips. "And with this news, the celebration might go on longer."

Caelan's eyes glittered. "Tomorrow then. Take the day off, and I'll be over in the morning."

I nodded again, feeling like a bobblehead doll.

One more kiss and he was out the door.

I sank onto the couch and let out a heavy sigh.

I was getting married. How had that happened?

What was wrong with me?

I wanted to marry Caelan before, but I had too many secrets to accept his proposal. Now, I was all in, and I couldn't help but feel like this was rushed, like maybe Caelan had seen a way to keep me from asking too many questions about Thalia and took the easy way out.

He'd gotten what he wanted, and I'd received no answers.

He was still lying to me, but he swore I'd get answers when we were married. But we weren't mated, and if the bond wasn't there, he could still lie to me whenever he wanted to. I wouldn't be able to sense when he was untruthful.

The thought didn't sit well with me.

Shaking my head, I got up to fix myself a sandwich. I wasn't hungry, but we'd be expending a lot of energy tonight, and I needed to refuel.

For now, I'd table his proposal and think about it tomorrow.

Tonight, I was about to break into a swan Keep.

"You didn't say the Keep was Rapunzel's tower," I hissed. "How the fuck are we supposed to get up there?"

Moira grinned. "It's an optical illusion. There are doors at the bottom. They're just hard to see. The main window is a balcony of sorts. It's where their sentries fly in and out. There's another lower one on the other side for the regular swans."

"That thing must be twenty stories tall. I wonder how many swans live inside."

"Not many." Moira dropped her binoculars. "There are two sentries tonight, but we can easily evade them if we time it right. They go to sleep by 10:30, and they're a little militant about their bedtime. It's 11:30 now, so everyone but the sentries should be asleep."

"I'm going to send some magic out to check the land. Keep an eye out?"

"Always."

I sank to the ground and pushed my fingers into the dirt, slowly inching my way forward until I crossed the land's boundary.

Sadness and grief. So much sadness. I sucked in a breath and had to force myself not to withdraw.

The land didn't speak to me the same way people did. Not usually. I received images and feelings, and these were overpowering. Underneath it, the land pulsed with health. Whatever faults the swans had, they cared for their land and took care of the earth. The soil was fertile, and in warmer weather, the Keep would be bursting with color. Dahlia and anemone bulbs rested under the soil. Seeds dropped from last year's perennials slept, awaiting springtime once more.

There were no signs of children or innocence. I loved reading land that hosted a lot of children. Joy resonated through the soil. The earth loved kids, and kids loved the earth back. They were still in awe of the land's bounties, where adults might have taken such for granted. But here, there was no such joy, only a deep longing.

I kept moving, closer and closer to the Keep and stopped, searching for any greenery inside.

There. Something in a hallway, I thought. I withdrew and touched the houseplant. A pothos. I grinned. The most common houseplant in the country always offered a way for me to spy.

Fat glossy leaves and moist soil filled with nutrition spoke to a healthy and mostly happy pothos. There was less grief here as houseplants were usually planted with store-bought dirt and not dirt from the land. This pothos hadn't experienced the land's grief. I waited, my conscience linked with the plant, but there was nothing but silence.

I stayed for several minutes until I was sure there was no activity. Moira was right, the Keep was asleep.

I came to with Moira still crouched beside me.

"Good?" she asked.

"Everything's quiet inside."

Moira grinned. "Let's go."

I followed Moira's cues, stopping when she said stop and moving when she said move, until we were at the door. Moira reached out and turned the handle.

It opened smoothly.

"No way," I whispered.

Even Moira seemed surprised. "They have no natural enemies within the shifter communities."

"Really? But they suck."

Moira snorted softly. "They do, but they've never been a real threat to anyone before."

"Where should we start?"

"We find either a library or an office and search through everything."

Moira opened the door, and we both slipped inside.

Two hours later, we'd found absolutely nothing.

"This is useless," I whispered. "How are we going to find anything in this mess?"

"Mess is right," Moira said as she looked around at the piles of paper and scattered books. "I don't even see a file cabinet."

"I hate swans."

Moira rose from the floor, wincing as straightened her back. "Maybe there's a basement."

"Why would Chimera info be in the basement?"

"Because every Keep usually has a mage. Chimeras are magical. We'll check there and if we can't find anything, we'll get the hell out of here."

We crept down the hallway, hand in hand. The inside was better than the austere gray of the outside, but the decorating was still sparse. Someone here had a green thumb, though. The plants they passed were well cared for and bright with color.

"Here," Moira whispered. "There's a staircase."

She cracked open the door, wincing when it made a loud creaking noise. We froze and waited for the calvary, but no one stirred.

Moira held the door open and motioned me inside. When the door shut, we were plunged into absolute darkness.

I froze, fear skittering up my spine, but Moira took my hand. "Relax. I've got amazing night vision. I'll lead you down."

As we walked, my vision got better, finally adjusting to the darkness. I'm not sure how long we walked, but the staircase was ridiculous, at least four stories down. When we got close to the bottom, Moira made a shh motion with her finger and crept down the rest of the way, motioning me to follow when she thought it was clear.

My eyes widened when I saw the room we'd ended up in.

A laboratory. Beakers and glass jars full of things I couldn't identify lay scattered all over scarred wooden tables. Books and papers were stacked on top of each other. Something bubbled in a large glass container without a heat source.

"Let's hurry," Moira whispered. "This place is used often, and we can't risk getting caught."

I nodded and went straight for the papers. Moira went to the other side of the lab.

My eyes skimmed over every piece of scrap paper I could find looking for anything that might identify how much information they had on me and how many people knew.

Logically, I knew it would never be that easy, but I hoped to find at least a scrap of information to help me figure this puzzle out.

The papers were mostly scribbled formula notes with measurements and ingredients, the books not much better. I shuffled through another pile on the other side of the table to no avail.

But Moira eventually walked around the corner holding a sheath of papers, her face paler than usual and her dark eyes wide with shock.

"What?" I whispered.

"We need to get the fuck out of here. Right now."

"You found something?"

"I'll tell you about it once we're away from this horror show."

She looked like someone had hit her over the head with a cast iron pan. I wanted to scream at her and rip those papers away, but Moira looked so shocked I couldn't bear to rattle her further.

"Come on," I whispered, taking her by the hand. "Let's hurry."

When we were by the front door, Moira had to monitor the sentries once more so we could sneak out without alerting them. We could never have done this in a normal Keep situation. Our scents would have given us away the moment we entered their land.

These damn swans didn't even have wards up. I almost felt bad for them in a twisted way. Yes, they were trying to breed me for their own nefarious purposes, but after seeing how they lived and seeing firsthand the lack of any normal security practices, I wondered for an amusing moment if they were too dumb to actually do anything about it.

The way it was now, I could wipe them out with a bare thought.

And, trust me, I'd thought about it.

"Go. Now," Moira hissed, yanking my hand to follow.

A few minutes later, we were off their land. Moira sank onto the ground and dragged in a shuddering breath. Without a word, she handed the sheaf of papers to me.

When I finally dragged my eyes up and met Moira's eyes, both of us slowly shook our heads.

This was far worse than we expected.

They knew the names and location of every Chimera left on earth, and they had already taken one of the males only a few days ago.

I needed to talk to Barrett immediately because my name was next on the list.

Thirty-Six

A loud honking noise greeted me when we pulled into the driveway.

Moira hit the brakes, jerking the vehicle to an abrupt stop. "Shit," she hissed. "How could they know this soon?"

I didn't believe in coincidences, but there was no way the swans had already discovered us and gotten to my property. But there was one shifter in the wind.

"Nadia," I said grimly.

Moira exhaled. "I'll get out with you."

"I don't see a knife," I said, trying to lighten the mood. "Or blade wings."

"Maybe they're retractable," Moira said with a quick grin.

She turned the car off, and we stepped out of the vehicle at the same time.

A flash of silver light lit up the night revealing a small, nude woman who resembled Gianna, Caelan's ex-fiancée.

"Would you like some clothes?" I asked.

Nadia blinked. "What?" Her fists were clenched tightly at her sides, and her slight frame shivered in the cold weather.

"It's freezing out here, and you're naked. Do you want something to wear?"

"I—" She frowned at me. "Yes, if you don't mind."

Moira hurried through the wards and inside the house. "We'll have you something in a minute."

I didn't make any sudden moves, but I'd primed my magic and sent it spiraling down into the earth until it was right underneath her feet. If she came at me, she'd get a surprise.

Moira came back out with a pair of sweatpants, a sweatshirt, and a pair of thick socks, none of them from my good stash. Moira was a good friend.

Nadia kept her eyes on me while she dressed. When she was finished, she straightened.

"You killed her, didn't you?"

Nadia might be a lot of things, but it didn't stop her from loving her family. Even the worst of us had someone who loved them. "No," I said honestly. "I had nothing to do with her death."

"But she was here."

I nodded. "Yes."

She closed her eyes. "Do you know how she died?"

I shook my head. "I don't know the circumstances surrounding her death."

"Do you know who killed her?"

"Yes. A woman named Rhona, and two men—Finn and Donovan."

Nadia sucked in a shocked gasp. "The Lord?"

"Yes. He was trying to destabilize Caelan's rule." I could have lied to her, but I was so tired of all the lies and subterfuge. This woman grieved for Gianna, and even though she wanted to take me and keep me in servitude, the first wrong had been served to her. It didn't lessen or offer forgiveness for what she planned to do to me, but I could, in a fucked-up kind of way, understand where the swans were coming from. I could understand their desperation and their longing for children and to continue their family tree.

Nadia slumped. "May I sit on your porch?"

I wanted to let her, but I shook my head. "No. I'm sorry. I

know what you've done to the Lords, and I know why you're interested in me."

Her eyes widened. "How—You—" She sighed. "You found Gianna's notebook, didn't you?"

"I did."

"This wasn't my idea," she said, a note of desperation in her voice. "We need help," she admitted. "And nothing is working."

"And you thought trying to kidnap a woman and force her to bear your offspring was the best way to go about it?"

A flicker of annoyance rolled over her face. "No one will help us. Swans are not popular because we aren't powerful." She took a step forward. "And you have so much power in your blood."

I couldn't let her know I knew she already had one of us. Playing dumb was the best way to delay her. Moira stood off to the side, watching carefully. She'd more than likely called someone when she went inside to get Nadia some clothes. All we had to do was delay a little while longer and someone would show up and take her.

I didn't want to kill Nadia. I felt sorry for her.

Which was all kinds of fucked up when I thought about it too hard.

"You can help us," she insisted. "Even if it's something small, like an egg donation or something we could use to try to boost our fertility."

An egg donation would mean whatever child was born would be...mine. "I can speak to Caelan and try to get you some assistance."

Nadia sneered. "We've already asked the Lords. They've refused our requests. Our kind will die if we can't breed."

"You're going about this all wrong. Find the reason for your problem first. Shifters always have low birth rates, so that's not abnormal in itself. Humans have high-tech labs and hire paranormals. We can find someone who's willing to help."

"It's not physical. We are under a curse."

Moira and I both stared at Nadia. "A curse," we said at the same time.

"A witch and a swan shifter mated hundreds of years ago, but the male was unfaithful."

I sucked in a breath. "They were truly mated?"

"Yes, but there was something wrong with the bond." Nadia looked down. "The witch tried everything to repair their bond, but it was no use. When they finally sundered, the witch swore our line would die with him. From that moment on, none of us ever conceived again. Not even outside of the clan."

Moira inhaled and shook her head. "You've tried with other species already."

Nadia nodded. "Everyone except for the Chimeras. Our mage believes there is something in their blood that may break our curse."

Caelan stepped onto my land, and I sensed another presence, so I quickly tweaked the words, allowing another Lord, maybe Thorvin or Ethan to follow. They were too far away to distinguish, and I wasn't completely familiar with their magical signatures yet.

Nadia sensed it at the same time. "You can kill me, but it won't stop us coming for you."

"How many know about me?"

A flash of glee in her eyes. "We all know about you. Your secret won't be safe for much longer if you refuse to cooperate with us."

"You're not asking for my cooperation. You want to steal my DNA to break your curse."

"I don't see you volunteering to help us."

"If you'd come to me and asked, I may very well have, but you're being kind of a bitch about it, so my answer is no."

Caelan and Ethan came around the corner.

Nadia shifted in a flash of light and launched herself up from the grass, throwing off my magic. Shit. I forgot she could fly.

She came right at me, bright yellow beak open with a honking cry.

And, goddammit, Moira was right, retractable blades on her wings.

She got me right in the shoulder, a deep slice rendering my right arm useless. Roots shot from the earth, but Nadia was an agile flyer. She rolled and dodged every attempt at spearing her ass, lunging toward me every time she saw an opening.

Moira couldn't help much, not with the roots and wing blades. But Ethan and Caelan had shifted into their wolf forms and circled me from behind.

I stiffened, uncomfortable with having Ethan at my back. Caelan would protect me from any opportunistic strikes on the other Lord's behalf, but I wouldn't relax until Ethan was off my land.

A screeching cry sent a thrill of victory through me. One of my roots punched right through her wing. Nadia's flight dipped, but she still kept coming.

She was keeping her strikes to my arms and sides, staying away from my face, or anything that might cause my death. Nadia didn't want me to die. She wanted me to suffer.

But she was one swan up against two Lords, a vampire, and a Floromancer, and the fight didn't last long. I didn't even have to shift.

Ethan leapt into the air, snatching Nadia by the neck. One shake, two shakes, and the third, the sound of a loud harsh crack, and the swan shifter went limp in Ethan's mouth as he landed on the ground in a crouch, his eyes glowing with power.

He dropped her body onto the ground and rose. I kept my eyes carefully above waist level and nodded to the Lord.

"Thank you for your timely intervention."

Ethan inclined his head. "Why was she so interested in you?"

Moira was right. The man had muscles for days. Damn. I would not have expected Ethan to be dead sexy underneath those tailored clothes, but he was.

"Evie?" Caelan questioned.

I blinked and dragged my mind out of the gutter. "Yes. Sorry. Um. She thought I had something to do with Gianna's death."

One of Ethan's eyebrows rose. "And did you?"

"Wouldn't you love it if I did? Always searching for some way to put me down, aren't you, Ethan?"

A small smile.

"But no," I growled. "My answer is the same as it's always been. I had nothing to do with Gianna's death."

I couldn't tell him about the real reason she was here, but Caelan would need to know. He stepped up beside me and winced as he touched my bloody collarbone. "Do you need to visit the Keep Healer?"

I shook my head. "No. I'll be fine in an hour or so."

He took my hand and interlaced our fingers. "Let me know if you change your mind."

Ethan watched us. "I hear there are congratulations in order, Evie."

Caelan had already started telling people. I slapped a smile on my face. "Yes, thank you."

"We will marry in a few weeks."

"What?" Moira screeched, her eyes wide in her face. "You're *engaged*?"

Caelan looked back and forth between us. "You went to dinner tonight to tell her, and you didn't say a word?"

"We got busy with other…things."

Moira looked shellshocked. "Evie. *Married*? Are you sure?"

"I'm right here," Caelan drawled.

I tugged my hand away and went over to Moira. She dragged me into a tight hug and whispered against my hair. "Are you sure about this? Were you under duress? Is everything okay?"

"We'll talk about it later," I whispered. "I'm sorry I forgot to tell you."

Moira sighed. "You should think more on why you forgot rather than feeling bad about not telling me."

"Stop being so wise," I hissed back.

"I want you to buy the most hideous bridesmaid dresses ever created."

I let out a wet laugh and stepped away. "We'll see."

Ethan walked up to us and held out his hand. "I know we have our differences, but it's not every day a Lord meets his match. Soon we will be…" He paused. "Not quite family, but close enough. Congratulations."

I shook his hand, surprised by the work-roughened feel of his palm. "Thank you, Lord Ethan."

He inclined his head and shifted once more before trotting off into the night.

Ethan being nice to me? The world really was about to go apocalyptic.

"A curse?" Caelan blurted. "On an entire shifter line?"

He'd said the same thing a few minutes before. The Lord was having a lot of trouble fathoming how a witch could have done such powerful magic. Our working hypothesis was her mating bond with the shifter. The bond allowed her to access the heart of the Pack's magic, allowing her to perform the curse and make it stick.

Information like that could be deadly if it got into the wrong hands. Mating bonds couldn't be faked, but if someone wanted to take a Pack out from the inside, accessing its magic could be effective.

We had not discussed the elephant in the room.

Our impending nuptials.

Caelan was too concerned about Nadia's plan for me and had been hard pressed to let me out of his sight lately.

It was getting extremely annoying.

Garrett and Thalia sat in the two chairs opposite Caelan's desk. I lounged on a couch on the other side, wishing I could sink into a deep and endless sleep. When Caelan brought me inside, I was surprised to find those two here, but Caelan told me they knew everything.

Everything being what happened and my Chimera heritage, something I'd chosen not to disclose to anyone, especially a stranger like her. But bringing it up in front of them would be in bad taste, so I tamped down my anger and tried to focus on the next steps with the swans and how we'd handle them now that they knew what I was. Their plans for me wouldn't come to fruition if I had anything to say about it, and I did. I'd wipe out the rest of their line if they came for me.

The last two weeks had been a whirlwind of wedding activities. Booking the flowers and the baker and the caterer and remembering all the tiny but necessary details was enough to make me scream.

I'd rather get married on my land in the spring, but when I brought it up, Caelan had vetoed the idea and insisted he couldn't wait to marry me and wanted to do it as soon as possible.

He prowled back and forth across the office, barely restrained energy leashed tightly to his body.

"Caelan?" I asked.

"Hmm?"

"Have you seen my father?"

The room went so silent, we could hear a pin drop.

"Why would I see Cernunnos?"

"Just curious." I glanced at Thalia, who wore a mysterious smile on her lips.

I wondered if I could find the spell she was supposedly under and break that rather than trying to break Caelan or my father.

But he was going to tell me about Thalia when we were married. I kept telling myself that, but the thought made me squirm. There were numerous other reasons for us to marry—the main one being I was in love with him.

"For fuck's sake, Caelan. Just tell her," Garrett snarled.

The Lord sent him a withering look. "You know I cannot."

Garrett's nostrils flared, but he stayed silent.

"You know what this is," I accused. "My father didn't swear you to an oath, either, did he?"

Garrett's cheeks colored. His jaw tightened.

"Don't you dare, Garrett." Caelan's voice held a touch of the wolf.

"She needs to know," his Second said.

"She will in a couple of weeks."

Garrett scoffed. "I'm not sure what's going on here, but I can't believe Evie is letting you string her along like this. Doesn't seem like her style."

I closed my eyes and let out a breath. "Garrett's right."

All eyes swung to me. Caelan stilled. "Evie."

"Going into a marriage with secrets will kill the marriage before it even starts. I need to know so I can walk into this with my head on straight."

Anger rolled over Caelan's eyes. "I've told you that I cannot tell you."

"Why?" I stood, my fingers trembling with anger. "This seems so stupid. Why are you clinging so hard to what might be a small secret? What does my father have on you?"

"Evie—"

"Thalia is your sister," Garrett blurted.

All the air was sucked out of my lungs. I snapped my attention to Garrett and Thalia. The seer's eyes were wide with stunned shock.

"Garrett!" she whispered.

"She's Cernunnos's child?" I asked.

Garrett nodded.

I turned to Caelan. "Is that why you were so eager to marry me before you told me? Because then I would look more appealing to my father to carry on his legacy?"

"Evie," Garrett said.

I held a hand up to silence him, screaming in my head that surely Caelan would deny this. He'd deny he'd manipulated me into marriage in order to claim the fae crown.

But he stayed silent, and my heart crashed to the earth.

"I see," I said quietly.

Caelan took a step forward. "Evie. This situation is a lot more complicated than your simplistic take."

"Simplistic." I laughed, a hoarse, croaking sound that sounded foreign coming from my throat.

He reached for me, but I stumbled back and hurried toward the door. From my peripheral, something large and green and orange launched itself through the air. With barely a thought, I reached out a hand and caught Seymour, snuggling him to my chest.

"Do not call me for a while," I said to Caelan. "And Garrett? Thank you. If your Lord kicks you out, you will have a place with me."

Garrett squeezed his eyes shut.

I met Thalia's eyes, but I couldn't read her expression. My sister.

I had a sister.

But the reveal of her heritage had revealed something uglier in my own relationship, and I couldn't take the time to process the fact that I had a living relative outside of my parents.

"Thalia," was all I said as I hurried out of the room.

I had a sister and a fiancé who'd just tried to trick me into marriage so he could claim half of my power.

And he hadn't even denied it.

There was nothing complicated about that.

The door rattled on its hinges as it slammed behind Evie on her way out. I sat there in the silence for a long moment before I turned my gaze to Garrett.

My Second threw his hands up. "Goddammit, Caelan. She deserved to know."

"I'm aware. Her father had me over a barrel, and I couldn't risk our people over the information."

"Yes, well, was this any better?" He gestured at the door.

My fists clenched in my lap. "She's overreacting."

Garrett blinked. "Don't you fucking dare say that to her if you get to see her again. Those words are equal to *'calm down'* in woman speak."

I pinched the space between my brows and sighed. Internally, the wolf prowled under my skin, itching to burst forth and race after Evie. The other part of the animal wanted to rip Garrett's face off. "Evie is under an immense amount of stress and has no idea who she can trust."

"You've been lying to her for months. She's right. There's no one she can truly trust."

I had to count to five in my head before I said something I regretted. "The lie was about something I have zero control over.

Thalia wasn't even in my orbit until Cernunnos brought her here. The seer does not affect our day-to-day operations or what's going on with Evie. When the chips are down, I have always had Evie's back. I've always been in her corner. She will calm down and realize this. Waiting it out is the only thing I can do."

Garrett shook his head. "I can see your wolf fighting to get out. It's killing you that Evie left."

"Of course it is," I snapped. "I'm caught in a game of gods and Chimera, and I can't possibly fucking win. Everywhere I turn, all I see are poor choices, and I have to decide if I hurt Evie or my people. Or both. None of those are good decisions."

I scrubbed a hand over my face. "And now Evie is being hunted by the swans."

Garrett's lips twitched. "It's almost comical."

In a way, yes. No one took the swans seriously, which was coming back to bite us in the ass. But especially Evie. "The fucking swans are often underestimated. How do you think they've survived so long?"

They could have come to me with their fertility issues, and I would have tried to help them. But the damn birds were notoriously tight-lipped when it came to the internal workings of their Pack.

Now they're after Evie. Gianna and Nadia might be dead, but this wasn't over. They wouldn't stop until their line was assured survival. And they were convinced Evie could help them.

As a Lord, I was in a tricky political situation. Wiping them out would destroy the trust the smaller shifter Packs had in my rule. But the threat to Evie could not go unanswered.

If we were married, I'd be well within my rights to wipe them out. But we weren't, and based on the slam of that door, my plans of marrying her within a couple of weeks had flown right out behind her.

"She's freaking out," I said more to myself than Garrett. "She feels like everyone is against her."

"The Lords have not done the best job in showing her otherwise," he drawled.

"I know." I stood up and went to the door. "And that stops right now."

"Want company?" Garrett asked.

The wolf inside me bared its teeth. "Always."

Epilogue

'm freaking out.

I shouldn't have walked out the door like that. I should have sat down and let Caelan explain. Regret filled me the moment I slammed the door behind me, but I couldn't go back inside with my tail tucked between my legs and beg for forgiveness.

Well, I could have, but I was too embarrassed and now I was back home sprawled on my couch like a teenager who didn't get asked to the prom, shoving ice cream in my pie hole.

What was worse was Caelan did not follow me. He didn't trail me back home, and my cell phone was silent. I had no idea I was so good at self sabotage. If there were an Emmy equivalent for self sabotagers, I'd be up on stage collecting the win.

Every time things were good, something ridiculous happened, and it was usually exacerbated by me.

"I suck," I lamented, right before I shoved another spoonful of rocky road in my mouth.

Freaking out was normal behavior, especially for someone like me who'd experienced profound trauma throughout my life. But my experiences didn't excuse me from the consequences of acting like an asshole to the people who loved me.

Caelan had never given me a reason to doubt him like this.

So what I was doing?

I groaned and shoved in another bite, my mind whirling with everything going on. There was one constant here, one person who'd come into my life late and who'd done nothing but meddle. He was the one responsible for Thalia, and knowing Cernunnos, he'd strong-armed Caelan into helping him.

What type of leverage did my father have on the Shifter Lord and why had he forced him to keep the secret of my sister from me?

Had Cernunnos wanted this outcome?

The thought struck a chord. I slowly sat up and put the spoon in my ice cream.

Breaking us up sounded exactly like something the Fae King might do if he wanted a more suitable match for his daughter, the heir slated to take over his kingdom.

"Sonofabitch," I growled.

Playing the game of the gods wasn't something I wanted to do, but once this particular god wormed his way into my good graces and used my kindness against me, I became a player whether he anticipated it or not.

Game on, *Dad*.

———

Keep reading for a look at Book Six
Shift of Rule

BOOK 6, SHIFTER LORDS

Evie finally said yes.
That's when the universe decided to laugh in her face.

After finally accepting Caelan's proposal, Evie was ready to put down true roots and start a life with the Shifter Lord. But nothing in Evie's life stays peaceful for too long.

When a beautiful and seductive female shifter from her fiancé's past slinks into town, she comes bearing grim tidings, splintering

Evie's happily ever after at the seams. Furious and heartbroken, Evie throws herself into training with her father to finally claim the fae crown and forget the shifter who shattered her heart.

Meanwhile, Moira's chaotic new powers are becoming a real problem. Between magical flare-ups in the shop and the accidental summoning of interdimensional beings, Evie has her hands full dealing with everything being dropped into her lap. Then her banshee disappears, and her mother shows up to declare open war, claiming Evie does not belong to the fae, the shifters, or the Chimeras. She belongs to her.

Once the ancient gods smell blood in the water, they come sniffing around seeking to ally with Evie during her darkest moments, but things are about to get so much worse. After all this time, Evie's darkest secret explodes into the light, and the fallout might destroy everything she's fought so hard to protect.

The Magical Soapmaker Mysteries

The Goddess Chronicles

Vikings of Virginia

The Deadicated Matchmaker

About the Author

Sheryl likes cake too much and can be found hoarding it while hiding from her children in the pantry closet.

Follow her on Amazon at: https://www.amazon.com/S-E-Babin/e/B00J1J236A

A small press bound by the belief that every voice matters.

Sign up for our newsletter to learn about new releases and more.
https://oliver-heberbooks.com/subscribe/

Follow us on social media:

facebook.com/oliverheberbooks
instagram.com/oliverheberbooks
amazon.com/oliverheberbooks
youtube.com/@OliverHeberBooksPublisher

9 789890 430607